M

One of Love's Jansenists

Hope Mirrlees

Alpha Editions

This edition published in 2022

ISBN : 9789356576964

Design and Setting By
Alpha Editions
www.alphaedis.com
Email - info@alphaedis.com

Contents

PREFACE

Fiction—to adapt a famous definition of law—is the meeting-point of Life and Art. Life is like a blind and limitless expanse of sky, for ever dividing into tiny drops of circumstances that rain down, thick and fast, on the just and unjust alike. Art is like the dauntless, plastic force that builds up stubborn, amorphous substance cell by cell, into the frail geometry of a shell. These two things are poles apart—how are they to meet in the same work of fiction?

One way is to fling down, *pêle-mêle*, a handful of separate acts and words, and then to turn on them the constructive force of a human consciousness that will arrange them into the pattern of logic or of drama.

Thus, in this book, Madeleine sees the trivial, disorderly happenings of her life as a momentous battle waged between a kindly Power who had written on tablets of gold before the world began that she should win her heart's desire, and a sterner and mightier Power who had written on tablets of iron that all her hopes should be frustrated, so that, finally, naked and bleeding, she might turn to Him. And having this conception of life all her acquaintances become minor *daimones*, friendly or hostile, according as they seem to serve one power or the other.

The other way is to turn from time to time upon the action the fantastic limelight of eternity, with a sudden effect of unreality and the hint of a world within a world. My plot—that is to say, the building of the shell—takes place in this inner world and is summed up in the words that dog the dreams of Madeleine—*per hunc in invisibilium amorem rapiamur*. In the outer world there is nothing but the ceaseless, meaningless drip of circumstances, in the inner world—a silent, ineluctable march towards a predestined climax.

I have had the epilogue printed in italics to suggest that the action has now moved completely on to the stage of the inner world. In the outer world Madeleine might with time have jettisoned the perilous stuff of youth and have sailed serenely the rough, fresh sea of facts. In the inner world, there was one thing and one thing only that could happen to her: life is the province of free-will, art the province of fate.

PART I

'En effet, si on laisse aller le Christianisme sans l'approfondir et le régénérer de temps en temps, il s'y fait comme une infiltration croissants de bon sens humain, de tolérance philosophique, de semi-Pélagianisme à quelque degré que ce soit: la "folie de la Croix" s'atténue.'

SAINTE-BEUVE.

CHAPTER I
THE DINNER AT MADAME PILOU'S

In the middle of the seventeenth century a family called Troqueville came from Lyons to settle in Paris. Many years before, Monsieur Troqueville had been one of the four hundred *procureurs* of the Palais de Justice. There were malicious rumours of disgraceful and Bacchic scenes in Court which had led to his ejection from that respectable body. Whether the rumours were true or not, Monsieur Troqueville had long ceased to be a Paris *procureur*, and after having wandered about from town to town, he had at last settled in Lyons, where by 'devilling' for a lawyer, writing bombastic love-letters for shop apprentices, and playing Lasquinet with country bumpkins, he managed to earn a precarious livelihood. When, a few months before the opening of this story, he had been suddenly seized with a feverish craving to return to Paris 'and once more wear the glove of my lady Jurisprudence in the tournay of the law-courts,' as he put it, his wife had regarded him with a frigid and sceptical surprise, as she had long since given up trying to kindle in him one spark of ambition. However, Madeleine, their only child, a girl of seventeen, expressed such violent despair and disappointment when Madame Troqueville pronounced her husband's scheme to be vain and impracticable, that finally to Paris they came—for to her mother, Madeleine's happiness was the only thing of any moment.

They had taken rooms above a baker's shop in the petite rue du Paon, in the East end of the University quarter—the *Pays Latin*, where, for many centuries, turbulent abstract youth had celebrated with Bacchic orgies the cherub Contemplation, and strutting, ragged and debonair on the razor's edge of most unprofitable speculation, had demonstrated to the gaping, well-fed burghers, that the intellect had its own heroisms and its own virtues. At that time it was a neighbourhood of dark, winding little streets, punctuated by the noble fabrics of colleges and monasteries, and the open spaces of their fields and gardens—a symbol, as it were, of contemporary learning, where crabbed scholasticism still held its own beside the spacious theories of Descartes and Gassendi.

Madame Troqueville had inherited a small fortune from her father, which made it possible to tide over the period until her husband found regular employment.

She was by birth and upbringing a Parisian, her father having been a Président de la Chambre des Comptes. As the daughter of a Judge, she was a member of 'la Noblesse de Robe,' the name given to the class of the high dignitaries of the *Parlement*, who, with their scarlet robes, their ermine, and their lilies, their Latin periods and the portentous solemnity of their manner, were at once ridiculous and awful.

It cannot be wondered at that on her return to Paris she shrank from renewing relations with old friends whose husbands numbered their legal posts by the score and who drove about in fine coaches, ruthlessly bespattering humble pedestrians with the foul mud of Paris. But for Madeleine's sake she put her pride in her pocket, and though some ignored her overtures, others welcomed her back with genial condescension.

The day that this story begins, the Troquevilles were going to dine with the celebrated Madame Pilou, famous in 'la Cour et la Ville' for her homespun wit and remarkably ill-favoured countenance—it would be difficult to say of which of these two distinctions she was most proud herself. Her career had been a social miracle. Though her husband had been only a small attorney, there was not a Princess or Duchess who did not claim her as an intimate friend, and many a word of counsel had she given to the Regent herself.

None of her mother's old acquaintanceships did Madeleine urge her so eagerly to renew as the one with Madame Pilou. In vain her mother assured her that she was just a coarse, ugly old woman.

'So also are the Three Fates,' said Jacques Tronchet (a nephew of Madame Troqueville, who had come to live with them), and Madeleine had looked at him, surprised and startled.

Madame Pilou dined at midday, so Monsieur Troqueville and Jacques were to go to her house direct from the Palais de Justice independently of Madame Troqueville and Madeleine. Madeleine had been ready a full half-hour before it was time to start. She had sat in the little parlour for a quarter of an hour absolutely motionless. She was dressed in her best clothes, a bodice of crimson serge, and an orange petticoat of *camelot de Hollande*, the slender purse's substitute for silk. A gauze neckerchief threw a transparent veil over the extreme *décolletage* of her bodice. On her head was one of the new-fashioned *ténèbres*, a square of black crape that tied under her chin, and took the place of a hat. She wore a velvet mask and patches, in spite of the Sumptuary Laws, which would reserve them for ladies of rank, and from behind the mask her clear gray eyes, that never smiled and seldom blinked, looked out straight in front of her. Her hands were folded on her lap. She had a remarkable gift for absolute stillness.

At the end of a quarter of an hour, she went to her mother, who was preparing a cress salad in the kitchen, and said in a quiet, tense voice:—

'Maybe you would liefer not go to Madame Pilou's this morning. If so, tell me, and I will abandon it,' then, with a sudden access of fury, 'You will make me hate you—you are for ever sacrificing matters of moment to trifles. An you were to weigh the matter rightly, my having some pleasure when I was young would seem of greater moment than there being a salad for supper!'

'Madame Pilou dines at twelve, and it is but a bare half-hour from our house to hers, and it is now eleven,' Madame Troqueville answered slowly, emphasising each word. 'But we will start now without fail, if 'tis your wish, and arrive like true Provincials half an hour before we are due;' irritation now made the words come tumbling out, one on the top of the other. Madeleine began to smile, and her mother went on with some heat, but no longer with irritation.

'But why in the name of Jesus do you lash yourself into so strange a humour before going to old Madame Pilou's? One would think you were off to the Palais Cardinal to wait on the Regent! She is but a plain old woman; now if she were very learned, or——'

'Oh, mother, let her be, and go and make your toilette,' and Madame Troqueville went off obediently to her room.

Madeleine paced about like a restive horse until her mother was ready, but did not dare to disturb her while she was dressing. It used to surprise Madeleine that she should take such trouble over such unfashionable toilettes.

It was not long before she came in quite ready. She began to put Madeleine's collar straight, which, for some reason, annoyed Madeleine extremely. At last they were out of the house.

Madame Pilou lived on the other side of the river, in the rue Saint Antoine, so there was a good walk before Madeleine and her mother, and judging from Madeleine's gloomy, abstracted expression, it did not promise to be a very cheerful one.

They threaded their way into the rue des Augustins, a narrow, cloistered street flanked on the left by the long flat walls of the Monastery, over which were wafted the sound of bells and the scent of early Spring. It led straight out on to the Seine and the peaceful bustle of its still rustic banks. They crossed it by the Pont-Neuf, that perennial Carnival of all that Paris held of most picturesque and most disreputable. The bombastic eloquence of the quacks extolling their panaceas and rattling their necklaces of teeth; the indescribable foulness of the topical songs in which hungry-looking bards celebrated to sweet ghostly airs of Couperin and Cambert the last practical joke played by the Court on the Town, or the latest extravagance of Mazarin; the whining litany of the beggars; the plangent shrieks of strange shrill birds caught in American forests—all these sounds fell unheard on at least one pair of ears.

On they hurried, past the booths of the jugglers and comedians and the stalls of the money-lenders, past the bronze equestrian statue of Henri IV., watching with saturnine benevolence the gambols of the Gothic vagabonds he had loved so dearly in life, cynically indifferent to the discreet threats of his rival the water-house of the Samaritaine, which, classical and chaste, hinted at a future little to the taste of the *Vert Gallant* and his vagabonds.

From time to time Madame Troqueville glanced timidly at Madeleine but did not like to break the silence. At last, as they walked down the right bank of the Seine, the lovely town at once substantial and aerial, taking the Spring as blithely as a meadow, filled her with such joy that she cried out:—

''Tis a delicate town, Paris! Are not you glad we came, my pretty one?'

'Time will show if there be cause for gladness,' Madeline answered gloomily.

'There goes a fine lady! I wonder what Marquise or Duchesse she may be!' cried Madame Troqueville, wishing to distract her. Madeleine smiled scornfully.

'No one of any note. Did you not remark it was a *hired* coach? "*Les honnêtes gens*" do not sacrifice to Saint Fiacre.'

Madame Troqueville gave rather a melancholy little smile, but her own epigram had restored Madeleine, for the time being, to good humour. They talked amicably together for a little, and then again fell into silence, Madeleine wearing a look of intense concentration.

Madame Pilou's house was on the first floor above the shop of a laundress. They were shown into her bedroom, the usual place of reception in those days. The furniture was of walnut, in the massive style of Henri IV., and covered with mustard-coloured serge. Heavy curtains of moquette kept out the light and air, and enabled the room to preserve what Madeleine called the 'bourgeois smell.' On the walls, however, was some fine Belgian tapestry, on which was shown, with macabre Flemish realism, the Seven Stations of the Cross. It had been chosen by the son Robert, who was fanatically devout.

Madame Pilou, dressed in a black dressing-gown lined with green plush, and wearing a chaperon (a sort of cap worn in the old days by every bourgeoise, but by that time rarely seen), was lying on the huge carved bed. Her face, with its thick, gray beard, looming huge and weather-beaten from under the tasselled canopy, was certainly very ugly, but its expression was not unpleasing. Monsieur Troqueville and Jacques had already arrived. Monsieur Troqueville was a man of about fifty, with a long beard in the doctor's mode, a very long nose, and small, excited blue eyes, like a child's. Jacques was rather a beautiful young man; he was tall and slight, and had a pale, pointed face and a magnificent chevelure of chestnut curls, and his light eyes slanting slightly up at the corners gave him a Faun-like look. He was a little like Madeleine, but he had a mercurial quality which was absent in her. Robert Pilou was there too, standing before the chimney-piece; he was dressed in a very rusty black garment, made to look as much like a priest's cassock as possible. Jacques said that with his spindly legs and red nose and spectacles, he was exactly like old Gaultier-Garguille, a famous actor of farce at the theatre of the Hôtel de Bourgogne, and as the slang name for the Hôtel de Bourgogne was, for some unknown reason, the 'Pois-Pilés,' Jacques, out of compliment to Robert's appearance and Madame Pilou's beard, called their house the 'Poil-Pilou.'

They were all sipping glasses of Hippocras and eating preserved fruit. Jacques caught Madeleine's eyes as she came in. His own slanting green ones were dancing with pleasure, he was always in a state of suppressed amusement at the Pilous, but there was no answering merriment in Madeleine's eyes. She gave one quick look round the room, and her face fell.

'Well, my friends, you are exceeding welcome!' bellowed Madame Pilou in the voice of a Musketeer. 'I am overjoyed at seeing you, and so is Robert Pilou.' Robert went as red as a turkey-cock, and muttered something about 'any one who comes to the house.' 'You see I have to say his *fleurettes* for him, and he does my praying for me; 'tis a bargain, isn't it, Maître Robert?' Robert looked as if he were going to have a fit with embarrassment, while Monsieur Troqueville bellowed with laughter, and exclaimed, 'Good! good! excellent!' then spat several times to show his approval. (This habit of his disgusted Madeleine: 'He doesn't even spit high up on the wall like a grand seigneur,' she would say peevishly.)

'Robert Pilou, give the ladies some Hippocras—Oh! I insist on your trying it. My apothecary sends me a bottle every New Year; it's all I ever get out of him, though he gets enough out of me with his draughts and clysters!' This sally was also much appreciated by Monsieur Troqueville.

Robert Pilou grudgingly helped each of them to as much Hippocras as would fill a thimble, and then sat down on the chair farthest removed from Madame Troqueville and Madeleine.

When the Hippocras had been drunk, Madame Pilou bellowed across to him: 'Now, Robert Pilou, it would be civil in you to show the young lady your screen. He has covered a screen with sacred woodcuts, and the design is most excellently conceived,' she added in a proud aside to Madame Troqueville. 'No, no, young man, you sit down, I'm not going to have the poor fellow made a fool of,' as Jacques got up to follow the other two into an adjoining closet. 'But you, Troqueville, I think it might be accordant with your humour—you can go.' Monsieur Troqueville, always ready to think himself flattered, threw a look of triumph at Jacques and went into the closet.

Madeleine was gazing at Robert with a look of rapt attention in her large, grave eyes, while he expounded the mysteries of his design. 'You see,' he said, turning solemnly to Monsieur Troqueville, 'I have so disposed the prints that they make an allegorical history of the Fronde and——'

'An excellent invention!' cried Monsieur Troqueville, all ready to be impressed, and at the same time to show his own cleverness. 'Were you a Frondeur yourself?'

Robert Pilou drew himself up stiffly. 'No, Monsieur, I—*was*—*not*. I was for the King and the Cardinal. Well, as I was saying, profane history is countenanced if told by means of sacred prints and moreover itself becomes sacred history.' Monsieur Troqueville clapped his hands delightedly.

'In good earnest it does,' he cried, 'and sacred history becomes profane in the same way—'tis but a matter of how you look at it—why, you could turn the life of Jesus into the history of Don Quixote—a picture of the woman who pours the ointment on his feet could pass for the grand lady who waits on Don Quixote in her castle, and the Virgin could be his niece——'

'Here you have a print of Judas Iscariot,' Robert went on, having looked at Monsieur Troqueville suspiciously. 'You observe he is a hunchback, and therefore can be taken for the Prince de Conti!' He looked round triumphantly.

Madeleine said sympathetically, ''Tis a most happy comparison!' but Monsieur Troqueville was smiling and nodding to himself, much too pleased with his own idea to pay any attention to Robert's.

'And here we have the Cardinal! By virtue of his holy office I need not find a sacred symbol for him, I just give his own portrait. This, you see, is St Michael fighting with the Dragon——'

'Why, that would do most excellently for Don Quixote fighting with the windmills!'

'Father, I beseech you, no more!' whispered Madeleine severely.

'But why? My conceit is every whit as good as his!' said Monsieur Troqueville sulkily. Fortunately Robert Pilou was too muddle-headed and too wrapt up in himself to understand very clearly what other people were talking about, so he went on:—

'It is a symbol of the King's party fighting with the Frondeurs. Now here is a picture of a Procession of the Confrérie de la Passion; needless to say, it shadows forth the triumphant entry of the King and Cardinal into Paris—you see the banners and the torches—'tis an excellent symbol. And here you have a picture of the stonemasons busy at the new buildings of Val de Grâce, that is a double symbol—it stands for the work of the King and Cardinal in rebuilding the kingdom; it also stands for the gradual re-establishment of the power of the Church. And this first series ends up with this'—and he pointed gleefully to a horrible picture of Dives in Hell—'this stands for the Prince de Condé in prison. And now we come to the second series———;' but just then Madame Pilou called them back to the other room.

'It is a most sweet invention!' said Madeleine in her low, soft voice, meeting Jacques's twinkle with unruffled gravity.

'A most excellent, happy conceit! but I would fain tell you the notion it has engendered in *my* mind!' cried Monsieur Troqueville, all agog for praise.

'Oh, I was of opinion it would accord with your humour,' nodded Madame Pilou, with rather a wicked twinkle.

'But what was *your* notion, Uncle?' asked Jacques, his mouth twitching.

'Well, 'tis this way———' began Monsieur Troqueville excitedly, but Madeleine felt that she would faint with boredom if her father were given an innings, so turned the attention of the company to the workmanship of a handsome clock on the chimney-piece.

'Yes, for Robert that clock is what the "Messieurs de Port Royal" (coxcombs all of them, *I* say!) would call the *grace efficace*, in that by preventing him from being late for Mass it saves his soul from Hell!' said Madame Pilou, looking at her son, who nodded his head in solemn confirmation. Jacques shot a malicious glance at Madeleine, who was looking rather self-conscious.

'Now, then, Monsieur Jacques,' went on Madame Pilou, thoroughly enjoying herself. 'You are a learned young man, and sustained your thesis in philosophy at the University, do you hold it can be so ordered that one person can get another into Paradise—in short, that one can be pious by proxy?'

'Madame Pilou!' piped Robert plaintively, flapping his arms as though they had been wings, then he crossed himself and pulled his face back into its usual expression of stolidity.

'Because,' went on Madame Pilou, paying not the slightest attention to him, 'it would be much to my liking if Robert could do all my church-going for me; I was within an ace of fetching up my dinner at Mass last Sunday, the stench was so exceeding powerful. I am at a loss to know why people are wont to smell worse in Church than anywhere else!'

'I suppose that is what is called the odour of sanctity,' said Jacques, with his engaging grin, looking at Madeleine to see if she was amused. Both Madeleine and Madame Troqueville smiled, but Robert was so busy seeing how long he could keep his cheeks blown out without letting out the breath that he did not hear, and Monsieur Troqueville was so occupied with planning how he could go one better that he had no time to smile. Jacques's sally, however, displeased Madame Pilou extremely. She was really very devout in the sane fashion of the old Gallican Church, and though she herself might make profane jokes, she was not going to allow them in a very young man.

'Odour of sanctity indeed!' she cried angrily. 'I warrant *you* don't smell any better than your neighbours, young man!' a retort which made up in vehemence what it lacked in point. Monsieur Troqueville roared with delight and Jacques made a face. He had a wonderful gift for making faces.

'Impudent fellow! One would think your face was Tabarin's hat by the shapes you twist it into! Anyway, you have more sense in your little finger than your uncle has in his whole body! and while we are on the matter of his shortcomings, I would fain know the *true* motive of his leaving Lyons?' and she shot a malicious look at the discomfited Monsieur Troqueville, while Madame Troqueville went quite white with rage. Fortunately, at this moment, the servant came to say that dinner was ready, and they all moved into the large kitchen, where, true to the traditions of the old bourgeoisie, Madame Pilou always had her meals.

'Well, well, Mademoiselle Marie, I dare swear you have not found that Paris has gained one ounce of wisdom during your sojourn in the provinces. Although the *Prince des Sots* no longer enters the gates in state on Mardi Gras, as was the custom in my young days, that is not to say that Folly has been banished the town. 'Do you frequent many of your old friends?' bellowed Madame Pilou, almost drowning the noise Monsieur Troqueville and Robert were making over their soup.

'Oh, yes, they have proffered me a most kindly welcome,' Madame Troqueville answered not quite truthfully.

'Have you seen the Coigneux and the Troguins?'

'We have much commerce with the Troguins.'

'And has not the *désir de parroistre* been flourishing finely since your day? All the Parliamentary families have got coats of arms from the herald Hozier since then, and have them tattooed all over their bodies like Chinamen.'

Monsieur Troqueville cocked an intelligent eye, he was always on the outlook for interesting bits of information.

'And you must know that there are no *families* nowadays, there are only "houses"! And they roll their silver up and down the stairs, hoping by such usage to give it the air of old family plate, instead of eating off decent pewter as their fathers did before them! And every year the judges grow vainer and more extravagant—great heavy puffed-out sacks of nonsense! There is *la cour* and *la ville*—and *la basse-cour*, and that's where the *gens de robe* live, and the judges are the turkey-cocks!' Every one laughed except Robert Pilou. 'And the sons with their plumes and swords like young nobles, and the daughters who would rather wear a velvet gown in Hell than a serge one in Paradise put me in a strong desire to box their ears!'

"Tis your turn now!' Jacques whispered to Madeleine, who was feeling terribly conscious of her mask and six patches. However, Madame Pilou abruptly changed the subject by turning to Madeleine and asking her what she thought of Paris.

'I think it is furiously beautiful,' she answered, at which Madame Pilou went off into a bellow of laughter.

'*Jésus!* Hark to the little Précieuse with her "furiously"! So "furiously" has reached the provinces, has it? Little Madeleine will be starting her "*ruelle*" next! Ha! Ha!' Madeleine blushed crimson, Jacques looked distressed, Robert Pilou gave a sudden wild whoop of laughter, then stopped dead, looked anxiously round, and pulled a long face again.

'That is news to me,' Monsieur Troqueville began intelligently; 'is "furiously" much in use with the Précieuses?' but Madame Troqueville, who was very indignant that Madeleine should be made fun of, broke in hurriedly with, 'I think my daughter learned it in Mademoiselle de Scudéry's *Grand Cyrus*; she liked it rarely; we read it through together from beginning to end.'

'Well, I fear me, I cannot confess to the same assiduity, and that though Mademoiselle de Scudéry brought me the volumes herself,' said Madame Pilou. 'I promised her I would read it if she gave me her word that that swashbuckler of a brother of hers should not come to the house for six months, but there he was that very evening, come to find out what I thought of the description of the battle of Rocroy! Are you a lover of reading, my child?' suddenly turning to Madeleine.

'No, 'tis most distasteful to me,' she answered emphatically, to her mother's complete stupefaction.

'But Madeleine——' she began. Madame Pilou, however, cut her short with 'Quite right, quite right, my child. You'll never learn anything worth the knowing out of books. I have lived nearly eighty years, and my Missal and Æsop his fables are near the only two books I have ever read. What you can't learn from life itself is not worth the learning——'

'But Madeleine has grown into such an excessive humour for books, that she wholly addicts herself to them!' cried Madame Troqueville indignantly. She was determined that an old barbarian like Madame Pilou should not flatter herself she had anything in common with her Madeleine. But Madame Pilou was too busy talking herself to hear her.

'Mademoiselle de Scudéry is writing a new romance, she tells me (it's all her, you know; Conrart tells me that all the writing in it that tedious, prolix, bombastic fop of a brother does is to put his name to the title page!) and she says that I am to be portrayed in it. Poor Robert is in a sad taking; he thinks you cannot be both in a romance and the Book of Life!' Robert Pilou looked at his mother with the eyes of an anxious dog, and she smiled at him encouragingly, and assured him that there were many devotees described in romances.

'I dare swear she will limn me as a beautiful princess, with Robert Pilou as my knight, or else I'll be—what d'ye call her—that heathen goddess, and Robert Pilou will be my owl!'

Madeleine had been strangely embarrassed for the last few minutes. When she was nervous the sound of her father's voice tortured her, and feeling the imminence of a favourite story of his about an old lady of Lyons, called Madame Hibou, who had found her gardener drunk in her bed, she felt she would go mad if she had to listen to it again, so to stop him, she said hurriedly, 'Could you tell us, Madame, whom some of the characters in the *Grand Cyrus* are meant to depict?'

'Oh! every one is there, every one of the Court and the Town. I should be loath to have you think I wasted my time in reading all the dozen volumes, but I cast my eye through some of them, and I don't hold with dressing up living men and women in all these outlandish clothes and giving them Grecian names. It's like the quacks on the Pont-Neuf, who call themselves "Il Signor Hieronymo Ferranti d'Orvieto," and such like, though they are only decent French burghers like the rest of us!'

'Or might it not be more in the nature of duchesses masquerading at the Carnival as Turkish ladies and shepherdesses?' suggested Madeleine in a very nervous voice, her face quite white, as though she were a young Quakeress, bearing testimony for the first time.

'Oh, well, I dare swear that conceit would better please the demoiselle,' said Madame Pilou good-humouredly. 'But it isn't only in romances that we aren't called by our good calendar names—oh, no, you are baptized Louise, or Marie, or Marguerite, but if you want to be in the mode, you must call yourself Amaryllis, or Daphne, or Phillis,' and Madame Pilou minced out the names, her huge mouth pursed up. 'I tell them that it is only actors and soldiers—the scum of the earth—who take fancy names. No, no, I am quite out of patience with the present fashion of beribboning and beflowering the good wood of life, as if it were a great maypole.'

'And I am clearly on the other side!' cried Madame Troqueville hotly, 'I would have every inch of the hard wood bedecked with flowers!'

'Well, well, Marie, life has dealt hardly with you,' said Madame Pilou, throwing a menacing look at Monsieur Troqueville, 'but life and I have ever been good friends; and the cause may be that we are not unlike one to the other, both strong and tough, and with little tomfoolery about us.' Madame Troqueville gazed straight in front of her, her eyes for the moment as chill as Madeleine's. This was more than she could stand, she, the daughter of an eminent judge, to be pitied by this coarse old widow of an attorney.

'Maybe the reason you have found life not unkind is because you are not like the dog in the fable,' said Madeleine shyly, 'who lost the substance out of greediness to possess the shadow.'

Madame Pilou was delighted. Any reference to Æsop's fables was sure to please her, for it brought her the rare satisfaction of recognising a literary allusion.

'That is very prettily said, my child,' and she chuckled with glee. Then she looked at Madeleine meditatively. 'But see here, as you are so enamoured of the *Grand Cyrus*, you had better come some day and make the acquaintance of Mademoiselle de Scudéry.'

'Oh, Madeleine, you would like that rarely, would you not?' cried Madame Troqueville, flushing with pleasure.

But Madeleine had gone deadly white, and stammered out, 'Oh—er—I am vastly obliged, Madame, but in truth I shouldn't ... the honour would put me out of countenance.'

'Out of countenance? Pish! Pish! my child,' laughed Madame Pilou, 'Mademoiselle de Scudéry is but a human being like the rest of us, she eats and drinks and is bled and takes her purges like any one else. Yes, you come and see her, and convey yourself towards her as if she were a *grande dame* who had never seen a goose's quill in her life, and you will gain her friendship on the spot.'

'The lady I would fainest in the world meet,' said Madeleine, and there was suppressed eagerness in her voice, 'is Madame de Rambouillet, she——'

'My child, your wish has something in't like rare wit and sense,' interrupted Madame Pilou warmly, 'she is better worth seeing than anything else in the world, than the Grand Turk or Prester John himself.'

'Was it not the late Monsieur Voiture that said of her, "I revere her as the most noble, the most beautiful, and the most perfect thing I have ever seen"?' said Madeleine, the ordeal of quoting making her burn with self-consciousness.

'I dare say it was. Poor Voiture, he was an impudent fellow, but his wit was as nimble as a hare. He always put me in mind of a performer there used to be on the Pont-Neuf—we called him the "Buveur d'Eau"—he would fill his mouth with ordinary cold water and then spout it out in cascades of different coloured scents. Some trick, doubtless, but it was wonderful. And in the same way Voiture would take some plain homespun sentiment and twist it and paint it and madrigalise it into something so fantastical that you would never recognise it as the same.'

'I remember me to have seen that "Buveur d'Eau" when I came to Paris as a young man, and——' began Monsieur Troqueville, in whom for some time the pleasures of the table had triumphed over the desire to shine. But Madeleine was not going to let the conversation wander to quacks and mountebanks. In a clear, though gentle voice, she asked if it were true that the Marquise de Rambouillet was in very delicate health.

'Yes, very frail but rarely in Paris nowadays. The last time I went to see her she said, smiling as is always her way, "I feel like a ghost in Paris these days, a ghost that died hundreds of years ago," and I much apprehend that she will in sober earnest be a ghost before long,' and Madame Pilou, who was deeply moved, blew her nose violently on a napkin.

'She must be a lady of great and rare parts,' said Madame Troqueville sympathetically. The remark about 'feeling like a ghost' had touched her imagination.

'Yes, indeed. She is the only virtuous woman I have ever known who is a little ashamed of her virtue—and that is perfection. There is but little to choose between a prude and a whore, *I* think ... yes, I do, Robert Pilou. Ay! in good earnest, she is of a most absolute behaviour. The Marquis has no need to wear *his* hair long. You know when this fashion for men wearing love-locks came in, I said it was to hide the horns!'

'Do the horns grow on one's neck, then?' Jacques asked innocently. Monsieur Troqueville was much tickled, and Madame Troqueville wondered wearily how many jokes she had heard in her life about 'horns' and 'cuckolds.'

'Grow on one's neck, indeed! You'll find *that* out soon enough, young man!' snorted Madame Pilou.

The substantial meal was now over, and Monsieur Troqueville had licked from his fingers the last crumbs of the last *Pasté à la mazarinade*, when Robert Pilou, who had been silent nearly all dinner-time, now said slowly and miserably, 'To appear in a romance! In a romance with Pagans and Libertins! Oh! Madame Pilou!' His mother looked round proudly.

'Hark to him! He has been pondering the matter; he always gets there if you but give him time!' and she beamed with maternal pride. Then Madame Troqueville rose and made her adieux, though Madeleine looked at her imploringly, as if her fate hung upon her staying a little longer. Madame Pilou was particularly affectionate in her good-bye to Madeleine. 'Well, we'll see if we can't contrive it that you meet Madame de Rambouillet.'

Madeleine's face suddenly became radiantly happy.

CHAPTER II
A PARTIAL CONFESSION

At supper that evening Madeleine seemed intoxicated with happiness. She laughed wildly at nothing and squeezed Jacques's hand under the table, which made him look pleased but embarrassed. Monsieur Troqueville was also excited about something, for he kept smiling and muttering to himself, gesticulating now and then, his nostrils expanding, his eyes flashing as if in concert with his own unspoken words. Jacques burst into extravagant praise of Madame Pilou, couched, as was his way, in abrupt adjectives, 'She is *crotesque* ... she is *gauloise* ... she is superb!'

'My dear Jacques,' said Madame Troqueville, smiling, 'You would find dozens of women every whit as *crotesque* and *gauloise* in the Halles. I'll take you with me when I go marketing some day.'

'Very well, and I'll settle down and build my harem there and fill it with Madame Pilous,' said he, grinning. 'If I had lived in the days of Amadis de Gaul she should have been my lady and I'd have worn ... a hair shirt made of her beard!'

Madeleine, who did not, as a rule, much appreciate Jacques's wit, laughed long and excitedly. Her mother looked at her, not sure whether to rejoice at or to fear this sudden change from languid gloom. Jacques went on with his jerky panegyric. 'She is like some one in Rabelais. She might have been the mother of Gargantua, she——'

'Gargamelle! Gargamelle was the mother of Gargantua!' cried Madeleine eagerly and excitedly.

'As you will, Gargamelle, then. Why doesn't she please you, Aunt? It is you that are *really* the Précieuse, and Madeleine is at heart a *franque gauloise*,' and he looked at Madeleine wickedly.

'That I'm not ... you know nothing of my humour, Jacques.... I know best about myself, I am abhorrent of aught that is coarse and ungallant.... I am to seek why you should make other people share your faults, you——' Madeleine had tears of rage in her eyes.

'You are a sprouting Madame Pilou, beard and all!' teased Jacques. 'No, you're not,' and he stopped abruptly. It was his way suddenly to get bored with a subject he had started himself.

'But Madeleine,' began Madame Troqueville, 'what, in Heaven's name, prompted you to refuse to meet Mademoiselle de Scutary?'

'De S-c-u-d-é-r-y,' corrected Madeleine, enunciating each letter with weary irritation.

'De Scudéry, then. You are such a goose, my child; in the name of Our Lady, how *can* you expect——' and Madame Troqueville began to work herself up into a frenzy, such as only Madeleine was able to arouse in her.

But Madeleine said with such earnestness, 'Pray mother, let the matter be,' that Madame Troqueville said no more.

Supper being over, Monsieur Troqueville, wearing an abstracted, important air, took his hat and cloak and went out, and Madame Troqueville went to her spinning-wheel.

Jacques and Madeleine went up to her bedroom, to which they retired nearly every evening, nominally to play Spelequins or Tric-trac. Madame Troqueville had her suspicions that little of the evening was spent in these games, but what of that? Jacques's mother had left him a small fortune, not large enough to buy a post in the *Parlement*, but still a competency, and if Madeleine liked him they would probably be able to get a dispensation, and Madame Troqueville would be spared the distasteful task of negotiating for a husband for her daughter. Her passion for Madeleine was not as strong as a tendency to shudder away from action, to sit spellbound and motionless before the spectacle of the automatic movement of life.

Jacques was now learning to be an attorney, for although his father had been an advocate, his friends considered that he would have more chance on the other side. Jacques docilely took their advice, for it was all one to him whether he eventually became an advocate or an attorney, seeing that from the clerks of both professions were recruited '*les Clercs de la Bazoche*'—a merry, lewd corporation with many a quaint gothic custom that appealed to Jacques's imagination.

They had a Chancellor—called King in the old days—whom they elected annually from among themselves, and who had complete authority over them. That year Jacques reached the summit of his ambition, for they chose him for the post.

He had never seen Madeleine till her arrival in Paris two months before. At that time he was fanning the dying embers of a passion for a little lady of the Pays-Latin of but doubtful reputation.

Then the Troquevilles had arrived, and, to his horror, he began to fall in love with Madeleine. Although remarkably cynical for his age, he was nevertheless, like all of his contemporaries, influenced by the high-flown chivalry of Spain, elaborated by the Précieuses into a code where the capital crime was to love more than once. In consequence, he was extremely surly with Madeleine at first and laid it on himself as a sacred duty to find out one fault in her every day. Her solemnity was unleavened by one drop of the mocking gaiety of France; in an age of plump beauties she seemed scraggy; unlike his previous love, she was slow and rather clumsy in her movements. But it was in vain, and he had finally to acknowledge that she was like one of the grave-eyed, thin-mouthed beauties Catherine de Médici had brought with her from Italy, that her very clumsiness had something beautiful and virginal about it, and, in fact, that he was deeply in love with her.

When he had told her of his new feelings towards herself she had replied with a scorn so withering as to be worthy of the most prudish Précieuse of the Marais. This being so, his surprise was as great as his joy when, about a week before the dinner described in the last chapter, she announced that he 'might take his fill of kissing her, and that she loved him very much.'

So a queer little relationship sprang up between them, consisting of a certain amount of kissing, a great deal of affectionate teasing on Jacques's side, endless discussions of Madeleine's character and idiosyncrasies—a pastime which never failed to delight and interest her—and a tacit assumption that they were betrothed.

But Jacques was not the gallant that Madeleine would have chosen. In those days, the first rung of the social ladder was *le désir de parroistre*—the wish to make a splash and to appear grander than you really were—and this noble aspiration of *'une âme bien née'* was entirely lacking in Jacques. Then his scorn of the subtleties of Dandyism was incompatible with being *un honnête homme*, for though his long ringlets were certainly in the mode, they had originally been a concession to his mother, and all Madeleine's entreaties failed to make him discard his woollen hose and his jerkin of Holland cloth, or substitute top boots for his short square shoes. Nor did he conform in his wooing to the code of the modish Cupid and hire the Four Fiddles to serenade her, or get up little impromptu balls in her honour, or surprise collations coming as a graceful climax to a country walk. Madeleine had too fine a scorn for facts to allow the knowledge of his lack of means to extenuate this negligence.

In short, the fact could not be blinked that Jacques was ignoble enough to be quite content with being a bourgeois.

Then again, in Metaphysics, Jacques held very different views from Madeleine, for he was an Atheistic follower of Descartes and a scoffer at Jansenism, while in other matters he was much in sympathy with the 'Libertins'—the sworn foes of the Précieuses. The name of 'Libertin' was applied—in those days with no pornographic connotation—to the disciples of Gassendi, Nandé, and La Motte le Vayer. These had evolved a new Epicurean philosophy, to some of their followers merely an excuse for witty gluttony, to others, a potent ethical incentive. The Précieuses, they held, had insulted by the diluted emotions and bombastic language their good goddess Sens Commun, who had caught for them some of the radiance of the Greek Σωφροσύνη. One taste, however, they shared with the Précieusues, and that was the love of the *crotesque*—of quaint, cracked brains and deformed, dwarfish bodies, and of colouring. It was the same tendency probably that produced a little earlier the architecture known as *baroque*, the very word *crotesque* suggesting the mock stalactitic grottoes with which these artists had filled the gardens of Italy. But this very thing was being turned by the Libertins, with unconscious irony, *via* the *genre burlesque* of the Abbé Scarron, into a sturdy Gallic realism—for first studying real life in quest of the *crotesque*, they fell in love with its other aspects too.

Madeleine resented that Jacques continued just as interested in his own life as before he had met her—in his bright-eyed vagabondage in Bohemia, his quest after absurdities on the Pont-Neuf and in low taverns. She hated to be reminded that there could be anything else in the world but herself. But in spite of her evident disapproval, he continued to spend just as much of his time in devising pranks with his subjects of La Bazoche, and in haunting the Pont-Neuf in quest of the *crotesque*.

Another thing which greatly displeased Madeleine was that Jacques and her father had struck up a boon-companionship, and this also she was not able to stop.

That same evening, when they got into her room, they were silent for a little. Jacques always left it to her to give the note of the evening's intimacy.

'What are you pondering?' he said at last.

''Twould be hard to say, Jacques.... I'm exceeding happy.'

'Are you? I'm glad of it! you have been of so melancholy and strange a humour ever since I've known you. There were times when you had the look of a hunted thing.'

'Yes, at times my heart was like to break with melancholy.'

Jacques was silent, then he said suddenly, 'Has it aught to do with that Scudéry woman?'

Madeleine gave a start and blushed all over. 'What ... what ... how d'you mean?'

'Oh! I don't know. I had the fancy it might in some manner refer to her ... you act so whimsically when mention is made of her.'

Madeleine laughed nervously, and examined her nails with unnecessary concentration, and then with eyes still averted from Jacques, she began in a jerky, embarrassed voice, 'I'm at a loss to know how you discovered it ... 'tis so foolish, at least, I mean rather 'tis so hard to make my meaning clear ... but to say truth, it *is* about her ... the humour to know her has come so furiously upon me *that I shall go mad if it cannot be compassed!*' and her voice became suddenly hard and passionate.

'There is no reason in nature why it should not. Old Pilou said she would contrive it for you, but you acted so fantastically and begged her not to, funny one!'

Madeleine once more became self-conscious. 'I know ... it's so hard to make clear my meaning.... 'Tis an odd, foolish fancy, I confess, but I am always having the feeling that things won't fall out as I would wish, except something else happens first. As soon as the desire for a thing begins to work on me, all manner of little fantastical things crop up around me, and I am sensible that except I compound with them I shall not compass the big thing. For example ... for example, if I was going to a ball and was eager it should prove a pleasant junketing, well, I might feel it was going to yield but little pleasure unless—unless—I were able to keep that comb there balanced on my hand while I counted three.'

'Don't!' cried Jacques, clasping his head despairingly. 'I shall get the contagion.... I *know* I shall!'

'Well, anyway,' she went on wearily, 'I was seized by the notion that ... that ... that it wouldn't ... that I wouldn't do so well with Mademoiselle de Scudéry unless I met her for the first time at the Hôtel de Rambouillet, and it *must* be there, and if the Marquise be of so difficult access, perchance it can't be compassed.... Oh! I would I were dead,' the last words came tumbling out all in one breath.

'Poor little Chop!' said Jacques sympathetically. (It was the fashion, brought to Paris by the exiled King of England, to call pets by English names, and Jacques had heard a bulldog called 'Chop,' and was so tickled by the name, that he insisted on giving it to Madeleine that he might have the pleasure of often saying it).

'"Tis a grievous thing to want anything sorely. But I am confident the issue will be successful.'

'Are you? Are you?' she cried, her face lighting up. 'When do you think the meeting will take place? Madame de Rambouillet is always falling ill.'

'Oh! Old Pilou can do what she will with all those great folk, and she has conceived a liking for you.'

'Has she? Has she? How do you know? What makes you think so?'

'Oh, I don't know ... however, she has,' he answered, suddenly getting distrait. 'Is it truly but as an exercise against the spleen that you pass whole hours in leaping up and down the room?' he asked after a pause, watching her curiously.

Madeleine blushed, and answered nervously:—

'Yes, 'tis good for the spleen—the doctor told me so—also, if you will, 'tis a caprice——'

'How ravishing to be a woman!' sighed Jacques. 'One can be as great a *visionnaire* as one will and be thought to have rare parts withal, whereas, if a man were to pass his time in cutting capers up and down the room, he'd be shut up in *les petites maisons*.[1] How comes it that you want to know Mademoiselle Scudéry more than any one else?'

'I cannot say, 'tis just that I do, and the wish has worked so powerfully on my fancy that 'tis become my only thought. It has grown from a little fancy into a huge desire. 'Tis like to a certain nightmare I sometimes have when things swell and swell.'

'When things swell and swell?'

'Yes, 'tis what I call my Dutch dream, for it ever begins by my being surrounded by divers objects, such as cheeses and jugs and strings of onions and lutes and spoons, as in a Dutch picture, and I am sensible that one of them presently, I never know which 'twill be, will start to swell. And then on a sudden one of them begins, and it is wont to continue until I feel that if it get any bigger I shall go mad. And in like manner, I hold it to be but chance that it was Mademoiselle de Scudéry that took to swelling, it might quite well have been any one else.'

Jacques smiled a little. 'It might always quite well have been any one else,' he said.

Madeleine looked puzzled for a minute and then went on unhappily, 'I feel 'tis all so unreal, just a "vision." Oh! How I wish it was something in accordance with other people's experiences ... something they could understand, such as falling in love, for example, but this——'

'It isn't the cause that is of moment, you know, it's the strength of the "passion" resulting from the cause. And in truth I don't believe any one *could* have been subject to a stronger "passion" than you since you have come to Paris.'

'So it doesn't seem to you extravagant then?' she asked eagerly.

'Only as all outside one's own desires do seem extravagant.' He sat down beside her and drew her rather timidly to him. 'I'm confident 'twill right itself in the end, Chop,' he whispered. She sprang up eagerly, her eyes shining.

'Do you think so, Jacques ... in sober earnest?'

'Come back, Chop!' In Jacques's eyes there was what Madeleine called the 'foolish expression,' which sooner or later always appeared when he was alone with her. It bored her extremely; why could he not be content with spending the whole time in rational talk? However, she went back with a sigh of resignation.

After a few minutes she said with a little excited giggle, 'What do you think ... er ... Mademoiselle de Scudéry will think of me?'

Jacques only grunted, the 'foolish expression' still in his eyes.

'Jacques!' she cried sharply, 'tell me!' and she got up.

'What will she think of you? Oh! that you're an ill-favoured, tedious little imp.'

'No, Jacques!'

'A scurvy, lousy, bombastic———'

'Oh! Jacques, forbear, for God's sake!'

'Provincial———'

'Oh! Jacques, no more, I'll *scream* till you hold your tongue ... *what* will she think of me, in sober earnest?'

'She'll think———' and he stopped, and looked at her mischievously. Her lips were moving, as if repeating some formulary. 'That you are ... that there is a "I know not what about you of gallant and witty."' Madeleine began to leap up and down the room, then she rushed to Jacques and flung her arms round his neck.

'I am furiously grateful to you!' she cried. 'I felt that had you not said something of good omen ere I had repeated "she'll think" twenty times, I would never compass my desires, and you said it when I had got to eighteen times!' Jacques smiled indulgently.

'So you know the language she affects, do you?' said Madeleine, with a sort of self-conscious pride.

'Alas! that I do! I read a few volumes of the *Grand Cyrus*, and think it the saddest fustian———'

'Madame Pilou said she had begun another ... do you think ... er ... do you think ... that ... maybe I'll figure in it?'

"'Tis most probable. Let's see. "Chopine is one of the most beautiful persons in the whole of Greece, as, Madame, you will readily believe when I tell you that she was awarded at the Cyprian Games the second prize for beauty.'" Madeleine blushed prettily, and gave a little gracious conventional smile. She was imagining that Mademoiselle de Scudéry herself was reading it to her. "'The *first* prize went, of course, to that fair person who, having learnt the art of thieving from Mercury himself, proceeded to rob the Graces of all their charms, the Muses of all their secrets. Like that of the goddess Minerva, hers is, if I may use the expression, a virile beauty, for on her chin is the thickest, curliest, most Jove-like beard that has ever been seen in Greece——'"

'Jacques! it's not——'

"'Madame, your own knowledge of the world will tell you that I speak of Madame Pilou!'" Madeleine stamped her foot, and her eyes filled with angry tears, but just then there was a discreet knock at the door, and Berthe, the Troqueville's one servant, came in with a cup and a jug of Palissy *faïence*. She was fat and fair, with a wall-eye and a crooked mouth. Her home was in Lorraine, and she was a mine of curious country-lore, but a little vein of irony ran through all her renderings of local legends, and there was nothing she held in veneration—not even '*la bonne Lorraine*' herself. Her tongue wagged incessantly, and Jacques said she was like the servant girl, Iambe—'the prattling daughter of Pan.' She had been with the Troquevilles only since they had come to Paris, but she belonged to the class of servants that become at once old family retainers. She took a cynically benevolent interest in the relationship between Jacques and Madeleine, and although there was no need whatever for the rôle, she had instituted herself the confidante and adviser of the 'lovers,' and from the secrecy and despatch with which she would keep the two posted in each other's movements, Monsieur and Madame Troqueville might have been the parental tyrants of a Spanish comedy. This attitude irritated Madeleine extremely, but Jacques it tickled and rather pleased.

'Some Rossoli for Mademoiselle, very calming to the stomach, in youth one needs such drafts, for the blood is hot, he! he!' and she nodded her head several times, and smiled a smile which shut the wall-eye and hitched up the crooked mouth. Then she came up to them and whispered, 'The master is not in yet, and the mistress is busy with her spinning!' and the strange creature with many nods and becks set the jug and cup on the table, and continuing to mutter encouragement, marched out with soft, heavy steps.

Madeleine dismissed Jacques, saying she was tired and wanted to go to bed.

CHAPTER III
A SUPPLEMENT TO THE CONFESSION

'On a oublié le temps où elle vivait et combien dans cette vie de luxe et de désœuvrement les passions peuvent ressembler à des fantaisies, de même que les manies y deviennent souvent des passions.'

SAINTE-BEUVE.—*Madame de Sévigné.*

It is wellnigh impossible for any one to be very explicit about their own nerves, for there is something almost indecently intimate in a nervous fear or obsession. Thus, although Madeleine's explanation to Jacques had given her great relief, it had been but partial. She would sooner have died than have told him the real impulse, for instance, that sent her dancing madly up and down the room, or have analysed minutely her feelings towards Mademoiselle de Scudéry.

The seeds of the whole affair were, I think, to be found in the fact that an ancestor of Madame Troqueville's had been an Italian lady of high family, who had left a strain, fine, fastidious, civilised—in the morbid way of Italy— to lie hidden in obscurity in the bourgeois stock, and to crop up from time to time with pathetic persistence, in a tragically aristocratic outlook, thin features, and the high, narrow forehead that had given to the pallid beauties of the sixteenth century a look of *maladif* intellect.

To Madeleine it had also brought a yearning from earliest childhood for a radiant, transfigured world, the inhabitants of which seemed first of all to be the rich merchant families of Lyons.

One of her most vivid memories was an occasion on which a strolling company of players had acted a comedy in the house of a leader among these merchants, a certain Maître Jean Prunier. Although the Troquevilles personally did not know the Pruniers, they had a common friend, and he had taken Madeleine and her parents to the performance. They went into an enormous room filled with benches, with a raised platform at one end. The walls and the ceiling were frescoed with various scenes symbolical of Maître Prunier's commercial prowess. He was shown riding on woolly waves on the back of a dolphin, presenting a casket of gloves to Marie de Médici, marching in crimson robes at the head of the six guilds of merchants. On the ceiling was his apotheosis. It showed him sitting, his lap full of gloves, on a Lyons shawl, which winged Cherubs were drawing through the air to a naked goddess on a cloud, who was holding out to him a wreath made of Dutch tulips. When Madame Troqueville saw it she shook with laughter, much to Madeleine's surprise.

Maître Prunier and his family sat on the stage during the performance, that they might be seen as well as see. He was a large stout man, and his nose was covered with warts, but his youngest daughter held Madeleine's eyes spellbound. She had lovely golden hair for one thing, and then, although she looked no older than Madeleine herself, who was about seven at the time, she was dressed in a velvet bodice covered with Genoese point, and— infinitely grander—she was actually wearing what to Madeline had always seemed one of the attributes of magnificent eld, to wit, a real stomacher, all stiff with busks and embroidered in brightly coloured silks with flowers and enchanting beasts—a thing as lovely and magical as the armour of Achilles in the woodcut that hung in the parlour at home.

Some years later Madeleine was sent to school at a Convent about a mile out of Lyons. One of the scholars was this very Jeanne Prunier. Madeleine would watch her stumbling through the Creed, her fat white face puckered with effort, her stumpy fingers fiddling nervously with her gold chain, and would wonder what great incomprehensible thoughts were passing behind that greasy forehead and as what strange phantasmagoria did she see the world. And that chain—it actually hung round her neck all day long, and when she went home, was taken through the great wooden door of Maître Prunier's house—the door carved with flowers and grinning faces—and perhaps in a drawer in her bedroom had a little box of its own. And Maître Prunier probably knew of its existence, as doubtless it had been his gift, and thus it had a place in the consciousness of that great man, while she, Madeleine ... he had never heard of her.

Lyons, like most rich provincial towns, was very purse-proud, and this characteristic was already quite apparent in its young daughters at the Convent. Their conversation consisted, to a great extent, in boastings about their fathers' incomes, and surmises as to those of the fathers of their companions. They could tell you the exact number of gold pieces carried on each girl's back, and when some one appeared in a new dress they would come up and finger the material to ascertain its texture and richness. Every one knew exactly how many pairs of Spanish gloves, how many yards of Venetian lace, how many pure silk petticoats were possessed by every one else, and how many Turkey carpets and Rouen tapestries and tables of marble and porphyry, how much gold and silver plate, and how many beds covered with gold brocade were to be found in each other's homes.

As Madeleine's dresses were made of mere serge, and contemptible *guese* was their only trimming, and as it was known that her father was nothing but a disreputable attorney, they coldly ignored her, and this made her life in the Convent agonising. Although subconsciously she was registering every ridiculous or vulgar detail about her passive tormentors, yet her boundless admiration for them remained quite intact, and to be accepted as one of their select little coterie, to share their giggling secrets, to walk arm in arm with one of them in the Convent garden would be, she felt, the summit of earthly glory.

One hot summer's day, it happened that both she and a member of the Sacred Circle—a girl called Julie Duval—felt faint in Chapel. A nun had taken them into the Refectory—the coolest place in the Convent—and left them to recover. Madeleine never quite knew how it happened, but she suddenly found herself telling Julie that her mother was the daughter of a Duke, and her father the son of an enormously wealthy merchant of Amsterdam; that he had been sent as quite a young man on a political mission to the Court of France, where he had met her mother; that they had fallen passionately in love with one another, and had been secretly married; when the marriage was announced the parents of both were furious, owing to her father's family being Protestant, her mother's Catholic, and had refused to have anything more to do with their respective offspring; that her father had taken the name of Troqueville and settled in Lyons; that some months ago a letter had come from her paternal grandfather, in which he told them that he was growing old and that, although a solemn vow prevented him from ever looking again on the face of his son, he would like to see his grandchild before he died, would she come to Amsterdam?; that she had refused, saying that she did not care to meet any one who had treated her father as badly as he; that the old man had written back to say that he admired her spirit and had made her his sole heir, 'which was really but a cunning device to take, without tendering his formal forgiveness, the sting from the act whereby he had disinherited my father, because he must have been well aware that I would share it all with him!' (Unconsciously she had turned her father into a romantic figure, to whom she was attached with the pious passion of an Antigone. In reality she gave all her love to her mother; but the unwritten laws of rhetoric commanded that the protagonists in this story should be *father* and daughter.)

Julie's eyes grew rounder and rounder at each word.

'*Jésus*, Madeleine Troqueville! what a fine lady you will be!' she said in an awed voice. Madeleine had not a doubt that by the next morning she would have repeated every word of it to her friends.

In the course of the day she half came to believing the whole story herself, and sailed about with measured, stately gait; on her lips a haughty, faintly contemptuous smile. She felt certain that she was the centre of attention. She was wearing her usual little serge dress and plain muslin fichu, but if suddenly asked to describe her toilette, she would have said it was of the richest velvet foaming with Italian lace. She seemed to herself four inches taller than she had been the day before, while her eyes had turned from gray to flashing black, her hair also was black instead of chestnut.

Mythology was one of the subjects in the Convent curriculum—a concession to fashion made most unwillingly by the nuns. But as each story was carefully expurgated, made as anterotic as possible, and given a neat little moral, Ovid would scarce have recognised his own fables. The subject for that day happened to be Paris's sojourn as a shepherd on Mount Ida. When the nun told them he was really the son of the King of Troy, Madeleine was certain that all the girls were thinking of her.

Several days, however, went by, and no overtures were made by the Sacred Circle. Madeleine's stature was beginning to dwindle, and her hair and eyes to regain their ordinary colour, when one morning Jeanne Prunier came up to her, took hold of the little medallion that hung round her neck on a fine gold chain, and said: 'Tiens! c'est joli, ça.'

This exclamation so often interchanged among the *élite*, but which Madeleine had never dreamed that any object belonging to her could elicit, was the prelude to a period of almost unearthly bliss. She was told the gallant that each of them was in love with, was given some of Jeanne's sweet biscuits and quince jam, and was made a member of their *Dévises* Society. The *dévise* designed for her was a plant springing out of a *tabouret* (the symbol of a Duchess); one of its stems bore a violet, the other a Dutch tulip, and over them both hovered the flowery coronet of a Duke—wherein was shown a disregard for botany but an imaginative grasp of Madeleine's circumstances.

At times she felt rather condescending to her new friends, for the old man could not live much longer, and when he died she would not only be richer than any of them, but her mother's people would probably invite her to stay with them in Paris, and in time she might be made a lady-in-waiting to the Regent ... and then, suddenly, the sun would be drowned and she would feel sick, for a Saint's day was drawing near, and they would all go home, and the girls would tell their parents her story, and their parents would tell them that it was not true.

The Saint's day came in due course, and after it, the awful return to the Convent. Had they been undeceived about her or had they not? It was difficult to tell, for during the morning's work there were few opportunities for social intercourse. It was true that in the embroidery class, when Madeleine absent-mindedly gave the Virgin a red wool nose instead of a white one, and the presiding nun scolded her, the girls looked coldly at her instead of sympathetically; then in the dancing lesson as a rule the sacred ones gave her an intimate grin from time to time, or whispered a pleasantry on the clumsy performance of some companion outside the Sacred Circle, but this morning they merely stared at her coldly. Still their indifference might mean nothing. Did it, or did it not?

'Un, deux, trois,

Marquez les pas,

Faites la ré-vé-ren-ce,'

chanted the little master.

How Madeleine wished she were he, a light, artificial little creature, with no great claims on life.

But her fears became a certainty, when going into the closet where they kept their pattens and brushes, Jeanne commanded her in icy tones to take her 'dirty brush' out of her, Jeanne's, bag. And that was all. If they had been boys, uproariously contemptuous, they would have twitted Madeleine with her lie, but being girls, they merely sneered and ignored her. She felt like a spirit that, suspended in mid-air, watches the body it has left being torn to pieces by a pack of wolves. Days of dull agony followed, but she felt strangely resigned, as if she could go on bearing it for ever and a day.

It was during the Fronde, and Jeanne and her friends had a cult for Condé and Madame de Longueville, the royal rebels. They taught their parrots at home to repeat lines of Mazarinades, they kept a print of Condé at the battle of Rocroy in their book of Hours, and had pocket mirrors with his arms emblazoned on the back, while Madame de Longueville simpered at them from miniatures painted on the top of their powder boxes or the backs of their tablets. As the nuns, influenced by the clergy, were strong Royalists, and looked upon Condé as a sort of Anti-Christ, the girls had to hide their enthusiasm.

Some weeks after Madeleine's fall, it was announced that on the following Wednesday there was to be a public demonstration in favour of Condé and the Frondeurs, and that there would be fireworks in their honour, and that some of the streets would be decorated with paper lanterns.

On Wednesday Jeanne and Julie came to Madeleine and ordered her to slip out of her window at about eight o'clock in the evening, go down to the gate at the end of the avenue, and when they called her from the other side, to unbolt it for them. They then went to one of the nuns and, pleading a headache, said they would like to go to bed, and did not want any supper.

During the last weeks Madeleine had lost all spirit, all personality almost, so she followed their instructions with mechanical submission, and was at the gate at the appointed time, opened it, let them in, and all three got back to bed in safety.

About a week later, all the girls were bidden to assemble in the Refectory, where the Reverend Mother was awaiting them with a look of Rhadamanthine severity.

'Most grievous news had been given her concerning a matter that must be dealt with without delay. She would ask all the demoiselles in turn if they had left their bedrooms on Wednesday evening.'

'No, Madame.'

'No, Madame,' in voices of conscious rectitude, as one girl after another was asked by name. It was also the answer of Jeanne and Julie. Then: 'Mademoiselle Troqueville, did you leave your bedroom on Wednesday evening?'

There was a pause, and then came the answer: 'Yes, Madame.'

All eyes were turned on her, and Julie, covertly, put out her tongue.

'Mesdemoiselles, you may all go, excepting Mademoiselle Troqueville.'

Madeleine noticed that the Reverend Mother had a small mole on her cheek, she had not seen it before.

Then came such a scolding as she had never before experienced. Much mention was made of 'obedience,' 'chastity,' 'Anti-Christ,' 'the enemies of the King and the Church.' What had they to do with walking across the garden and opening a gate? Perhaps she had shown too much leg in climbing out of the window—that would, at least, account for the mention of chastity.

The Reverend Mother had asked *if any one had left their bedroom*—that was all—and Madeleine had. And to her mind, dulled, and, as is often the case, made stupidly literal by sheer terror, this fact had lost all connection with Jeanne's and Julie's escapade, and seemed, by itself, the cause of this mysterious tirade. It certainly was wrong to have left her bedroom—but why did it make her 'an enemy of the King'?

She found herself seizing on a word here and there in the torrent and spelling it backwards.

'Example' ... elpmaxe ... rather a pretty word! *la chastité* ... étitsahc al ... it sounded like Spanish ... who invented the different languages? Perhaps a prize had once been offered at a College for the invention of the best language, and one student invented French and got the prize, and another nearly got the second, but it was discovered in time that he had only turned his own language backwards, and that was cheating.... *Jésus!* there was a little bit of wood chipped out of the Reverend Mother's crucifix! But these thoughts were just a slight trembling on the surface of fathoms of inarticulate terror and despair.

Then she heard the Reverend Mother telling her that it would be a sign of grace if she were to disclose the names of her companions.

In a flash she realised that she was supposed to have done whatever it was that Jeanne and Julie had done on Wednesday evening.

'But, Madame, I didn't ... 'twas only——'

'Mademoiselle, excuses and denials will avail you nothing. Who was the other lady with you?'

'Oh, it isn't that ... there were no others, at least ... ah! I am at a loss how I can best make it clear, but we are, methinks, at cross-purposes.'

But her case was hopeless. She could not betray Jeanne and Julie, and even if she had wished to, she was incapable just then of doing so, feeling too light-headed and rudderless to make explanations. Finally she was dismissed, and walked out of the room as if in a trance.

She was greeted by a clamour of questions and reproaches from the girls. Jeanne and Julie were in hysterics. When they discovered that she had not betrayed them, they muttered some sheepish expressions of gratitude, and to save their faces they started badgering her in a half-kindly way for having got herself into trouble so unnecessarily; why could she not have said 'No' like the rest of them? Madeleine had no satisfactory answer to give, because she did not know why herself. In sudden crises it seemed as if something stepped out from behind her personality and took matters into its own hands, and spite of all her good-will it would not allow her to give a false answer to a direct question. And this although, as we have seen, she could suddenly find herself telling gratuitous falsehoods by the gross.

Of course Madeleine was in terrible disgrace, and penance was piled on penance. The Sacred Circle was friendly to her again, but this brought no comfort now, and the severe looks of the nuns put her in a perpetual agony of terror.

About a week went by, and then one day, when she was sitting in the little room of penance, the door was thrown open and in rushed Julie turned into a gurgling, sniffing whirlwind of tears.

'The Reverend Mother' ... sob ... 'says I must' ... sob ... 'ask your forgiveness' ... scream, and then she flopped down on the floor, overcome by the violence of her emotion. It was clear to Madeleine that in some miraculous way all had been discovered, but she did not feel particularly relieved. The 'movement of the passions' seemed to have been arrested in her. She sat watching Julie with her clear, wide-open eyes, and her expression was such as one might imagine on the face of an Eastern god whose function is to gaze eternally on a spectacle that never for an instant interests or moves him. She did not even feel scorn for Julie, just infinite remoteness.

Julie began nervously to shut and open one of her hands; Madeleine looked at it. It was small and plump and rather dirty, and on one of its fingers there was a little enamelled ring, too tight for it, and pressing into the flesh. It looked like a small distracted animal; Madeleine remembered a beetle she had once seen struggling on its back. Its smallness and dirtiness, and the little tight ring and its suggestion of the beetle, for some reason touched Madeleine. A sudden wave of affection and pity for Julie swept over her. In a second she was down beside her, with her arms around her, telling her not to cry, and that it didn't matter. And there she was found some minutes later by the Reverend Mother, from whom she received a panegyric of praise for her forgiving spirit and a kiss, which she could well have dispensed with.

Then the whole thing was explained; an anonymous letter had been sent to the Reverend Mother saying that the writer had seen, on the evening of the demonstration in favour of Condé, two girls masked and hooded, evidently of position, as they had attendants with them, and that they were laughing together about their escape from the Convent. The Reverend Mother had never thought of connecting with the affair Jeanne's and Julie's early retirement that evening. Now she had just got a letter from Maître Prunier informing her that it had come to his knowledge that his daughter and her great friend had been walking in the town that same evening. He had learned this distressing news from one of his servants whom Jeanne had got to accompany her on her escapade. He bade the Reverend Mother keep a stricter watch on his daughter. She had sent for Jeanne and Julie and they had told her that it was only through coercion that Madeleine had played any part in the escapade.

Then the Reverend Mother and Julie went away, and Jeanne came in to offer her apologies. She also had evidently been crying, and her mouth had a sulky droop which did not suggest that her self-complacency had shrivelled up, like that of Julie. Madeleine found herself resenting this; how *dare* she not be abject?

The two following sentences contained Jeanne's apology:—

(*a*) 'The Reverend Mother is a spiteful old dragon!' and she sniffed angrily.

(*b*) 'Will you come home for my Fête Day next month? There is to be a Collation and a Ball and a Comedy,' and she gave the little wriggle of her hips, and the complacent gesture of adjusting her collar, which were so characteristic.

A few weeks ago, this invitation would have sent Madeleine into an ecstasy of pleasure. To enter that great fantastic door had seemed a thing one only did in dreams. As Jeanne gave her invitation she saw it clearly before her, cut off from the house and the street and the trees, just itself, a finely embossed shield against the sky. It was like one of the woodcuts that she had seen in a booth of the Fair that year by a semi-barbarian called Master Albert Dürer. Woodcuts of one carrot, or a king-fisher among the reeds, or, again, a portion of the grassy bank of a high road, shown as a busy little commonwealth of bees and grasses, and frail, sturdy flowers, heedless of and unheeded by the restless stream of the high road, stationary and perfect like some obscure island of the Ægean. The world seen with the eyes of an elf or an insect ... how strange! Then she looked at Jeanne, and suddenly there flashed before her a sequence of little ignoble things she had subconsciously registered against her. She had a provincial accent and pronounced *volontiers, voulentiers*; she had a nasty habit of picking her nose; Madeleine had often witnessed her being snubbed by one of the nuns, and then blushing; there was something indecently bourgeois in the way she turned the pages of a book.

The ignoble pageant took about two seconds for its transit, then Madeleine said, 'I am much beholden to you, albeit, I fear me I cannot assist at your Fête,' and dropping her a curtsey she opened the door, making it quite clear that Jeanne was to go, which she did, without a word, as meek as a lamb.

In Madeleine's description of this scene to Jacques long afterwards she made herself say to Jeanne what actually she had only thought; many young people, often the most sensitive, hanker after the power of being crudely insolent: it seems to them witty and mature.

That night Madeleine was delirious, and Madame Troqueville was sent for. It was the beginning of a long illness which, for want of a better name, her doctor called a sharp attack of the spleen.

CHAPTER IV
THE SIN OF NARCISSUS

In time she recovered, or at least was supposed to have recovered, but she did not return to the Convent, and her mother still watched her anxiously and was more than ever inclined to give in to her in everything.

The doctor had advised her to continue taking an infusion of steel in white wine, and to persist in daily exercise, the more violent the better. So at first she would spend several hours of the day playing at shuttlecock with her mother, but Madame Troqueville's energy failing her after the first few weeks, Madeleine was forced to pursue her cure by herself.

She found the exercise led to vague dreaming of a semi-dramatic nature— imaginary arguments with a nameless opponent dimly outlined against a background of cloth of gold—arguments in which she herself was invariably victorious. In time, she discarded the shuttlecock completely, finding that this semi-mesmeric condition was reached more easily through a wild dance, rhythmic but formless.

In the meantime her social values had become more just, and she realised that rank is higher than wealth, and that she herself, as the granddaughter of a Judge of the Paris *Parlement*, and even as the daughter of a *procureur*, was of more importance socially than the daughters of merchants, however wealthy.

Round the Intendant of the province and his wife there moved a select circle, dressed in the penultimate Paris fashion, using the penultimate Paris slang, and playing for very high stakes at Hoc and Reversi. It was to this circle that Madeleine's eyes now turned with longing, as they had formerly done to the Sacred Circle at the Convent.

In time she got to know some of these Olympians. Those with whom she had the greatest success were the Précieuses, shrill, didactic ladies who by their unsuccessful imitation of their Paris models made Lyons the laughing-stock of the metropolis. Some of them would faint at the mention of a man's name; indeed, one of them, who was also a *dévote*, finding it impossible to reconcile her prudishness with the idea of a male Redeemer, started a theory that Christ had been really a woman—"'Tis clear from His clothes,' she would say—and that the beard that painters gave Him, was only part of a plot to wrest all credit from women. They spoke a queer jargon, full of odd names for the most ordinary objects and barely intelligible to the uninitiated. Madeleine talked as much like them as self-consciousness would permit. Also, she copied them in a scrupulous care of her personal appearance, and in their attention to personal cleanliness, which was considered by the world at large as ridiculous as their language. Madame Troqueville feared she would ruin her by the expensive scents—*poudre d'iris, musc, civette, eau d'ange*—with which she drenched herself.

In the meantime she had got to know a grubby, smirking old gentleman who kept a book-shop and fancied himself as a literary critic. He used to procure the most recent publications of Sercy and Quinet and the other leading Paris publishers, and his shop became a favourite resort of a throng of poetasters and young men of would-be fashion who came there to read and criticise in the manner of the Paris *muguets*. Hither also came Madeleine, and in a little room behind the shop, where she was safe from ogles and insolence, she would devour all the books that pleased and modelled the taste of the day.

Here were countless many-volumed romances, such as the *Astrée* of Honoré d'Urfé, La Calprenède's *Cassandre*, and that flower of modernity, Mademoiselle de Scudéry's *Grand Cyrus*. *Romans à clef*, they were called, for in them all the leaders of fashion, all the *bels esprits* of the day were dressed up in classical or Oriental costumes, and set to the task of fitting the fashions and fads of modern Paris into the conditions of the ancient world or of the kingdom of the Grand Turk. But the important thing in these romances was what Madeleine called to herself, with some complacency at the name, '*l'escrime galante*'—conversations in which the gallant, with an indefatigable nimbleness of wit, pays compliment after compliment to the prudishly arch belle, by whom they are parried with an equal nimbleness and perseverance. If the gallant manages to get out a declaration, then the belle is *touchée*, and in her own eyes disgraced for ever. Then, often, paragons of *esprit* and *galanterie*, and the other urbane qualities necessary to *les honnêtes gens*, give long-winded discourses on some subtle point in the psychology of lovers. And all this against a background of earthquakes and fires and hair-breadth escapes, which, together with the incredible coldness of the capricious heroine, go to prove that nothing can wither the lilies and roses of the hero's love and patience and courage. Then there were countless books of *Vers Galants*, sonnets, and madrigals by beplumed, beribboned poets, who, like pedlars of the Muses, displayed their wares in the *ruelles* and alcoves of great ladies. There were collections of letters, too, or rather, of *jeux d'esprit*, in which verse alternated with prose to twist carefully selected news into something which had the solidity of a sonnet, the grace of a madrigal. Of these letters, Madeleine was most dazzled by those of the late Vincent Voiture, Jester, and spoilt child of the famous Hôtel de Rambouillet, and through his letters she came to feel that she almost knew personally all those laughing, brilliant people, who had made the Hôtel so famous in the reign of Louis XIII.—the beautiful touchy 'Lionne,' with her lovely voice and burnished hair; the Princess Julie, suave and mocking, and, like all her family, an incorrigible tease; and the great Arthénice herself, whimsical and golden-hearted, with a humorous, half-apologetic chastity. She knew them all, and the light fantastic world in which they lived, a world of mediæval romance *pour rire*, in which magic palaces sprang up in the night, and where ordinary mortals who had been bold enough to enter were apt to be teased as relentlessly as Falstaff by the fairies of Windsor Forest.

But what Madeleine pored over most of all was the theory of all these elegant practices, embodied in species of guide-books to the polite world, filled with elaborate rules as to the right way of entering a room and of leaving it, analyses of the grades of deference or of insolence that could be expressed by a curtsey, the words which must be used and the words that must not be used, and all the other tiny things which, pieced together, would make the paradigm of an *honnête homme* or a *femme galante*. There Madeleine learned that the most heinous crime after that of being a bourgeois, was to belong to the Provinces, and the glory speedily departed from the Lyons Précieuses to descend on those of Paris. Her own surroundings seemed unbearable, and when she was not storming at the Virgin for having made her an obscure provincial, she was pestering her with prayers to transplant her miraculously to some higher sphere.

The craze for Jansenism—that Catholic Calvinism deduced from the writings of Saint Augustine by the Dutch Jansen, and made fashionable by the accomplished hermits of Port-Royal—already just perceptibly on the wane in Paris, had only recently reached Lyons. As those of Paris some years before, the haberdashers of Lyons now filled their shops with collars and garters *à la Janséniste*, and the booksellers with the charming treatises on theology by '*les Messieurs de Port-Royal.*' Many of the ladies became enamoured of the 'furiously delicious Saint Augustine,' and would have little debates, one side sustaining the view that his hair had been dark, the other that it had been fair. They raved about his Confessions, vowing that there was in it a 'Je ne sais quoi de doux et de passionné.'

Madeleine also caught the craze and in as superficial a manner as the others. For instance, the three petticoats worn by ladies which the Précieuses called '*la modeste,*' '*la friponne,*' and '*la secrète,*' she rechristened '*la grâce excitante,*' '*la grâce subséquente,*' and '*la grâce efficace.*' She gained from this quite a reputation in Lyons.

That Lent, the wife of the Intendant manœuvred that a priest of recognised Jansenist leanings should preach a sermon in the most fashionable Church of the town. He based his sermon on the Epistle for the day, which happened to be 2 Timothy, iii. 1. 'This know also, that in the last days perilous times shall come. *For men shall be lovers of their own selves.*' The whole sermon was a passionate denunciation of *amour-propre*—*self-love* according to its earliest meaning—that newly-discovered sin that was to dominate the psychology of the seventeenth century. By a certain imaginative quality in his florid rhetoric, he made his hearers feel it as a thing loathly, poisonous, parasitic. After a description of the awful loneliness of the self-lover, cut off for ever from God and man, he thundered out the following peroration:—

'Listen! This Narcissus gazing into the well of his own heart beholds, not that reflection which awaits the eyes of every true Christian, a Face with eyes like unto swords and hair as white as wool, a King's head crowned with thorns, no, what meets *his* eyes is his own sinful face. In truth, my brethren, a grievous and unseemly vision, but anon his face will cast a shadow a thousand-fold more unsightly and affrighting—to wit, the fiery eyes and foaming jowl of the Dragon himself. For to turn into a flower is but a pretty fancy of the heathen, to turn into the Dragon is the doom of the Christian Narcissus.'

Madeleine left the Church deeply moved. She had realised that *she* was such a Narcissus and that '*amour-propre*' filled every cranny of her heart.

She turned once more to the publications of Port-Royal, this time not merely in quest of new names for petticoats, and was soon a convinced Jansenist.

Jansenism makes a ready appeal to egotists ... is it not founded on the teaching of those two arch-egotists, Saint Paul and Saint Augustine? And so Madeleine found in Jansenism a spiritual pabulum much to her liking. For instance, grace comes to the Jansenist in a passion of penitence, an emotion more natural to an egotist than the falling in love with Christ which was the seal of conversion in the time of Louis XIII., with its mystical Catholicism *à l'espagnole*, touched with that rather charming *fadeur* peculiar to France. Then to the elect (among whom Madeleine never doubted she was numbered) there is something very flattering in the paradox of the Jansenists that although it is from the Redemption only that Grace flows, and Christ died for all men, yet Grace is no vulgar blessing in which all may participate, but it is reserved for those whom God has decided shall, through no merit of their own, eventually be saved.

Above all, Jansenism seemed made for Madeleine in that it promised a remedy for man's 'sick will,' a remedy which perhaps would be more efficacious than steel and white wine for the lassitude, the moral leakage, the truly 'sick will' from which she had suffered so long. The Jansenist remedy was a complete abandonment to God, 'an oarless drifting on the full sea of Grace,' and at first this brought to her a sense of very great peace.

Her favourite of the Port-Royal books was *La Fréquente Communion*, in which the Père Arnauld brought to bear on Theology in full force his great inheritance, the Arnauld legal mind, crushing to powder the treatise of a certain Jesuit priest who maintained that a Christian can benefit from the Eucharist without Penitence.

Influenced by this book, very few Jansenists felt that they had reached the state of grace necessary for making a good Communion.

So, what with self-examination, self-congratulation, and abstaining from the Eucharist, for a time Jansenism kept Madeleine as happy and occupied as a new diet keeps a *malade imaginaire*. Her emotions when she danced became more articulate. She saw herself the new abbess of Port-Royal, the wise, tender adviser of the 'Solitaires,' Mère Angélique with a beautiful humility having abdicated in her favour, 'for here is one greater than I.' She went through her farewell address to her nuns, an address of infinite beauty and pathos. She saw herself laid out still and cold in the Chapel, covered with flowers culled by royal fingers in the gardens of Fontainebleau, with the heart-broken nuns sobbing around her. Finally the real Madeleine flung herself on her bed, the tears streaming from her eyes. Her subtle enemy, *amour-propre*, had taken the veil.

She had started a diary of her spiritual life, in which she recorded the illuminations, the temptations, the failures, the reflections, the triumphs, of each day. The idea suddenly occurred to her of sending the whole to Mère Agnès Arnauld, who was head of the Paris Port-Royal. She wrote her also a letter in which she told her of certain difficulties that had troubled her in the Jansenist doctrine, suggested by the Five Propositions. These were conclusions of an heretical nature, drawn from Jansen's book and submitted to the Pope. The Jansenists denied that they were fair conclusions, but in their attempt to prove this, they certainly laid themselves open to the charge of obscurantism. She included in her letter the following *énigme* she had written on *amour-propre*, on the model of those of the Abbé Cotin, whose fertile imagination was only equalled by his fine disregard of the laws of prosody.

Je brûle, comme Narcisse, de ma propre flamme,

Quoique je n'aie pas

L'excuse des doux appas

De ce jeune conquérant des cœurs de dames.

Selon mon nom, de Vénus sort ma race;

Suis-je donc son joli fils

Qui rit parmi les roses et lys?

Moi chez qui jamais se trouve *la Grâce?*

The pun on 'Grace' seemed to her a stroke of genius. She was certain that Mère Agnès could not fail to be deeply impressed with the whole communication, and to realise that Madeleine was an instrument exquisitely tempered by God for fine, delicate work in His service. Madeleine planned beforehand the exact words of Mère Agnèse's answer:—

'Your words have illumined like a lamp for myself and my sister many a place hitherto dark.' 'My dearest child, God has a great work for you.' 'My brother says that the Holy Spirit has so illumined for you the pages of his book, that you have learned from it things he did not know were there himself,'

were a few of the sentences. In the actual letter, however, none of them occurred. Mère Agnès seemed to consider Madeleine's experiences very usual, and irritated her extremely by saying with regard to some difficulty that Madeleine had thought unutterably subtle and original:—

'Now I will say to you what I always say to my nuns when they are perplexed by that difficulty.'

The letter ended with these words of exhortation:—

'Remember that pride of intellect is the most deadly and difficult to combat of the three forms of Concupiscence, and that the pen, although it can be touched into a shining weapon of God's, is a favourite tool of the Evil One, for *amour-propre* is but too apt to seize it from behind and make it write nothing but one's own praises, and that when one would fain be writing the praises of God. Are you certain, my dear child, that this has not happened to you? Conceits and *jeux d'esprit* may sometimes without doubt be used to the Glory of God, as, for example, in the writings of the late Bishop of Geneva of thrice blessed memory. But by him they were always used as were the Parables of Our Lord, to make hard truths clear to simple minds, but you, my child, are not yet a teacher. Examine your heart as to whether there was not a little vanity in your confessions. I will urgently pray that grace may be sent you, to help you to a *true* examination of your own heart.'

In Madeleine's heart rage gave way to a dull sense of failure. She would not be a Jansenist at all if she could not be an eminent one. It was quite clear to her that her conversion had merely reinforced her *amour-propre*. What was to be done?

Jansenism had by no means destroyed her hankerings after the polite society of Paris, it had merely pushed them on to a lower shelf in her consciousness. One night she dreamed that she was walking in a garden in thrillingly close communion with the Duc de Candale. Their talk was mainly about his green garters, but in her dream it had been fraught with passionate meaning. Suddenly he turned into Julie de Rambouillet, but the emotion of the intimacy was just as poignant. This dream haunted her all the following day. Then in a flash it occurred to her that it had been sent from above as a direct answer to prayer. Obviously love for some one else was the antidote to *amour-propre*. This was immediately followed by another inspiration. Ordinary love was gradually becoming a crime in the code of the Précieuses, and '*l'amitié tendre*' the perfect virtue. But would it not be infinitely more 'gallant' and distinguished to make a *woman* the object of that friendship? It seemed to her the obvious way of keeping friendship stationary, an elegant statue in the discreet and shady groves of Plato's Academe which lies in such dangerous contiguity to the garden of Epicurus. Thus did she settle the demands at once of Jansenism and of the Précieuses.

The problem that lay before her now was to find an object for this Platonic tenderness. Julie de Rambouillet, as a wife, mother, and passionately attached daughter, could scarcely have a wide enough emotional margin to fit her for the rôle. After first choosing and then discarding various other ladies, she settled on Madeleine de Scudéry. Unmarried and beyond the age when one is likely to marry (she was over forty), evidently of a romantic temperament, very famous, she had every qualification that Madeleine could wish. Then there was the coincidence of the name, a subject for pleasant thrills. Madeleine soon worked up through her dances a blazing pseudo *flamme*. The sixth book of Cyrus, which treats of Mademoiselle de Scudéry herself, under the name of Sappho, and of her own circle, seemed full of tender messages for *her*.

'Moreover, she is faithful in her friendships; and she has a soul so tender, and a heart so passionate, that one may certainly place the supreme felicity in being loved by Sappho.'

'I conceive that beyond a doubt there is nothing so sweet as to be loved by a person that one loves.'

She pictured herself filling the rôle of Phaon, whom she had heard was but an imaginary character, Mademoiselle de Scudéry having as yet made no one a '*Citoyen de Tendre.*'

'And the most admirable thing about it was that in the midst of such a large company, Sappho did not fail to find a way of giving Phaon a thousand marks of affection, and even of sacrificing all his rivals to him, without their remarking it.'

Oh, the thrill of it! It would set Madeleine dancing for hours.

The emotions of her dances were at first but a vague foretasting of future triumphs and pleasures, shot with pictures of wavering outlines and conversations semi-articulate. But she came in time to feel a need for a scrupulous exactitude in details, as if her pictures acquired some strange value by the degree of their accuracy. What that value was, she could not have defined, but her imaginings seemed now to be moulding the future in some way, to be making events that would actually occur.... It was therefore necessary that they should be well within the bounds of probability.

This new conviction engendered a sort of loyalty to Mademoiselle de Scudéry, for previously a stray word or suggestion would fire her with the charms of some other lady, whom she would proceed to make for the time the centre of her rites—la Comtesse de la Suze, after having read her poetry, the Marquise de Sévigné, when she had heard her praised as a witty beauty— but now, with the fortitude of a Saint Anthony, she would chase the temptresses from her mind, and firmly nail her longings to Mademoiselle de Scudéry. And soon the temptation to waver left her, and Mademoiselle de Scudéry became a corroding obsession. She began to crave feverishly to go to Paris. Lyons turned into a city of Hell, where everything was a ghastly travesty of Heaven. The mock Précieuses with their grotesque graces, the vulgar dandies, so complacently unconscious of their provincialism, the meagre parade of the Promenade, it was all, she was certain, like the uncouth Paris of a nightmare. If she went to Paris, she would, of course, immediately meet Mademoiselle de Scudéry, who, on the spot, would be fatally wounded by her *esprit* and air gallant, and the following days would lead the two down a gentle slope straight to *le Pays de Tendre*. But how was she to get to Paris?

Then, as if by a miracle, her father was also seized by a longing to go to Paris, and finally a complete *déménagement* was decided upon. What wonder if Madeleine felt that the gods were upon her side?

But once in Paris, she was brought face to face with reality. It had never struck her that a meeting with Mademoiselle de Scudéry might be a thing to need manœuvring. Days, weeks, went by, and she had not yet met her. She began to realise the horror of time, as opposed to eternity. Her meeting with Mademoiselle de Scudéry could only be the result of a previous chain of events, not an isolated miracle. To fit it into an air-tight compartment of causality and time, seemed to require more volition than her 'sick will' could compass.

Then there was the maddening thought that while millions of people were dead, and millions not yet born, and millions living at the other side of the world, Mademoiselle de Scudéry was at that very moment alive, and actually living in the same town as herself, and yet she could not see her, could not speak to her. What difference was there in her life at Paris to that at Lyons?

They had settled, as we have seen, in the Quartier de l'Université, as it was cheap, and not far from the Île Notre-Dame, where Jacques and Monsieur Troqueville went every day, to the Palais de Justice. It was a quarter rich in the intellectual beauty of tradition and in the tangible beauty of lovely objects, but—it was not fashionable and therefore held no charm for Madeleine.

The things she valued were to be found in the quarters of Le Marais, of the Arsenal, of the Faubourg Saint-Honoré, of the Place Royale. She hated the Rambouillets for not begging her to live with them, she hated the people in the streets for not acclaiming her with shouts of welcome every time she appeared, she hated Mademoiselle de Scudéry for never having heard of her. Whenever she passed a tall, dark lady, she would suddenly become very self-conscious, and raising her voice, would try and say something striking in the hopes that it might be she.

She was woken every morning by the cries of the hawkers:—

'Grobets, craquelines; brides à veau, pour friands museaux!'

'Qui en veut?'

'Salade, belle Salade!'

'La douce cerise, la griotte à confire, cerises de Poitiers!'

'Amandes nouvelles, amandes douces; amendez-vous!'

And above these cries from time to time would rise the wail of an old woman carrying a basket laden with spoons and buttons and old rags,

'Vous désirez quelque cho-o-se?'

Was it Fate come to mock her?

There is no position so difficult to hold for any length of time as a logical one. Even before leaving Lyons, in Madeleine's mind the steps had become obliterated of that ruthless argument by which the Augustinian doctors lead the catechumen from the premises set down by Saint Paul to conclusions in which there is little room for hope. She struggled no longer in close mental contact—according to Jansenius's summing up of the contents of Christianity—with:—

'Hope or Concupiscence, or any of the forms of Grace; or with the price or the punishment of man, or with his beatitude or his misery; or with free-will and its enslavage; or with predestination and its effect; or with the love and justice and mercy and awfulness of God; in fact, with neither the Old nor the New Testament.'

But, without any conscious 'revaluing of values,' the kindly god of the Semi-Pelagians, a God so humble as to be grateful for the tiniest crumb of virtue offered Him by His superb and free creatures, this God was born in her soul from the mists made by expediency, habit, and the 'Passions.'

But when she had come to Paris and no miracle had happened, she began to get desperate, and Semi-Pelagianism cannot live side by side with despair. The kind Heavenly Father had vanished, and His place was taken by a purblind and indifferent deity who needed continual propitiation.

These changes in her religious attitude took place, as I have said, unconsciously, and Madeleine considered herself still a sound Jansenist.

As a consequence of this spiritual slackening, the imaginary connection had been severed between her obsession and her religion. She had forgotten that her love for Mademoiselle de Scudéry had originally been conceived as a remedy for *amour-propre*. But, about a week before the dinner at Madame Pilou's, she had come upon these lines of Voiture:—

'De louange, et d'honneur, vainement affamée,

Vous ne pouvez aimer, et voulez estre aymée.'

To her fevered imagination these innocent words hinted at some mysterious law which had ordained that the spurner of love should in his turn be spurned. She remembered that it was a commonplace in the writings of both the ancients and the moderns that it was an ironical lawgiver who had compiled the laws of destiny. And if this particular law were valid, the self-lover was on the horns of a horrible dilemma, for, while he continued in a condition of *amour-propre*, he was shut off from the love of God, but if he showed his repentance by falling in love, he was bringing on himself the appointed penalty of loving in vain. And here her morbid logic collapsed, and she thought of a very characteristic means of extricating herself. She would immediately start a love affair that it might act as a buffer between the workings of this law and her future affair with Mademoiselle de Scudéry.

It was this plan that had sent her to Jacques with the startling announcement I have already mentioned, that she loved him very much, and that he might take his fill of kissing her.

CHAPTER V
AN INVITATION

A few days after the dinner at Madame Pilou's Madeleine was dancing Mænad-like up and down her little room. Then with eyes full of a wild triumph she flung herself on her bed.

Beside her on the table lay the sixth volume of *Le Grand Cyrus*, which she had taken to using as a kind of *Sortes Virgilianæ*. She picked it up and opened it. Her eyes fell on the following words:—

'For with regard to these ladies, who take pleasure in being loved without loving; the only satisfaction which lies in store for them, is that which vanity can give them.'

She shut it impatiently and opened it again. This time, it was these words that stood out:—

'Indeed,' added she, 'I remember that my dislike came near to hatred for a passably pleasant gentlewoman——'

Madeleine crossed herself nervously, got down from her bed, and took several paces up and down the room, and then opened the book again.

'Each moment his jealousy and perturbation waxed stronger.'

Three attempts, and not one word of good omen. She had the sense of running round and round in an endless circle between the four walls of a tiny, dark cell. Through the bars she could see one or two stars, and knew that out there lay the wide, cool, wind-blown world of causality, governed by eternal laws that nothing could alter. But knowing this did not liberate her from her cell, round which she continued her aimless running till the process made her feel sick and dizzy.

She opened the book again. This time her eyes fell on words that, in relation to her case, had no sense. She looked restlessly round the room for some other means of divination. The first thing she noticed was her comb. She seized it and began counting the teeth, repeating:—

'Elle m'aime un peu, beaucoup, passionément, pas de tout.' 'Passionément' came on the last tooth. She gave a great sigh of relief; it was as if something relaxed within her.

Then the door opened, and Berthe padded in, smiling mysteriously.

'A lackey has brought Mademoiselle this letter.' Madeleine seized it. It had not been put in an envelope, but just folded and sealed. It was addressed in a very strange hand, large and illegible, to:—

Mademoiselle Troqueville,
Petite Rue du Paon,
Above the baker Paul,
At the Sign of the Cock,
Near the Collège de Bourgogne.

'He wore a brave livery,' Berthe went on, 'the cloth must have cost several *écus* the yard, and good strong shoes, but no pattens. I wouldn't let him in to stink the house, I told him——'

'Would you oblige me by leaving me alone, Berthe?' said Madeleine. Berthe chuckled and withdrew.

A letter brought to her by a lackey, and in a strange writing! Her heart stood still. It must either be from Mademoiselle de Scudéry or Madame de Rambouillet, it did not much matter which. She felt deadly sick. Everything danced before her. She longed to get into the air and run for miles—away from everything. She rushed back into her room, and locked the door. She still was unable to open the letter. Then she pulled herself together and broke the seal. Convinced that it was from Mademoiselle de Scudéry, she threw it down without reading it, and, giggling sheepishly, gave several leaps up and down the room. Then she clenched her hands, drew a deep breath, picked it up and opened it again. Though the lines danced before her like the reflection of leaves in a stream, she was able to decipher the signature. It was: 'Votre obéissante à vous faire service, M. Cornuel.' Strange to say, it was with a feeling of relief that Madeleine realised that it was not from Mademoiselle de Scudéry. She then read the letter through.

'MADEMOISELLE,—My worthy friend, Madame Pilou, has made mention of you to me. Mademoiselle de Scudéry and I intend to wait on Madame de Rambouillet at two o'clock, Thursday of next week. An you would call at a quarter to two at my Hôtel, the Marais, rue St-Antoine, three doors off from the big butcher's, opposite *Les Filles d'Elizabeth*, I shall be glad to drive you to the Hôtel de Rambouillet and present you to the Marquise.'

The Lord was indeed on her side! So easily had He brushed aside the hundreds of chances that would have prevented her first meeting

Mademoiselle de Scudéry at the Hôtel de Rambouillet, on which, as we have seen, she had set her heart.

In a flash God became once more glorious and moral—a Being that cares for the work of His hands, a maker and keeper of inscrutable but entirely beneficent laws, not merely a Daimon of superstitious worship. Then she looked at her letter again. So Madame Cornuel had not bothered to tie it round with a silk ribbon and put it in an envelope! She was seized by a helpless paroxysm of rage.

'In my answer I'll call her *Dame* Cornuel,' she muttered furiously. Then she caught sight of the Crucifix above her bed, and she was suddenly filled with terror. Was this the way to receive the great kindness of Christ in having got her the invitation? Really, it was enough to make Him spoil the whole thing in disgust. She crossed herself nervously and threw herself on her knees. At first there welled up from her heart a voiceless song of praise and love ... but this was only for a moment, then her soul dropped from its heights into the following Litany:—

'Blessed Virgin, Mother of Our Lord, make me shine on Thursday.

Guardian Angel, that watchest over me, make me shine on Thursday.

Blessed Saint Magdalene, make me shine on Thursday.

Blessed Virgin, Mother of Our Lord, give me the friendship of Mademoiselle de Scudéry.

Guardian Angel, that watchest over me, give me the friendship of Mademoiselle de Scudéry.

Blessed Saint Magdalene, give me the friendship of Mademoiselle de Scudéry.'

She gabbled this over about twenty times. Then she started a wild dance of triumphant anticipation. It was without plot, as in the old days; just a wallowing in an indefinitely glorious future. She was interrupted by her mother's voice calling her. Feeling guilty and conciliatory, as she always did when arrested in her revels, she called back:—

'I am coming, Mother,' and went into the parlour. Madame Troqueville was mending a jabot of Madeleine's. Monsieur Troqueville was sitting up primly on a chair, and Jacques was sprawling over a chest.

'My love, Berthe said a lackey brought a letter for you. We have been impatient to learn whom it was from.'

'It was from Madame Cornuel, asking me to go with her on Thursday to the Hôtel de Rambouillet.... Mademoiselle de Scudéry is to be there too.'

(Madeleine would much rather have not mentioned Mademoiselle de Scudéry at all, but she felt somehow or other that it would be 'bearing testimony' and that she *must*.)

Madame Troqueville went pink with pleasure, and Jacques's eyes shone.

'Madame de Rambouillet! The sister of Tallemant des Réaux, I suppose. Her husband makes a lot of cuckolds. Madame *Cornuel*, did you say? If she's going to meet young Rambouillet, it will be her husband that will have the *cornes*! hein, Jacques? *hein*? It will be he that has the *cornes*, won't it?' exclaimed Monsieur Troqueville, who was peculiarly impervious to emotional atmosphere, chuckling delightedly, and winking at Jacques, his primness having suddenly fallen from him. Madeleine gave a little shrug and turned to the door, but Madame Troqueville, turning to her husband, said icily:—

''Twas of the *Marquise* de Rambouillet that Madeleine spoke, no kin whatever of the family you mention. Pray, my love, tell us all about it. Which Madame Cornuel is it?'

Monsieur Troqueville went on giggling to himself, absolutely intoxicated by his own joke, and Madeleine began eagerly:—

'Oh! the famous one ... "Zénocrite" in the *Grand Cyrus*. She's an exceeding rich widow and a good friend of Mademoiselle de Scudéry. She is famed in the Court and in the Town, for her quaint and pungent wit. 'Twas she who stuck on the malcontents the name of "*les Importants*," you know, she——'

'I had some degree of intimacy with her in the past,' said Madame Troqueville, then in a would-be careless voice, 'I wonder if she has any sons!' Madeleine shut her eyes and groaned, and Jacques with his eyes dancing dragged up Monsieur Troqueville, and they left the house.

So her mother had known Madame Cornuel once; Madeleine looked round the little room. There was a large almanac, adorned, as was the custom, with a woodcut representing the most important event in the previous year. This one was of Mazarin as a Roman General with Condé and Retz as barbarian prisoners tied to his chariot; her mother had bound its edges with saffron ribbon. The chairs had been covered by her with bits of silk and brocade from the chest in which every woman of her day cherished her sacred hoard. On the walls were samplers worked by her when she had been a girl.

What was her life but a pitiful attempt to make the best of things? And Madeleine had been planning to leave her behind in this pathetically thin existence, while she herself was translated to unutterable glory. It suddenly struck her that her *amour-propre* had sinned more against her mother than any one else. She threw her arms round her neck and hugged her convulsively, then ran back to her own room, her eyes full of tears. She flung herself on her knees.

'Blessed Virgin, help me to show that I am sensible to your great care over me by being more loving and dutiful to my mother, and giving her greater assistance in the work of the house. Oh, and please let pleasant things be in store for *her also*. And oh! Blessed Lady, let me cut an exceeding brave figure on Thursday. Give me occasions for airing all the conceits I prepare beforehand. Make me look furiously beautiful and noble, and let them all think me *dans le dernier galant*, but mostly *her*. *Give me the friendship of Mademoiselle de Scudéry*.' She had not meant to add this long petition about herself, but the temptation had been too great.

And now to business. She must ensure success by being diligent in her dancing, thus helping God to get her her heart's desire.

Semi-Pelagianism does not demand the blind faith of the Jansenists. Also, it implicitly robs the Almighty of omnipotence. Thus was Madeleine a true Semi-Pelagian in endeavouring to assist God to effect her Salvation (we know she considered her Salvation inextricably bound up with the attainment of the friendship of Mademoiselle de Scudéry), for:—

'The differentia of semi-Pelagianism is the tenet that in regeneration, and all that results from it, the divine and the human will are co-operating, co-efficient (synergistic) factors.'

In the train of the shadowy figure of Madame Cornuel, Madeleine mounts the great stairs of the Hôtel de Rambouillet. The door is flung open; they enter the famous *Salle Bleue*. Lying on a couch is an elderly lady with other ladies sitting round her, at whose feet sit gallants on their outspread cloaks.

'Ah! dear Zénocrite, here you come leading our new *bergère*,' cries the lady on the couch. 'Welcome, Mademoiselle, I have been waiting with impatience to make your acquaintance.'

Madeleine curtseys and says with an indescribable mixture of modesty and pride:—

'Surely the world-famed amiability of Madame is, if I may use the expression, at war with her judgment, or rather, for two such qualities of the last excellence must ever be as united as Orestes and Pylades, some falsely flattering rumour has preceded me to the shell of Madame's ear.'

'Say rather some Zephyr, for such always precede Flora,' one of the gallants says in a low voice to another.

'But no one, I think,' continues Madeleine, 'will accuse me of flattery when I say that the dream of one day joining the pilgrims to the shrine of Madame was the fairest one ever sent me from the gates of horn.'

'Sappho, our *bergère* has evidently been initiated into other mysteries than those of the rustic Pan,' says Arthénice, smiling to Mademoiselle de Scudéry, whom Madeleine hardly dares to visualise, but feels near, a filmy figure in scanty, classic attire.

Madeleine turns to Sappho with a look at once respectful and gallant, and smiling, says:—

'That, Madame, is because being deeply read in the Sibylline Books— which is the name I have ventured to bestow on your delicious romances— I need no other initiation to *les rites galants*.'

'I fear, Mademoiselle, that if the Roman Republic had possessed only the Books that you call Sibylline, it would have been burned to the ground by the great Hannibal,' says Sappho with a smile.

'Madame, it would have been of no consequence, for the Sibyl herself would have taken captive the conqueror,' answers Madeleine gallantly.

'Ah, Sappho!' cries the Princess Julie, 'I perceive that we Nymphs are being beaten by the Shepherdess in the battle of flowers.'

'Ah, no, Madame!' Madeleine answers quickly. 'Say rather that the Shepherdess knows valleys where grow wild flowers that are not found in urban gardens, and these she ventures to twine into garlands to lay humbly at the feet of the Nymphs.' She pauses. Sappho, by half a flicker of an eyelid, shows her that she knows the garlands are all meant for her.

'But, Mademoiselle, if you will pardon my curiosity, what induced you to leave your agreeable prairies?' asks Mégabate.

'Monsieur,' answers Madeleine, smiling, 'had you asked Aristæus why he left the deserts of Libya, his answer would have been the same as mine: "There is a Greece."'

'Was not Aristæus reared by the Seasons themselves and fed upon nectar and ambrosia?' asks Sappho demurely.

'To be reared by the Seasons! What a ravishing fate!' cries one of the gallants. 'It is they alone who can give the *real* roses and lilies, which blossom so sweetly on the cheeks of Mademoiselle.'

'Monsieur, one of the Seasons themselves brings the refutation of your words. For Lady Winter brings ... *la glace*,' says Madeleine, with a look of delicious raillery.

'But, indeed,' she continues, 'I must frankly admit that my distaste for Bœotia (for that is what I call the Provinces!) is as great as that felt for pastoral life by Alcippe and Amaryllis in the *Astrée*. There is liberty in the prairies, you may say, but any one who has read of the magic palaces of Armide or Alcine in *Amadis de Gaule*, would, rather than enjoy all the liberty of all the sons of Boreas, be one of the *blondines* imprisoned in the palace of the present day Armide,' and she bows to Arthénice.

'I do not care for *Amadis de Gaule*,' says Sappho a little haughtily. Madeleine thrills with indescribable triumph. Can it be possible that Sappho is jealous of the compliment paid to Arthénice?

CHAPTER VI
THE GRECIAN PROTOTYPE

During the days that followed, Madeleine wallowed in Semi-Pelagianism. With grateful adoration, she worshipped the indulgent God, who had hung upon a Cross that everything she asked might be given her.

As a result of this new-found spiritual peace, she became much more friendly and approachable at home. She even listened with indulgence to her father's egotistical crudities, and to her mother's hopes of her scoring a great success on the following Wednesday when the Troguins were giving a ball. Seeing that her imprisonment in the bourgeois world of pale reflections was so nearly over, and that she would so soon be liberated to the plane of Platonic ideas and face to face with the *real* Galanterie, the *real* Esprit, the *real* Fashion, she could afford a little tolerance.

Then, in accordance with her promise to the Virgin, she insisted on helping her mother in the work of the house. Madame Troqueville would perhaps be sewing, Madeleine would come up to her and say in a voice of resigned determination: 'Mother, if you will but give me precise instructions what to do, I will relieve you of this business.' Then, having wrested it from her unwilling mother, she would leave it half finished and run off to dance—feeling she had discharged her conscience. The virtue did not lie in a thing accomplished, but in doing something disagreeable—however useless. The boredom of using her hands was so acute as to be almost physical pain. It was as if the fine unbroken piece of eternity in which her dreams took place turned into a swarm of little separate moments, with rough, prickly coats that tickled her in her most tender parts. The prickly coats suggested thorns, and—the metaphor breaking off, as it were, into a separate existence of its own—she remembered that in the old story of her childhood, it was thorns that had guarded the palace of the hidden Princess. This association of ideas seemed full of promise and encouraged her to persevere.

Many were the winks and leers of Berthe over this new domesticity, which she chose to interpret in a manner Madeleine considered unspeakably vulgar. 'Ho! Ho!' ... wink ... 'Mademoiselle is studying to be a housewife! Monsieur Jacques will be well pleased.' And when Madeleine offered to help her wash some jabots and fichus, she said, with a mysterious leer, that she was reminded of a story of her grandmother's about a girl called Nausicaa, but when Madeleine asked to be told the story, she would only chuckle mysteriously.

One evening she made a discovery that turned her hopes into certainty.

After supper, she had given Jacques a signal to follow her to her own room. It was not that she wanted his society, but it was incumbent on her to convince the gods that she loved him. She sat down on his knee and caressed him. He said suddenly:—

'I could scarce keep from laughing at supper when my uncle was descanting on his diverse legal activities and reciting the fine compliments paid him by judges and advocates by the score! *Malepest!* So you do not drive him to a nonplus with too close questionings, but let him unmolested utter all his conceit, why then his lies will give you such entertainment as——'

'Have a care what you say, Jacques,' she cried, 'I'll not have my father called a liar. It may be that he paints the truth in somewhat gaudy colours, but all said, 'tis a good-natured man, and I am grateful to him in that being exercised as to the material welfare of my mother and myself, he came to Paris to better our fortunes. Jacques! Have done with your foolish laughter!'

But Jacques continued cackling with shrill, mocking glee.

'My aunt's and your material welfare, forsooth! This is most excellent diversion! If you but knew the true cause of his leaving Lyons! If you but knew!'

'Well, tell me.'

'That I will not, sweet Chop! Oh, 'tis a most fantastic nympholeptic! As passionate after dreams as is his daughter.'

'I am to seek as to your meaning, Jacques,' said Madeleine very coldly, and she slipped down from his knee.

Jacques went on chuckling to himself: 'To see him standing there, nonplussed, and stammering, and most exquisitely amorous.

'Lingua sed torpet, tenuis sub artus

Flamma demanat, sonitu suopte

Tintinant aures, gemina teguntur

Lumina nocte.'

'What's that you are declaiming, Jacques?'

'Some lines of the Grecian Sappho, turned into Latin by Catullus, that figure, with an exquisite precision, the commingling in a lover of passion and of bashfulness.'

The look of cold aloofness suddenly vanished from Madeleine's face.

'The Grecian Sappho!' she cried eagerly. 'She is but a name to me. Tell me of her.'

'She was a poetess. She penned amorous odes to diverse damsels, and then leapt into the sea,' he answered laconically, looking at her with rather a hostile light in his bright eyes.

'Repeat me one of her odes,' she commanded, and Jacques began in a level voice:—

'Deathless Dame Venus of the damasked throne, daughter of Jove, weaver of wiles, I beseech thee tame not my soul with frets and weariness, but if ever in time past thou heard'st and hearkened to my cry, come hither to me now. For having yoked thy chariot of gold thou did'st leave thy father's house and fair, swift swans, with ceaseless whirring of wings over the sable earth did carry thee from heaven through the midmost ether. Swift was their coming, and thou, oh, blessed one, a smile upon thy deathless face, did'st ask the nature of my present pain, and to what new end I had invoked thee, and what, once more, my frenzied soul was fain should come to pass.

'"Who is she now that thou would'st fain have Peitho lead to thy desire? Who, Sappho, does thee wrong? *For who flees, she shall pursue; who spurns gifts, she shall offer them; who loves not, willy-nilly she shall love.*"

'Now, even now, come to me! Lift from me the weight of hungry dreams, consummate whatever things my soul desires, and do thou thyself fight by my side.'

He looked at her, his eyes screwed up into two hard, bright points. Madeleine continued to gaze in front of her—silent and impassive.

'Well, is it to your liking?' he asked.

'What?' she cried with a start, as if she had been awakened from a trance. 'Is it to my liking? I can scarcely say. To my mind 'tis ... er ... er to speak ingenuously, somewhat blunt and crude, and lacking in *galanterie*.'

He broke into a peal of gay laughter, the hostile look completely vanished.

'*Galanterie*, forsooth! Oh, Chop, you are a rare creature! Hark'ee, in the "smithy of Vulcan," as you would say, weapons are being forged of the good iron of France—battle-axes *à la Rabelais*, and swords *à la Montaigne*—and they will not tarry to smash up your fragile world of *galanterie* and galimatias into a thousand fragments.'

Madeleine in answer merely gave an abstracted smile.

Madame Troqueville came in soon afterwards to turn out Jacques and order Madeleine to bed. Madeleine could see that she wanted to talk about the Troguin's ball, but she was in no mood for idle conjectures, and begged her to leave her to herself.

As soon as she was alone she flung herself on her knees and offered up a prayer of solemn triumphant gratitude. That of her own accord she should have come to the conclusion reached centuries ago by the Paris Sappho's namesake—that the perfect *amitié tendre* can exist only between two women—was a coincidence so strange, so striking, as to leave no doubt in her mind that her friendship with Mademoiselle de Scudéry was part of the ancient, unalterable design of the universe. Knowing this, how the Good Shepherd must have laughed at her lack of faith!

CHAPTER VII
THE MERCHANTS OF DAMASCUS AND DAN

Madeleine woke up the following morning to the sense of a most precious new possession.

She got out of bed, and, after having first rubbed her face and hands with a rag soaked in spirit, was splashing them in a minute basin of water—her thoughts the while in Lesbos—when the door opened and in walked Madame Troqueville.

'*Jésus!* Madeleine, it *cannot* be that you are *again* at your washing!' she cried in a voice vibrant with emotion. 'Why, as I live, 'twas but yesterday you did it last. Say what you will, it will work havoc with your sight and your complexion. I hold as naught in this matter the precepts of your Précieuses. You need to sponge yourself but once a week to keep yourself fresh and sweet, a skin as fine and delicate as yours——'

But Madeleine, trembling with irritation that her mother should break into her pleasant reverie with such prosaic and fallacious precepts, cried out with almost tearful rage: 'Oh, mother, let me be! What you say is in the last of ignobility; 'tis the custom of all *honnêtes gens* to wash their hands and face *each day*.... I'll not, not, *not* be a stinking bourgeoise!'

It was curious how shrill and shrewish these two outwardly still and composed beings were apt to become when in each other's company.

Madame Troqueville shrugged her shoulders: 'Well, if you won't be ruled! But let that go—I came to say that we should do well to go to the Foire Saint-Germain this morning to provide you with some bravery for the Troguin's ball——'

'The Troguin's ball, forsooth! Ever harping on that same string! Are you aware *that I am for the Hôtel de Rambouillet* on Thursday? That surely is a more staid and convenient event on which to hang your hopes!'

'Is it?' said Madame Troqueville, with a little smile. 'Well, what shall you wear on that most pregnant day? Your flowered ferrandine petticoat and your crimson sarge bodice?'

Madeleine went rather pale; she rapped out in icy tones: '*Les honnêtes gens* pronounce it *serge*. Leave me, please ... I have the caprice to dress myself unaided this morning.'

Once alone, Madeleine flung herself on her bed, clutched her head in her hands and gave little, short, sharp moans.

The truth of the matter was this—that when, in her dances, she rehearsed her visit to the Hôtel de Rambouillet, she pictured herself dressed in a very *décolleté* bodice of *céladon* velvet sparkling with jewels and shrouded in priceless Italian lace, a petticoat of taffetas dotted with countless knots of ribbon, and green silk stockings with rose-coloured clocks. Until this moment, when her mother, with her irritating sense of reality, had brought her face to face with facts, it had never so much as occurred to her that nothing of this bravery existed outside her own imagination. Yes, it was true! a serge bodice and a ferrandine petticoat were all the finery her wardrobe could provide. Was she then to make her début at the Palace of Arthénice as a dingy little bourgeoise? What brooked the Grecian Sappho and her conceits, what brooked the miraculous nature of Madame Cornuel's invitation if the masque of reality was to lack the 'ouches and spangs' of dreams? Well, God had made the path of events lead straight to Mademoiselle de Scudéry, could He not too turn her mother's purse into that of Fortunatus? She could but go to the Fair—and await a miracle.

As they made their way along the bank of the Seine, Madame Troqueville was wrapt in pleasant reverie. None of the wealthy young bourgeoises at the ball would look as delicate and fine as her Madeleine ... what if she took the fancy of some agreeable young magistrate, with five or six different posts in the *Parlement*, and a flat, red house with white facings in the Place Dauphine, like the Troguins? Then he would 'give the Fiddles' for a ball, and offer Madeleine a bouquet in token that it was in her honour, then Madeleine would 'give the Fiddles' for a return ball.... The Troguins would lend their house ... and then ... why not? stranger things had happened.

'A fragment of Lyons silk ... some *bisette* and some *camelot de Hollande* ... a pair of shoes that you may foot it neatly ... yes, you will look rare and delicate, and 'twill go hard but one gold coin will furnish us with all we need.'

Madeleine smiled grimly—unless she were much mistaken, not even one *silver* coin would be squandered on the Troguins's ball.

They were now making their way towards two long rows of wooden buildings in which was held the famous Fair.

In the evenings it was a favourite haunt of beauty and fashion, but in the mornings it was noisy with all the riff-raff of the town—country cousins lustily bawling 'Stop, thief!'; impudent pages; coarse-tongued musketeers; merchant's wives with brazen tongues and sharp, ruthless elbows; dazzled Provincials treating third-rate courtesans to glasses of *aigre de cèdre* and the delicious cakes for which the Fair was famous.

Through this ruthless, plangent, stinking crowd, Madame Troqueville and Madeleine pushed their way, with compressed lips and faces pale with disgust.

Of a sudden, their ears were caught by the cry:—

'Galants pour les dames! Faveurs pour les galants! Rubans d'écarlate, de cramoisie, et de Cé-la-don!'

It came from a little man of Oriental appearance, sitting at a stall that contained nothing but knots of ribbon of every colour, known as *galants*.

When he caught sight of Madeleine, he waved before her one of pale green.

'A *céladon galant* for the young lady—a figure of the perfect lover,' he called out. 'Mademoiselle cannot choose but buy it!' Céladon, the perfect lover, in the famous romance called *Astrée*, had given his name to a certain shade of green.

Madeleine, thinking the words of good omen, pinched her mother's arm and said she *must* have it. After a good deal of bargaining, they got it for more than Madame Troqueville had intended spending on a pair of shoes, and with a wry little smile, she said:—

'Enough of these childish toys! Let us now to more serious business,' and once more began to push her way through the hateful, seething crowd.

Suddenly, Madeleine again pinched her mother's arm, and bade her stop. They were passing the stall of a mercer—a little man with black, beady eyes, leering at them roguishly from among his delicate merchandise.

'Here is most rare Italian lace,' said Madeleine, with a catch in her voice.

'Ay, here, for example, is a piece of *point de Gênes* of most exquisite design,' broke in the mercer's wife—an elegant lady, with a beautifully dressed head of hair, 'I sold just such a piece, a week come Thursday, to the Duchesse de Liancourt.'

'Ah! but if one be fair and young and juicy 'tis the transparent *point de Venise* that is best accordant with one's humour,' interrupted the mercer, with a wink at Madeleine. ''Tis the *point de Venise* that discovers the breasts, Mademoiselle! Which, being so, I vow the names should be reversed, and the *transparent* fabric be called *point de Gênes*, hein? *Point de gêne!*' and he gleefully chuckled over his own wit, while his wife gave him a good-natured push and told him with a grin not to be a fool.

'Whatever laces you may stock, good sir, no one can with truth affirm that you have—*point d'Esprit*,' said Madeleine graciously.

'Come, my child!' said Madame Troqueville, with a smile, and prepared to move away. This put the mercer on his mettle.

'Ladies, you would be well advised to tarry a while with me!' he cried, in the tones of a disinterested adviser. 'Decked in these delicate toys you would presently learn how little serves, with the help of art, to adorn a great deal. Let a lady be of any form or any quality, after a visit to my stall she'd look a Marquise!'

'Nay, say rather that she'd look a Duchesse,' amended his wife.

'Come, my child!' said Madame Troqueville again.

'Nay, lady, there is good sense in what I say!' pleaded the mercer, 'the very pith of modishness is in my stall. A *galant* of gay ribbons, and a fichu of fine point—such as this one, for example—in fact the trifling congeries which in the dress of *gallants* is known as "*petite oie*" will lend to the sorriest *sarge* the lustre of velvet!'

Madeleine's eyes were blazing with excitement. God had come to her rescue once again, and forgoing, with the economy of the true artist, the meretricious aid of a material miracle, had solved her problem in the simplest manner by the agency of this little mercer. To cut a brave figure on Thursday, there was no need of Fortunatus's purse. Her eyes had been opened. Of course, as in manners, so in dress, the days of solidity were over. Who now admired the heavy courtesy of the school of the Admiral de Bassompière in comparison with the careless, mocking grace of the *air galant*? In the same way, she, twirling a little cane in her hand, motley with ribbons, her serge bodice trimmed with the *pierreries du Temple* (of which, by the way, more anon), with some delicate trifles from the mercer's stall giving a finish to the whole, could with a free mind, allow three-piled velvet and strangely damasked silk to feed the moths in the brass-bound, leather chests that slumber in châteaux, far away mid the drowsy foison of France.

With strange, suppressed passion, she pleaded with her mother, first, for a Holland handkerchief, edged with Brussels lace, and caught up at the four corners by orange-coloured ribbon; then for a pair of scented gloves, also hung with ribbons; then for a bag of rich embroidery for carrying her money and her Book of Hours. And Madame Troqueville, under the spell of Madeleine's intense desire, silently paid for one after another.

They left the mercer's stall, having spent three times over the coin that Madame Troqueville had dedicated to the Troguins's ball. Suddenly, she realised what had happened, and cried out in despair:—

'I have done a most inconsiderate, rash, weak thing! How came it that I countenanced such shameless, such fantastic prodigality? I fear——'

'Mother, by that same prodigality I have purchased my happiness,' said Madeleine solemnly.

'Oh, my foolish love! 'Tis only children that find their happiness in toys,' and her mother laughed, in spite of herself. 'Well, our purse will not now rise above a piece of ferrandine. We must see what we can contrive.'

They walked on, Madeleine in an ecstasy of happiness—last night, the Grecian Sappho, this morning, God's wise messenger, the mercer—the Lord was indeed on her side!

They were passing the stall of a silk merchant. He was a tight-lipped, austere-looking old man, and he was listening to an elderly bourgeoise, whose expression was even more severe than his own. The smouldering fire in her eye and the harsh significance of her voice, touched their imagination, and they stopped to listen.

'Ay, as the Prophet tells us, the merchants of Damascus and Dan and Arabia brought in singing ships to the fairs of Tyre, purple, and broidered work, and fine linen, and coral, and agate, and blue clothes in chests of rich apparel, bound with cords and made of cedar. And where now is Tyre, Master Petit?'

'Tyre, with its riches and its fairs, and its merchandise and its mariners fell into the midst of the seas in the day of its ruin,' solemnly chanted in reply Master Petit. Evidently neither he nor the lady considered the words to have any application either to himself or to the costly fabrics in which he was pleased to traffic.

'Vanity of vanities! 'Tis a lewd and sinful age,' said the lady, with gloomy satisfaction, 'I know one old vain, foolish fellow who keeps in my attic a suit of tawdry finery in which to visit bawdy-houses, as if, forsooth, all the purple and fine linen of Solomon himself could add an ounce of comeliness to his antic, foolish face! He would be better advised to lay up the white garment of salvation with sprigs of the lavender of grace, in a coffer of solid gold, where neither moth nor rust doth corrupt, and where thieves do not break through and steal. I do oft-times say to him: "Monsieur Troqueville——"'

'Come, my child,' said Madame Troqueville quietly, moving away.

So this was what Jacques had meant by his mysterious hints the night before! Madeleine followed her mother with a slight shudder.

CHAPTER VIII
'RITE DE PASSAGE'

At about six o'clock on Wednesday evening a hired coach came to take them to the Troguin's. To a casual eye it presented a gorgeous appearance of lumbering gilt, but Madeleine noticed the absence of curtains, the straw leaking out of the coachman's cushion, and the jaded, shabby horses. Jacques had arranged that a band of his devoted clerks of *la Bazoche*, armed with clubs, should follow the coach to the Île Notre Dame, for the streets of Paris were infested by thieves and assassins, and it did not do to be out after dusk unarmed and unattended. On ordinary occasions this grotesque parody of the state of a Grand Seigneur—a hired coach, and grinning hobbledehoys instead of lackeys, strutting it, half proud, half sheepish, in their quaint blue and yellow livery—would have nearly killed Madeleine with mortification. To-night it rather pleased her, as a piquant contrast to what was in store for her to-morrow and onwards. For were not *all* doors to open to her to-morrow—the doors of the Hôtel de Rambouillet, the doors of the whole fashionable world, as well as the doors of Mademoiselle de Scudéry's heart? The magical *petite-oie*, hidden away in her drawer at home, and the miraculous manner in which her eyes had been opened to its efficacy were certain earnests of success. The whole universe was ablaze with good omens—to-morrow 'the weight of hungry dreams' would drop from her, and her soul would get what it desired.

She found herself remembering with some perplexity that in romances the siege of a lady's heart was a very long affair. Perhaps the instantaneous yielding of the fortress, which she felt certain would be the case with Mademoiselle de Scudéry when they met, was not quite in the best traditions of *Galanterie*. It was annoying, but inevitable, for she felt that any further delay would kill her.

The Troguins lived in the new, red-brick triangle of houses called la Place Dauphine, facing the bronze statue of Henri IV., and backed by Notre-Dame.

Lackeys holding torches were standing on the steps of their house, that the guests might have no trouble in finding it.

After having taken off their cloaks and pattens, the Troquevilles went into the ball-room. Here were countless belles and gallants, dressed in white, carnation, and sea-water green, which, on the authority of a very grave writer, we know to be the colours that show best by candle-light. Here and there this delicate mass of colour was freaked with the sombre *soutanes* of magistrates and the black silk of dowagers. The Four Fiddles could be heard tuning up through the hubbub of mutual compliments. Madeleine felt as if she were gazing at it all from some distant planet. Then Madame Troguin bustled up to them.

'Good-evening, friends, you are exceeding welcome. You must all have a glass of Hippocras to warm you. It operates so sweetly on the stomach. I am wont to say a glass of Hippocras is better than any purge. I said as much to Maître Patin—our doctor, you know—and he said——'

Madeleine heard no more, for she suddenly caught sight of her father's shining, eager eyes and anxious smile, 'his vanity itching for praise,' she said to herself scornfully. She saw him make his way to where the youngest Troguin girl was sitting on a *pliant* with several young men on their cloaks at her feet. How could he be such an idiot, Madeleine wondered, he *must* know that the Troguin girl did not want to talk to *him* just then. But there he stood, hawking and spitting and smirking. Now he was sitting down on a *pliant* beside her ... how angry the young men were looking ... Madeleine was almost certain she saw the Troguin girl exchange a look of despair with one of them. Now, from his arch gesture, she could see that he was praising the outline of her breasts and regretting the jabot that hid them.... *Jésus!* his provinciality! it was at least ten years ago since it had been fashionable to praise a lady's breasts! So her thoughts ran on, while every moment she felt more irritated.

Then the fiddles struck up the air of 'Sur le pont d'Avignon,' and the whole company formed up into circles for the opening *Branle*.

There was her father, grimacing and leaping like a baboon in a nightmare, grave magistrates capering like foals, and giving smacking kisses to their youthful partners, young burghers shouting the words at the top of their voices. The whole scene seemed to Madeleine to grow every minute more unreal.

Then the fiddles stopped and the circles broke up into laughing, breathless groups. A young bourgeois, beplumed and beribboned, and wearing absurd thick shoes, came up to her, and taking off his great hat by the crown, instead of, in the manner of '*les honnêtes gens*,' by the brim, made her a clumsy bow. He began to '*galantise*' her. Madeleine wondered if he had learned the art from the elephant at a fair. She fixed him with her great, still eyes. Then she found herself forced to lead him out to dance a *Pavane*. The fiddles were playing a faint, lonely tune, full of the sadness of light things bound to a ponderous earth, for these were the days before Lulli had made dance tunes gay. The beautiful pageant had begun—the *Pavane*, proud and preposterous as a peacock or a Spaniard. Then some old ladies sitting round the room began in thin, cracked voices to sing according to a bygone fashion, the words of the dance:—

'Approche donc, ma belle,

Approche-toi, mon bien;

Ne me sois plus rebelle,

Puisque mon cœur est tien;

Pour mon âme apaiser,

Donne mois un baiser.'

They beat time with their fans, and their eyes filled with tears. Gradually the song was taken up by the whole room, the words rising up strong and triumphant:—

'Approche donc, ma belle,

Approche-toi, mon bien————'

Madeleine's lips were parted into a little smile, and her spellbound eyes filled with tears; then she saw Jacques looking at her and his eyes were bright and mocking. She blushed furiously.

'He is like Hylas, the mocking shepherd in the *Astrée*,' she told herself. 'Hylas, hélas, Hylas, hélas,' she found herself muttering.

After another pause for *Galanterie* and preserved fruits, the violins broke into the slow, voluptuous rhythm of the Saraband. The old ladies again beat time with their fans, muttering 'vraiment cela donne à rêver.'

Madeleine danced with Jacques and he never took his eyes from her face, but hers were fixed and glassy, and the words of the Sapphic Ode, 'that man seems to me the equal of the gods' ... clothed itself, as with a garment, with the melody.

She was awakened from her reverie by feeling Jacques's grasp suddenly tighten on her hand. She looked at him, he was white and scowling. A ripple of interest was passing over the dancers, and all eyes were turned to the door. Two or three young courtiers had just come in, attracted by the sound of the fiddles. For in those days courtiers claimed a vested right to lounge uninvited into any bourgeois ball, and they were always sure of an obsequious welcome.

There was the Président Troguin puffily bowing to them, and the Présidente bobbing and smirking and offering refreshment. Young Brillon, the giver of the fiddles, had left his partner, Marguerite Troguin, and was standing awkwardly half-way to the door, unable to make up his mind whether he should doff his hat to the courtiers before they doffed theirs to him; but they rudely ignored all three, and, swaggering up to the fiddles, bade them stop playing.

'*Foi de gentilhomme*, I vow that it is of the last consequence that this Saraband should die. It is really ubiquitous,' lisped one of them, a little *muguet*, with a babyish face.

'It must be sent to America with the Prostitutes,' said another.

'That is furiously well turned, Vicomte. Really it deserves to be put to the torture.'

'Yes, because it is a danger to the kingdom, it debases the coinage.'

'Why?'

'Because it generates tender emotions in so many vulgar bosoms turning thus the fine gold of Cupid into a base alloy!'

'Bravo! Comte, tu as de l'esprit infiniment.'

During this bout of wit, the company had been quite silent, trying hard to look amused, and in the picture.

'My friends, would you oblige us with the air of a *Corante*?' the Vicomte called out with a familiar wink to the 'Four Fiddles,' with whom it behoved every fashionable gallant to be on intimate terms. The 'Fiddles' with an answering wink, started the tune of this new and most fashionable dance.

'Ah! I breathe again!' cried the little Marquis. They then proceeded to choose various ladies as partners, discussing their points, as if they had been horses at a Fair. The one they called Comte, a tall, military looking man, chose Marguerite Troguin, at which Brillon tried to assert himself by blustering out that the lady was *his* partner. But the Comte only looked him up and down, with an expression of unutterable disgust, and turning to the Marquis, asked: 'What *is* this *thing*?' Brillon subsided.

Then they started the absurd *Corante*. The jumping steps were performed on tip-toe, and punctuated by countless bows and curtseys. There was a large audience, as very few of the company had yet learned it. When it was over, it was greeted with enthusiastic applause.

The courtiers proceeded to refresh themselves with Hippocras and lemonade. Suddenly the little Marquis seized the cloak of the Comte, and piped out in an excited voice:—

'Look, Comte, over there ... I swear it is our old friend, the ghost of the fashion of 1640!'

'It is, it is, it's the black shadow of the white Ariane! The *crotesque* and importunate gallant!' They made a dash for Monsieur Troqueville, who was trying hard to look unconscious, and leaping round him beset him with a volley of somewhat questionable jests. All eyes were turned on him, eyebrows were raised, questioning glances were exchanged. Madame Troqueville sat quite motionless, gazing in front of her, determined not to hear what they were saying. She would *not* be forced to see things too closely.

When they had finished with Monsieur Troqueville, they bowed to the Présidente, studiously avoiding the rest of the company in their salutation, and, according to their picture of themselves, minced or swaggered out of the room. Jacques followed them.

This interlude had shaken Madeleine out of her vastly agreeable dreams. The *muguets* had made her feel unfinished and angular, and they had not even asked her to dance. Then, their treatment of her father had been a sharp reminder that after all she was by birth nothing but a contemptible bourgeoise. But as the evening's gaiety gradually readjusted itself, so did her picture of herself, and by the time of the final *Branle*, she was once more drunk with vanity and hope.

The Troguins sent them back in their own coach, and the drive through the fantastic Paris of the night accentuated Madeleine's sense of being in a dream. There passed them from time to time troops of tipsy gallants, their faces distorted by the flickering lights of torches, and here and there the *lanternes vives* of the pastry-cooks—brilliantly-lighted lanterns round whose sides, painted in gay colours, danced a string of grimacing beasts, geese, and apes, and hares and elephants—showed bright and strange against the darkness.

Then the words:—

La joie! la joie! Voilà des oublies! echoed melancholy in the distance. It was the cry of the *Oublieux*, the sellers of wafers and the nightingales of seventeenth century Paris, for they never began to cry their wares before dusk.

La joie! la joie! Voilà des oublies!

Oublie, oublier! The second time that evening there came into Madeleine's head a play on words.

La joie! la joie! Voilà des oublies! Could it be that the secret of *la joie* was nothing but this dream-sense and—*l'oubli?*

They found Jacques waiting for them, pale but happy. He would not tell them why he had left the ball-room, but he followed Madeleine to her room. He was limping. And then, with eyes bright with triumph, he described how, at their exit from the ball-room, he had rallied the *Clercs* of the *Bazoche* (they had stayed to play cards with the Troguin's household), how they had followed the courtiers, and, taking them by surprise, had given them the soundest cudgelling they had probably ever had in their lives. 'Though they put up a good fight!' and he laughed ruefully and rubbed his leg.

'How came it that they knew my father?' Madeleine asked. Jacques grinned.

'Oh, Chop, should I tell you, it would savour of the blab ... yet, all said, I would not have you lose so good a diversion ... were I to tell you, you would keep my counsel?'

'Yes.'

Then he proceeded to tell her that her father had fallen in love in Lyons with a courtesan called Ariane. She had left Lyons to drive her trade in Paris, and that was the true cause of his sudden desire to do the same. On reaching Paris, his first act was to buy from the stage wardrobe of the Hôtel de Bourgogne, an ancient suit of tawdry finery, which long ago had turned a courtier into the Spirit of Spring in a Royal Ballet. This he had hidden away in the attic of an old Huguenot widow who kept a tavern on the Mont Sainte-Geneviève, and had proceeded to pester Ariane with letters and doggerel imploring an interview—but in vain! Finally, he had taken his courage in both hands, and donning his finery—'which he held to have the virtue of the cestus of Venus!' laughed Jacques—he had boldly marched into Ariane's bedroom, only to be received by a flood of insults and ridicule by that lady and her gallants.

Madeleine listened with a pale, set face. Why had she been so pursued these last few days by her father's sordid *amours*?

'So this ... Ariane ... rejected my father's suit?' she said in a low voice.

'Ay, that she did! How should she not?' laughed Jacques.

'And you gave your suffrage to the foolish enterprise?'

Jacques looked rather sheepish.

'I am not of the stuff that can withstand so tempting a diversion—why, 'twill be a jest to posterity! His eager, foolish, obsequious face; *and* his tire! I'faith, I would not have missed it for a kingdom!' and he tossed back his head and laughed delightedly.

Hylas, *hélas*!... Jacques was limping ... Vulcan was lame, wasn't he? 'In the smithy of Vulcan weapons are being forged that will smash up your world of *galanterie* and galamatias into a thousand fragments!'

'Why, Chop, you look sadly!' he cried, with sudden contrition. ''Tis finished and done with, and these coxcombs' impudence bred them, I can vouch for it, a score of bruises apiece! Chop, come here! Why, the most modish and *galant* folk have oftentimes had the strangest *visionnaires* for fathers. There is Madame de Chevreuse—who has not heard of the *naïvetés* and *visions* of her father? And 'twas a strange madman that begot the King himself!' he said, thinking to have found where the shoe pinched. But Madeleine remained silent and unresponsive, and he left her.

Yes, why had she been so pursued these last few days by her father's *amours*? It was strange that love should have brought him too from Lyons! And he too had set his faith on the magical properties of bravery! What if.... Then there swept over her the memory of the Grecian Sappho, driving a host of nameless fears back into the crannies of her mind. Besides—*to-morrow* began the new era!

She smiled ecstatically, and, tired though she was, broke into a triumphant dance.

CHAPTER IX
AT THE HÔTEL DE RAMBOUILLET

When Madeleine awoke next morning, the feeling she had had over night of being in a dream had by no means left her.

From the street rose the cries of the hawkers:—

'Ma belle herbe, anis fleur.'

'A la fraîche, à la fraîche, qui veut boire?'

'A ma belle poivée à mes beaux épinards! à mon bel oignon!'

And then shrill and plaintive:—

'Vous désirez quelque cho-o-o-se?'

It was no longer a taunt but the prayer of a humble familiar asking for its mistress's orders, or, rather, of Love the Pedlar waiting to sell her what she chose. She opened her window and looked out. The length of the narrow street the monstrous signs stuck out from either side, heraldic lions, and sacred hearts, and blue cats, and mothers of God, and *Maréchales* looking like Polichinelle. It was as incongruous an assortment as the signs of the Zodiac, as flat and fantastic as a pack of cards——

'*Vous désirez quelque cho-o-ose?*' She laughed aloud. Then she suddenly remembered her vague misgivings of the night before. She drew in her head and rushed to her divination book. These were the lines her eyes fell upon:—

' ... and she seemed in his mind to have said a thousand good things, which, in reality, she had not said at all.'

For one moment Madeleine's heart seemed to stop beating. Did it mean that she was not going to get in her prepared mots? No, the true interpretation was surely that Mademoiselle de Scudéry would think her even more brilliant than she actually was. She fell on her knees and thanked her kind gods in anticipation.

However, she too must do her part, must reinforce the Power behind her, so over and over again she danced out the scene at the Hôtel de Rambouillet, trying to keep it exactly the same each time. '*Ah! dear Zénocrite! here you come, leading our new Bergère.*'

All the morning she seemed in a dream, and her mother, father, Jacques, and Berthe hundreds of miles away. She could not touch a morsel of food. 'Ah! the little creature with wings. I know, I know,' Berthe kept muttering.

With her throat parched, and still in a strange, dry dream, she went to dress. The magical *petite-oie* seemed to her to take away all shabbiness from the serge bodice and the petticoat of *camelot de Hollande*. Then, in a flash, she remembered she had decided to add to her purchases at the Fair a trimming of those wonderful imitation jewels known as the *pierreries du Temple*. The *petite-oie* had taken on the exigency of a magic formulary, and its contents, to be efficacious, had to conform as rigidly to the original conception as a love-potion must to its receipt. In a few minutes she would have to start, and the man who sold the stones lived too far from Madame Cornuel for her to go there first. She was in despair.

At that moment the door opened, and in walked Jacques; as a rule he did not come home till evening. He sheepishly brought out of his hose an elaborate arrangement of green beads.

'Having heard you prate of the *pierreries du Temple*, I've brought you these glass gauds. I fear me they aren't from the man in the Temple, for I failed to find the place ... but these seemed pretty toys. I thought maybe they would help you to cut a figure before old Dame Scudéry.'

It was truly a strange coincidence that he should have brought her the very thing that at that very moment she had been longing for. But was it the very thing? For the first time that morning, Madeleine felt her feet on earth. The beads were hideous and vulgar and as unlike the *pierreries du Temple* as they were unlike the emeralds they had taken as their model. She was almost choked by a feeling of impotent rage.

How dare Jacques be such a ninny with so little knowledge of the fashion? How dare he expect a belle to care for him, when he was such a miserable gallant with such execrable taste in presents? The idea of giving *her* rubbish like that! She would like to kill him!

Always quick to see omens, her nerves, strung up that morning to their highest pitch, felt in the gift the most malignant significance. *Timeo Danaos et dona ferentes*—I fear the Greeks even when they bear gifts. She blanched, and furtively crossed herself. Having said, in a dead voice, some words of thanks, she silently pinned the bead trimming on to her bodice and slowly left the room.

It was time to start; she got into the little box-like sedan. There was her mother standing at the door, waving her hand, and wishing her good luck. She was soon swinging along towards the Seine.

When the house was out of sight, with rude, nervous fingers she tore off the beads, and they fell in a shower about the sedan. Though one could scarcely move in the little hole, she managed to pick them all up, and pulling back the curtain she flung them out of the window. They were at that moment crossing the Pont-Neuf, and she caught a glimpse of a crowd of beggars and pages scrambling to pick them up. Recklessly scattering jewels to the rabble! It was like a princess in *Amadis*, or like the cardinal's nieces, the two Mancini, whose fabulous extravagance was the talk of the town. Then she remembered that they were only glass beads. Was it an omen that her grandeur would be always a mere imitation of the real thing? Also—though she had got rid of the hateful trimming, her *petite-oie* was still incomplete. Should she risk keeping Madame Cornuel waiting and go first to the man in the Temple? No, charms or no charms, she was moving on to her destiny, and felt deadly calm. What she had prayed for was coming and she could not stop it now. Its inevitableness frightened her, and she began to feel a poignant longing for the old order, the comforting rhythm of the rut she was used to, with the pleasant feeling of every day drawing nearer to a miraculous transformation of her circumstances.

She pulled back the curtain again and peeped out, the Seine was now behind them, and they were going up la rue de la Mortellerie. Soon she would be in the clutches of Madame Cornuel, and then there would be no escape. Should she jump out of the sedan, or tell the porters to take her home? She longed to; but if she did, how was she to face the future? And what ingratitude it would be for the exquisite tact with which the gods had manipulated her meeting with Sappho! the porters swung on and on, and Madeleine leaned back and closed her eyes, hypnotised by the inevitable.

The shafts of the sedan were put down with a jerk, and Madeleine started up and shuddered. One of the porters came to the window. 'Rue Saint-Antoine, Mademoiselle.' Madeleine gave him a coin to divide with his companion, opened the door, and walked into the court. Madame Cornuel's coach was standing waiting before the door.

She walked in and was shown by a valet into an ante-room. She sat down, and began mechanically repeating her litany. Suddenly, there was a rich rustle of taffeta, the door opened, and in swept a very handsomely-dressed young woman. Madeleine knew that it must be Mademoiselle le Gendre, the daughter of Monsieur Cornuel's first wife. In a flash Madeleine took in the elegant continence of her toilette. While Madeleine had seven patches on her face, she had only three. Her hair was exquisitely neat, and she was only slightly scented, while her deep, plain collar *à la Régente*, gave an air of puritanic severity to the bright, cherry-coloured velvet of her bodice. Also, she was not nearly as *décolletée* as Madeleine.

Madeleine felt that all of a sudden her *petite-oie* had lost both its decorative and magical virtue and had become merely incongruous gawds on the patent shabbiness of her gown. For some reason there flashed through her head the words she had heard at the Fair: 'As if all the purple and fine linen of Solomon himself could add an ounce of comeliness to his antic, foolish face.'

'Mademoiselle Troqueville? My step-mother awaits us in the coach, will you come?' said the lady. Her manner was haughty and unfriendly. Madeleine realised without a pang that it would all be like this. But after all, nothing in this dull reality really mattered.

'Bestir yourself! 'Tis time we were away!' shouted a voice from the *carrosse*. Mademoiselle le Gendre told Madeleine to get in.

'Mademoiselle Troqueville? I am glad to make your acquaintance—pray get in and take the back seat opposite me.' Madeleine humbly obeyed, indifferent to what in her imaginings she would have looked upon as an unforgivable insult, the putting her in the back seat.

'Hôtel de Rambouillet,' Madame Cornuel said to a lackey, who was waiting for orders at the window. The words left Madeleine quite cold.

Madame Cornuel and her step-daughter did not think it necessary to talk to Madeleine. They exchanged little remarks with each other at intervals, and laughed at allusions which she could not catch.

'Are we to fetch Sappho?' suddenly asked the younger woman.

'No, she purposes coming later, and on foot.'

Madeleine heard the name without a thrill.

The coach rolled on, and Madeleine sat as if petrified. Suddenly she galvanised herself into activity. In a few minutes they would be there, and if she allowed herself to arrive in this condition all would be lost. Why should she let these two horrid women ruin her chance of success? She muttered quickly to herself:—

'Oh! blessed Virgin, give me the friendship of Mademoiselle de Scudéry,' and then started gabbling through her prepared scene.

"'Ah, dear Zénocrite, here you come, leading our new *bergère!*" cries the lady on the bed. "Welcome, Mademoiselle, I have been waiting with impatience to make your acquaintance.'"

Would she get it finished before they arrived? She felt all her happiness depended on it.

"'Madame, it would have been of no consequence, for the Sibyl herself would have taken the conqueror captive.... But, Mademoiselle, what, if you will pardon my curiosity, induced you to leave your agreeable prairies?'"

They were passing the Palais Cardinal—soon they would turn down the rue St Thomas du Louvre—she had not much time.

The coach was rolling into the court of the Hôtel de Rambouillet and she had not finished. They got out. A tall woman, aged about thirty, with reddish hair and a face badly marked by smallpox, but in spite of these two blemishes of an extremely elegant and distinguished appearance, came towards them, screwing up her eyes in the manner of the near-sighted. Her top petticoat was full of flowers; she was too short-sighted to recognise Madame Cornuel till she was quite close, then she dropped a mock-low curtsey, and drawled 'Ma-a-a-dame.' Madame Cornuel laughed: evidently she had imitated a mutual acquaintance. With a sudden sense of exclusion Madeleine gave up hope.

'Are you following the example of our friend of the Faubourg St-Germain, may I inquire?' asked Madame Cornuel, with a little smile, pointing to the flowers, at which her step-daughter laughed, and the tall red-haired lady made a *moue* and answered with a deep sigh:—

'Ah! the wit of the Marais!' The meaning of this esoteric persiflage was entirely lost on Madeleine, and she sat with an absolutely expressionless face, trying to hide her own embarrassment.

'Ah! pardon me, I had forgotten,' Madame Cornuel exclaimed. 'Mademoiselle de Rambouillet, allow me to present to you Mademoiselle Troqueville.' (It may have been Madeleine's imagination, but it seemed to her that Madame Cornuel paused before calling her Mademoiselle.) Mademoiselle de Rambouillet screwed up her eyes at her and smiled quite pleasantly, while Madeleine, absolutely tongue-tied, tried to perform the almost impossible task of curtseying in a coach. They got out, and went inside, the three others continuing their mystifying conversation.

They went up a staircase and through one large splendid room after another. So here was Madeleine, actually in the famous 'Palais de Cléomire,' as it was called in *Cyrus*, but the fact did not move her, indeed she did not even realise it. Once Mademoiselle de Rambouillet turned round and said to her:—

'I fear 'tis a long journey, Mademoiselle,' but the manner in which she screwed up her eyes both terrified and embarrassed her, so instead of answering she merely blushed and muttered something under her breath.

Finally they reached Madame de Rambouillet's bedroom (she had ceased for some years to receive in the *Salle Bleue*). She was lying on a bed in an alcove and there were several people in the *ruelle*; as the thick velvet curtains of the windows were drawn Madeleine got merely an impression of rich, rare objects glowing like jewels out of the semi-darkness, but in a flash she took in the appearance of Madame de Rambouillet. Her face was pale and her lips a bright crimson, which was obviously not their natural colour; she had large brown eyes with heavy pinkish eyelids, and the only sign that she was a day over fifty was a slight trembling of the head. She was wearing a loose gown of some soft gray material, and on her head were *cornettes* of exquisite lace trimmed with pale yellow ribbons. One of her hands was lying on the blue coverlet, it was so thin that its veins looked almost like the blue of the coverlet shining through. The fingers were piled up with beautiful rings.

There was a flutter round the bed, and then Madeleine found herself being presented to the Marquise.

'Ah! Mademoiselle Toctin, I am ravished to make your acquaintance,' she said in a wonderfully melodious voice, with a just perceptible Italian accent. 'You come from delicious Marseilles, do you not? You will be able to recount to us strange Orient romances of orange-trees and Turkish soldiers. Angélique, bring Mademoiselle Touville a *pliant*, and place it close to me, and I will warm myself at her Southern *historiettes*.'

'It is from Lyons that I come, not from Marseilles,' was the only repartee of which at the moment Madeleine was capable. Her voice sounded strange and harsh, and she quite forgot a 'Madame.' However, the Marquise did not hear, as she had turned to another guest. But Angélique de Rambouillet heard, and so did another lady, with an olive complexion and remarkably bright eyes, whom Madeleine guessed to be Madame de Montausier, the famous 'Princesse Julie.' They exchanged glances of delight, and Madeleine began to blush, and blush, though, as a matter of fact, it was by their mother they were amused.

In the meantime a very tall, elderly man, with a hatchet face, came stumbling towards her.

'You have not a chair, have you, Mademoiselle?'

'Here it is, father,' said Angélique, who was bringing one up.

'Ah! that is right, Mademoiselle er ... er ... er ... will sit here.'

Madeleine took to this kind, polite man, and felt a little happier. He sat down beside her and made a few remarks, which Madeleine, full of the will to be agreeable, answered as best she could, endeavouring to make up by pleasant smiles for her sudden lack of *esprit*. But, unfortunately, the Marquis was almost stone-blind, so the smiles were lost upon him, and before long Madeleine noticed by his absent laugh and amused expression that his attention was wandering to the conversation of the others.

'I am of opinion you would look inexpressibly *galant* in a scarlet hat, Marquis,' Madame de Rambouillet was saying to a short, swarthy man with a rather saturnine expression. They all looked at him mischievously. 'Julie would be obliged to join Yvonne in the Convent, but there would be naught to hinder you from keeping Marie-Julie at your side as your *adopted* daughter.' The company laughed a little, the laugh of people too thoroughly intimate to need to make any effort. 'Monsieur de Grasse is wearing his episcopal smile—look at him, pray! Come, Monseigneur, you *must* confess that a scarlet hat would become him to a marvel,' and Madame de Rambouillet turned her brilliant, mischievous eyes on a tiny prelate with a face like a naughty schoolboy's.

He had been called Monsieur de Grasse. Could he, then, be the famous Godeau, bishop and poet? It seemed impossible. For Saint Thomas is the patron saint of provincials when they meet celebrities in the flesh.

'I fear Monsieur's head would be somewhat too *large* to wear it with comfort,' he answered.

'Hark to the episcopal *fleurette*! Marquis, rise up and bow!' but the only answer from the object of these witticisms was a surly grunt. Another idle smile rippled round the circle, and then there fell a silence of comfortable intimacy. If Madeleine had suddenly found herself in the kingdom of Prester John she could not have understood less of what was going on around her.

'Madame Cornuel has a furiously *galante historiette* she is burning to communicate to us,' said Mademoiselle de Rambouillet, screwing up her eyes at Madame Cornuel.

'Julie, bid Monsieur de Grasse go upstairs to play with Marie-Julie, and then Madame Cornuel will tell it.'

'Monsieur de Grasse——'

'Madame la Marquise come to my rescue! I too would fain hear the *historiette!*'

'Nolo episcopari, hein?'

'Now, then, be obedient, and get you to Marie-Julie!'

'Where can I take refuge?'

'If there were a hazel-nut at hand, 'twould serve your purpose.'

'No, Madame la Marquise, permit me to hide within your locket.'

'As you will. Now, Madame, we are all attention.'

Throughout this fooling, Madeleine had sat with aching jaws stretched into a smile, trying desperately hard not to look out of it. They all looked towards Madame Cornuel, who sat smiling in unruffled silence.

'Madame?'

'Well, Mademoiselle, tell me who is to be its heroine, who its hero, and what its plot, and then I will recount it to you,' she said. They seemed to think this very witty, and laughed heartily. There was another pause, and Madeleine again made an attempt to engage the Marquis's attention.

'The ... the ... the houses in Paris ... seem to me most goodly structures,' she began. He gave his nervous laugh.

'Yes, yes, we have some rare architects these days. Have you been to see the new buildings of the Val de Grâce?'

'No, I have not ... er ... it is a Convent, is it not?'

'Yes. Under the patronage of Notre Dame de la Crêche.'

His attention began to wander again; she made a frantic effort to rekindle the flames of the dying topic.

'What a strange name it is—Val de Grâce, what do you think can be its meaning?'

'Yes, yes,' with his nervous laugh, 'Val de Grâce, doubtless there is some legend connected with it.'

Madeleine gave up in despair.

The languid, intimate talk and humorous silences had suddenly turned into something more animated.

'Madame de Sablé vows that she saw her there with her own eyes, and that she was dressed in a *justaucorps*.'

'Sophie has seen more things than the legendary Argos!'

'Well, it has been turned into a Vaudeville in her quarter.'

'In good earnest, has it? What an excellent diversion! Julie, pray ask Madame d'Aiguillon about it and tell us. Go to-day.'

'I daren't; "my dear, my dear, *cela fait dévotion* and that puts me in mind, the Reine-Mère got a special chalice of Florentine enamel and I must———" Roqueten, Roqueten, Roquetine.'

'Upon my life, the woman's talk has less of meaning than a magpie's!' growled Madeleine to herself.

At that moment the door opened and in came a tall, middle-aged woman, swarthy, and very ugly. She was dressed in a plain gown of gray serge. Her face was wreathed in an agreeable smile, that made her look like a civil horse.

Madeleine had forgotten all about Mademoiselle de Scudéry, but when this lady came in, it all came rushing back; she got cold all over, and if before she had longed to be a thousand miles away, she now longed to be ten thousand.

There was a general cry of:—

'Mademoiselle: the very person we were in need of. You know everything. Tell us all about the Présidente Tambonneau, but avoid, in your narration, an excessive charity.'

'If you talk with the tongues of men and of Angels and yet *have* Charity, ye are become as sounding brass and as a tinkling cymbal,' said Madame Cornuel in her clear, slow voice. She spoke rarely, but when she did it was with the air of enunciating an oracle.

'Humph! That is a fault that *you* are rarely guilty of!' growled Montausier quite audibly.

'The Présidente Tambonneau? No new extravagance of hers has reached my ears. What is there to tell?' said the new-comer. She spoke in a loud, rather rasping voice, and still went on smiling civilly.

'Oh, you ladies of the Marais, every one is aware that you are omniscient, and yet you are perfect misers of your *historiettes*!'

'Sappho, we must combine against the *quartier du Palais Cardinal*, albeit they *do* call us "omniscient." It sounds infinitely *galant*, but I am to seek as to its meaning,' said Madame Cornuel.

'Ask Mademoiselle, she is in the last intimacy with the *Maréchal des mots*; it is reported he has raised a whole new company to fight under his *Pucelle*.'

'From all accounts, she is in sore need of support, poor lady. Madame de Longueville says she is *"parfaitement belle mais parfaitement ennuyeuse,"*' said Mademoiselle de Rambouillet very dryly.

'That would serve as an excellent epitome of divers among our friends,' murmured Madame de Montausier.

'Poor Chapelain! all said, he, by merely being himself, has added infinitely more to our diversion than the wittiest person in the world,' said Madame de Rambouillet, looking mischievously at Mademoiselle de Scudéry, who, though still wearing the same smile, was evidently not pleased.

'Yes, Marquis, when you are made a duke, you would do well to employ Monsieur Chapelain as your jester. Ridiculous, solemn people are in reality much more diverting than wits,' said Mademoiselle de Rambouillet to Montausier, who looked extremely displeased, and said in angry, didactic tones:—

'Chapelain a des sentiments fins et delicats, il raisonne juste, et dans ses œuvres on y trouve de nobles et fortes expressions,' and getting up he walked over to Mademoiselle de Scudéry, and they were soon talking earnestly together.

Madeleine all this time had been torn between terror of being introduced to Mademoiselle de Scudéry, and terror of not being introduced. Her face was absolutely impassive, and she had ceased to pretend to take any interest in what was going on around her.

Suddenly she heard Madame de Rambouillet saying to Monsieur de Grasse:—

'You remember Julie's and her sister's *vision* about night-caps?'

'Ah, yes, and the trick played on them by Voiture, and the poor, excellent Marquis de Pisani.'

'Yes,' she answered, with a little sigh and a smile. 'Well, it has been inherited by little Marie-Julie, whenever she beholds one she becomes transfixed by terror. *Visions* are strange things!'

Madeleine for the first time that afternoon felt happy and pleased. She herself had always loathed night-caps, and as a child had screamed with terror whenever she had seen any one wearing one. What a strange coincidence that this *vision* should be shared by Madame de Rambouillet's daughters! She turned eagerly to the Marquis.

'Monsieur, I hear Madame la Marquise telling how Mesdames her daughters were wont to be affrighted by night-caps; when I was a child, they worked on me in a like manner, and to speak truth, to this day I have a dislike to them.'

'Indeed, indeed,' he answered, with his nervous laugh. 'Yes, my daughters had quite a *vision* as to night-caps. Doubtless 'twas linked in their memory with some foolish, monstrous fable they had heard from one of their attendants. 'Tis strange, but our little granddaughter has inherited the fear and she refuses to kiss us if we are wearing one.'

Alas! There was no crack through which Madeleine could get in her own personality! The Marquis got up and stumbled across the room to Mademoiselle de Scudéry, and Montausier, having to give up his chair, sat down by Madeleine. There was a cry of 'Ah! here she comes!'

The door opened and a little girl of about seven years old walked into the room, followed by a *gouvernante* who stood respectfully in the doorway. The child was dressed in a miniature Court dress, cut low and square at the neck. She had a little pointed face, and eyes with a slight outward squint. She made a beautiful curtsey, first to her grandmother and then to the company.

'My dearest treasure,' Madame de Rambouillet cried in her beautiful husky voice. 'Come and greet your friend, Monsieur de Grasse.'

Every one had stopped talking and were looking at the child with varying degrees of interest. Madeleine felt suddenly fiercely jealous of her; she stole a glance at Mademoiselle de Scudéry, and saw on her face the universal smile of tolerant amusement with which grown-up people regard children. The child went up to Godeau, kissed his ring, and then busily and deliberately found a foot-stool for herself, dragged it up to Madame de Rambouillet's bed, and sat down on it.

'The little lady already has the *tabouret chez la reine*,'[2] said Mademoiselle de Scudéry, smiling and bowing to Madame de Rambouillet. The child, however, did not understand the witticism; she looked offended, frowned, and said severely:—

'I am working a *tabouret* for myself,' and then, as if to soften what she evidently had meant for a snub, she added: 'It has crimson flowers on it, and a blue saint feeding birds.'

Montausier went into fits of proud laughter.

'There is a bit of hagiology for you to interpret, Monsieur de Grasse,' he cried triumphantly, suddenly in quite a good temper, and looking round to see if the others were amused. Godeau looked interested and serious.

'That must be a most rare and delicate *tabouret*, Mademoiselle,' he said; 'do you know what the saint's name is?'

'No, I thank you,' she answered politely, but wearily, and they all again went into peals of laughter.

'My love,' said Madame de Rambouillet. 'I am certain Monsieur de Grasse and that lady,' nodding towards Mademoiselle de Scudéry, 'would be enchanted by those delicious verses you wrote for my birthday, will you recite them?'

But the child shook her head, backwards and forwards, the more she was entreated, the more energetically she shook her head, evidently enjoying the process for its own sake. Then she climbed on to her grandmother's bed and whispered something in her ear. Madame de Rambouillet shook with laughter, and after they had whispered together for some minutes the child left the room. Madame de Rambouillet then told the company that Marie-Julie's reason for not wishing to recite her poem was that she had heard her father say that all *hommes de lettres* were thieves and were quite unprincipled about using each other's writings, and she was afraid that Mademoiselle de Scudéry or Monsieur de Grasse might, if they heard her poem, publish it as their own. There was much laughter, and Montausier was in ecstasies.

'I am impatient for you to hear the poem,' said Madame de Rambouillet. 'It is quite delicious.'

'Yes, my daughter promises to be a second Neuf-germain!'[3] said Madame de Montausier, smiling.

'What a Nemesis, that a mother who has inspired so many delicious verses, and a father——' began Mademoiselle de Scudéry, but just then the child came back with her head disappearing into a large beplumed man's hat, and carrying a shepherd's crook in her hand.

'I am a Muse,' she announced, and the company exchanged delighted, bewildered glances.

'Now, I will begin.'

'Yes, pray do, my dear love,' said Madame de Rambouillet, trying to compose her face.

'The initial letters form my grandmother's name: Cathérine,' she explained, and then, taking her stand in the middle of the room, began to declaim with great unction:—

'Chérie, vous êtes aimable et

Aussi belle que votre perroquet,

Toujours souriante et douce.

Hélas! j'ai piqué mon pouce

En brodant pour votre jour de fête

Rien qu'une bourse qui n'est pas bête.

J'aime ma Grandmère, c'est ma chatte,

Nellie, mon petit chien, donne lui ta patte,

Et lèche la avec ta petite langue.'

She then made a little bow to the company, and sat down again on her *tabouret*, quite undisturbed by the enthusiastic applause that had followed her recitation.

'Mademoiselle,' began Godeau solemnly, 'words fail me, to use the delicious expression of Saint Amant, with which to praise your ravishing verses as they deserve. But if the Abbé Ménage were here, I think he might ask you if the *qui* in ... let me see ... the sixth line, refers to the *bourse* or to the act of pricking your finger. Because if, as I imagine, it is to the latter, the laws of our language demand the insertion of a *ce* before the *qui*, while the unwritten laws of universal experience assert that the action of pricking one's finger should be called *bête* not *pas bête*. We writers must be prepared for this sort of ignoble criticism.'

'Of course the *qui* refers to *bourse*,' said Madame de Montausier, for the child was looking bewildered. 'You will pardon me but what an exceeding foolish question from a Member of the Academy! It was *bête* to prick one's finger, but who, with justice, could call *bête* a *bourse* of most quaint and excellent design? Is it not so, *ma chatte?*' The child nodded solemnly, and Monsieur de Grasse was profuse in his apologies for his stupidity.

Madeleine had noticed that the only member of the company, except herself, who had not been entranced by this performance, was Mademoiselle de Scudéry. Though she smiled the whole time, and was profuse in her compliments, yet she was evidently bored. Instead of pleasing Madeleine, this shocked her, it also made her rather despise her, for being out of it.

She turned to Montausier and said timidly:—

'I should dearly love to see Mademoiselle *votre fille* and the Cardinal's baby niece together. They would make a delicious pair.' But Montausier either really did not hear, or pretended not to, and Madeleine had the horrible embarrassment of speaking to air.

'Who is that *demoiselle*?' the child suddenly cried in a shrill voice, looking at Madeleine.

'That is Mademoiselle Hoqueville, my love.'

'Hoqueville! *what* a droll name!' and she went into peals of shrill laughter. The grandparents and mother of the child smiled apologetically at Madeleine, but she, in agony at being humiliated, as she considered, before Mademoiselle de Scudéry, tried to improve matters by looking haughty and angry. However, this remark reminded Madame de Rambouillet of Madeleine's existence, and she exclaimed:—

'Oh! Mademoiselle Hoqueville, you have, as yet, seen naught of the hôtel. Marie-Julie, my love, go and say *bon-jour* to that lady and ask her if she will accompany you to the *salle bleue*.'

The child obediently went over to Madeleine, curtseyed, and held out her hand. Madeleine was not certain whether she ought to curtsey back or merely bow without rising from the chair. She compromised in a cross between the two, which made her feel extremely foolish. On being asked if she would like to see *la salle bleue*, she had to say yes, and followed the child out of the room.

She followed her through a little *cabinet*, and then they were in the famous room, sung by so many poets, the scene of so many gay and brilliant happenings.

Madeleine's first feeling was one of intense relief at being freed from the strain of the bedroom, then, as it were, she galvanised into activity her demand upon life, and felt in despair at losing even a few moments of Mademoiselle de Scudéry's company. The child walked on in front humming a little tune to herself. Madeleine felt she must pull herself together, and make friends with her.

'What rare and skilful verses those were you recited to us,' she began, her voice harshly breaking the silence of the huge room. The child looked at her out of her crab-eyes, pursed up her mouth, and went on humming.

'Do you dearly love your little dog?'

'Haven't got one.' This was startling.

'But you made mention of one in your poem,' said Madeleine in an aggrieved tone.

The child screamed with scornful laughter:—

'She isn't *mine*, she's Aunt Angélique's!' she cried, and looked at Madeleine as if she must be mad for having made such a mistake. There was another pause. Madeleine sighed wearily and went to look at the famous tapestry, the child followed her.

Its design consisted of groups of small pastoral figures disporting themselves in a blue Arcady. In one group there was a shepherdess sitting on a rustic bench, surrounded by shepherds; a nymph was offering her a basket of flowers. The child pointed to the shepherdess: 'That is my grandmother, and that is me bringing her flowers, and that is my father, and that is Monsieur Sarrasin, and that is my dear Maître Claude!' ... This was better. Madeleine made a violent effort to be suitably fantastic.

'It may be when you are asleep you do in truth become that nymph and live in the tapestry.' The child stared at her, frowned, and continued her catalogue:—

'And that is my mother, and that is Aunt Angélique, and that is Madame de Longueville, and that is Madame de Sablé, and that is Monsieur de la Rochefoucauld, and that is my little friend Mademoiselle de Sévigné,' and so on.

When she had been through the list of her acquaintances, she wandered off and began to play with a box of ivory puzzles. Madeleine, in a final attempt to ingratiate herself, found for her some of the missing pieces, at which her mouth began to tremble, and Madeleine realised that all the pleasure lay in doing it by herself, so she left her, and with a heavy heart crept back to the bedroom.

She found Madame Cornuel and Mademoiselle Legendre preparing to go, and supposing they had already said good-bye, solemnly curtseyed to all the company in turn. They responded with great friendliness and kindness, but she suddenly noticed Madame Cornuel exchanging glances with her step-daughter, and realised in a flash that by making her *adieux* she had been guilty of a provincialism. She smiled grimly to herself. What did it matter?

Madame Cornuel dropped her in the rue Saint-Honoré, and she walked quietly home.

She had not exchanged a single word with Mademoiselle de Scudéry.

CHAPTER X
AFTERWARDS

Madeleine walked up the petite rue du Paon, in at the baker's door, and upstairs. She still felt numbed, but knew that before her were the pains of returning circulation; Madame Troqueville heard her come in and ran out from the kitchen, full of smiles and questions. Madeleine told her in a calm voice that it had all been delightful, praised the agreeable manners of the Rambouillets, and described the treasures of the *salle bleue*. She repeated the quaint sayings of the child, and Madame Troqueville cried '*Quel amour!* Oh, Madeleine, I would like you to have just such another little daughter!'

Madeleine smiled wearily.

'And what of Mademoiselle de Scu-tary?' her mother asked rather nervously.

'De Scudéry,' corrected Madeleine, true to habit. 'She was furiously *spirituelle* and very ... civil. I am a trifle tired.... I think I will away and rest,' and she dragged herself wearily off to her own room. Madame Troqueville, who had watched her very unhappily, made as if she would follow her, but thought better of it.

When Madeleine got into her room, she sat down on her bed, and clasped her head. She could not, she would not think. Then, like a wave of ecstasy there swept over her little points she had noticed about Mademoiselle de Scudéry, but which had not at the time thrilled her in the slightest. Her teeth were rather long; she had a mole on her left cheek; she was not as grandly dressed as the others; the child had snubbed her; Montausier had been very attentive to her; she was a great celebrity; Madame de Rambouillet had teased her. This medley of recollections, each and all of them made her feel quite faint with pleasure, so desirable did they make her love appear. But then ... she had not spoken to her ... she had been humiliated before her.... Oh! it was not to be faced! Her teeth were rather long. Montausier had been attentive to her ... oh, how thrilling! And yet ... she, Madeleine had not even been introduced to her. The supernal powers had seemed to have a scrupulous regard for her wishes. They had actually arranged that the first meeting should be at the Hôtel de Rambouillet ... and she had not even been introduced to her! Could it be possible that the Virgin had played her a trick? Should she turn and rend in mad fury the whole Heavenly Host? No; that would be accepting defeat once for all, and that must not be, for the past as well as the future was malleable, and it was only by emotionally accepting it that a thing became a fact. This strange undercurrent of thought translated itself thus in her consciousness: God and the Virgin must be trusted; they had only disclosed a tiny bit of their design, what madness then, to turn against them, thus smashing perhaps their perfect scheme for her happiness! Or perhaps her own co-operation had not been adequate—she had perhaps not been instant enough in dancing—but still ... but still ... the visit to the Hôtel de Rambouillet was over, she had seen Mademoiselle de Scudéry, and was still not one inch nearer to her heart's desire. She *could* not face it.

She came down to supper. Her father was silent and gloomy, shaking his head and twisting his lips. His visit to *his* lady had been a failure. Was there ... could there be ... some mystical connection? And there was Jacques still limping ... and he had given her that horrid bead trimming.... *No, no, no* ... these were insane, goblin ideas that must be crushed.

Her mother was trying hard to be cheerful, and Jacques kept looking at her anxiously. When supper was over she went up to her room, half hoping, half fearing that he would follow.

Shortly there was a scratch at the door (with great difficulty she had persuaded him to adopt the fashionable scratch—to knock was *bourgeois*).

He came in, and gave her a look with his bright eyes, at once compassionate and whimsical. She felt herself dully hoping that he would not ask why she was not wearing the bead trimming. He did not, but began to tell her of his day, spent mostly at the Palais and a tavern. But all the time he watched her; she listened languidly. 'How went the *fête galante?*' he asked, after a pause.

'It was furiously *galante,*' she answered with a tragic smile. He walked slowly up to her, half smiling all the time, sat down on her bed, and put his arm around her.

'You are cruelly unhappy, my poor one, I know. But 'twill pass, in time all caprices yield to graver things.'

'But it is no caprice!' she cried passionately. 'Oh, Jacques, it is hard to make my meaning clear, but they be real live people with their own pursuits ... they are all square like little fat boxes ... oh, how can I make you understand?'

Jacques could not help laughing. 'I'm sure, 'tis hateful of them to be like boxes; though, in truth, for my part, I am to seek ... oh, Madeleine, dear life, it's dreadful to be miserable ... the cursed *phantasia*, what tricks it plays us ... 'tis a mountebank, don't heed it but put your faith in the good old *bourgeois* intellect,' but Madeleine, ignoring this comfort from Gassendi, moaned out,—

'Oh! Jacques! I want to die ... you see, 'tis this way—they've got their own lives and memories, folded up all tight around them. Oh! can no one ever get to know any one else?'

He began to understand.

'Indeed one can, but it takes time. One has to hew a path through the blood, through the humours, up to the brain, and, once there, create the Passion of Admiration. How can it be done at once?'

'I can't wait ... I can't wait ... except things come at once I'll have none of them ... at least that's not quite my meaning,' she added hurriedly, looking furtively round and crossing herself several times. 'Oh! but I don't feel that I am of a humour that can wait.... Oh! I feel something sick and weak in me somewhere.'

'It's but those knavish old animal spirits playing tricks on the will, but I think that it is only because one is young,' and he would have launched out on a philosophical dissertation, only Madeleine felt that she could not stand it.

'*Don't*, Jacques!' she screamed. 'Talk about *me*, or I shall go mad!'

'Well, then, recount to me the whole matter.'

'Oh! there is nothing worth the telling, but they *would* make dædal pleasantries—pleasantries one fails to understand, except one have a clue— and they would talk about people with whom I was not acquainted.... Oh! it seems past human compassing to make friends with a person except one has known them all one's life! How *could* I utter my conceit if they would converse of matters I did not understand?' she repeated furiously. Jacques smiled.

'I admit,' he said dryly, 'to be show man of a troupe of marionettes is an agreeable profession.' She looked at him suspiciously for a second, and then catching his hands, cried desperately:—

'Is it beyond our powers ever to make a *new* friend?'

'That it is not, but it can't be effected at once. I am sure that those *Messieurs de Port-Royal* would tell you that even Jesus Christ finds 'tis but a slow business worming His way into a person's heart. There He stands, knocking and knocking, and then——' Madeleine saw that he was on the point of becoming profane, and as her gods did not like profanity, she crossed herself and cut in with:—

'But even admitting one can't come to any degree of intimacy with a person at once, the *beginning* of the intimacy must happen at once, and I'm at a loss to know how the beginning can happen at once any more than the whole thing.'

She had got into one of her tight knots of nerves, when she craved to be reasoned with, if only for the satisfaction of confounding the reasons offered her. Jacques clasped his head and laughed.

'You put me in mind of the philosophy class and old Zeno! It's this way, two people meet, nothing takes place perhaps. They meet again, and one gives a little look, it may be, that sets the bells of the other's memory pleasantly ringing, or says some little thing that tickles the humours of the other, and thus a current is set up between them ... a fluid, which gradually reaches the heart and solidifies into friendship.'

'But then, there might never be the "little look," or the "little word," and then ... there would be no friendship' (she crossed herself) ' ... it all seems at the mercy of Chance.'

'Of chance ... and of harmony. 'Tis a matter beyond dispute that we are more in sympathy with some souls than with others—

'Il est des nœuds secrets, il est des sympathies,

Dont par le doux rapport les âmes assorties ...

you know these lines in *Rodogune*?'

'And do you hold that sympathy can push its way past ... obstacles ... such as bashfulness, for example?'

Jacques smiled.

'In good earnest it can.' Suddenly her nerves relaxed.

'Then it is *not* contrary to natural laws to make a new friend?' she cried joyfully.

'That it is not. And who knows, the rôles may be reversed ere long and we shall see old Mother Scudéry on her knees, while Chop plays the proud spurner! What said that rude, harsh, untaught Grecian poetess whose naked numbers brought a modest blush to your "precious" taste?

'Who flees—she shall pursue;

Who spurns gifts—she shall offer them;

Who loves not—willy-nilly, she shall love.'

Madeleine gave a little sob of joy and flung her arms round Jacques's neck. Oh, he was right, he was right! Had she not herself feared that immediate success would be *bourgeois*? 'Twould be breaking every law of *galanterie* were Sappho to yield without a struggle. It took Céladon twelve stout volumes before he won his Astrée, and, as Jacques had pointed out, Christ Himself, with all the armaments of Heaven at His disposal, does not at once break through the ramparts of a Christian's heart. But yet ... but yet ... her relationship with Mademoiselle de Scudéry that afternoon could not, with the most elastic poetic licence, be described as that of 'the nymph that flees, the faun that pursues!' Also ... she was not made of stuff stern enough to endure repeated rebuffs and disappointments. Already, her nerves were worn to breaking-point. A one-volumed romance was all her fortitude could face.... God grant the course of true love to run smooth from now.

Jacques shortly left her, and she went to bed.

Outside Jacques ran into Madame Troqueville, who said she wished to speak to him. They went into her room.

'Jacques,' she began, 'I am uneasy about Madeleine. I greatly fear things fell not out as she had hoped. Did she tell you aught of what took place?'

'I think she is somewhat unhappy because they didn't all call her *tu* right away ... oh, I had forgotten, she holds it *bourgeois* to *tutoier*,' he answered, smiling. Madame Troqueville smiled a little too.

'My poor child, she is of so impatient a humour, and expects so much,' and she sighed. 'Jacques, tell me about your uncle. Are you of opinion he will make his way in Paris?' She looked at him searchingly. Her eyes were clear and cold like Madeleine's.

Jacques blushed and frowned; he felt angry with her for asking him. But her eyes were still fixed on his face.

'How can I tell, aunt? It hangs on all ... on all these presidents and people.'

Madame Troqueville gave a little shrug, and her lips curled into a tiny, bitter smile. 'I wonder why men always hold women to be blind, when in reality their eyes are so exceeding sharp. Jacques, for my sake, and for Madeleine's, for the child's future doth so depend on it, won't you endeavour to keep your uncle from ... from all these places.... I know you take your pleasure together, and I am of opinion you have some influence with him.' Jacques was very embarrassed and very angry; it was really, he felt, expecting too much of a young man to try and make him responsible for his middle-aged uncle.

'I fear I can do nothing, aunt. 'Tis no business of mine,' he said coldly, and they parted for the night.

CHAPTER XI
REBUILDING THE HOUSE OF CARDS

All next day Madeleine had the feeling of something near her which she must, if she wished to live, push away, away, right out of her memory. Her vanity was too vigilant to have allowed her to give to Jacques a *full* account of the scene at the Hôtel de Rambouillet. The fixed smile, the failure to interest the Marquis, that awful exit, for instance, were too indecent to be mentioned. Even her thoughts blushed at their memory, and shuddered away from it—partly, perhaps, because at the back of her consciousness there dwelt always the imaginary Sappho, so that to recall these things was to be humiliated anew in her presence.

In fact, the whole scene at the Hôtel de Rambouillet must be forgotten, and that quickly, for it had been a descent into that ruthless world of reality in which Madeleine could not breathe. That world tyrannised over by the co-sovereigns Cause and Effect, blown upon by sharp, rough winds, and—most horrible of all—fretted with the counter-claims on happiness of myriads of individuals just as 'square' and real as she. In such a world how could she—with such frightful odds against her—hope for success, for *here* she was so impotent, merely a *gauche* young girl of no position?

There were times, as I have shown, when she felt a *nostalgie* for the world of reality, as a safe fresh place, but now ... in God's name, back to her dreams.

———

Madeleine is entering the door of Sappho's house. Sappho is lying on her bed, surrounded by her demoiselles. (This time Madeleine visualises her quite clearly. She is swarthy and plain.) When she sees Madeleine, she gives a little blush, which caresses the motion of Madeleine's passions, and fills her with as sweet an expectancy as the rhythm of a Saraband. Madeleine comes forward, and kissing her hand says, with the most gallant air in the world: 'I am well aware, Madame, that poets are exempt from the tax to *la Dame Vérité*, and that they have set up in her place another Sovereign. So when you gave me the other day the gracious permission to wait on you, I had, I admit, a slight fear that you were speaking as the subject of this sovereign, whose name, I believe, is *le joli Mensonge*, and that by taking you at your word, I would prove myself an eager, ignorant Scythian, unable to understand what is said, and—more important still—what is not said, by the citizens of the polite hemisphere. Madame, I would ten times rather earn such a reputation, I would ten times rather be an unwelcome visitor, than to wait another day before I saw you.' It is a bold speech, and which, if made by any one else would surely have aroused all Sappho's pride and prudishness. At first she colours and seems slightly confused, and then, she lets a smile have its own way. She changes the subject, however.

'Do you consider,' she asks, 'that the society of Lesbos compensates, if I may use the expression, for the enamelled prairies and melodious brooks of Bœotia? For my own part, I know few greater pleasures than to sojourn in a rustic place with my lyre and a few chosen friends.' These last two words awake the lover's gadfly, jealousy, and causes it to give Madeleine a sharp sting.

'I should imagine, Madame,' she says coldly, 'that by this means you must carry Lesbos with you wherever you go, and although it is one of the most agreeable spots on earth, this must deprive you of many of the delights of travel.'

'I see that you take me for a provincial of the metropolis,' says Sappho with a smile full of delicious raillery and in which Madeleine imagines she detects a realising of her jealousy and a certain pleasure in it, so that, in spite of herself, smiling also, she answers,—

'One has but to read your ravishing verses, which are as fresh, as full of pomp, and as flowery as a summer meadow, to know that your pleasure in pastoral joys is as great as your pleasure in intercourse with *les honnêtes gens*, and the other attractions of the town. And this is combined with such marvellous talent that in your poetry, the trees offer a pleasanter shade, the flowers a sweeter odour, the brooks a more soothing lullaby than in earth's most agreeable glades.'

'If you hold,' answers Sappho smiling, 'that my verses make things fairer than they really are, you cannot consider them really admirable, for surely the closer art resembles nature the more excellent it becomes.'

'Pardon me, Madame,' says Madeleine, also smiling, 'but we who believe that there are gods and goddesses ten times fairer than the fairest person on earth, must also believe that somewhere there exist for these divine beings habitations ten times fairer than the fairest of earth's meadows. And you, Madame, have been carried to these habitations on the wings of the Muses, and in your verses you describe the delicious visions you have there beheld.'

Sappho cannot keep a look of gratification from lighting up her fine eyes.

'You think, then, that I have visited the Elysian Fields?' she asks.

'Most certainly,' rejoins Madeleine quickly. 'Did I not call you the other day, in the Palais de Cléomire, the Sybil of Cumæ?' She pauses, and draws just the eighth of an inch closer to Sappho. 'As such, you are the authorised guide to the Elysian Fields. May I hope that some day you will be *my* conductress there?'

'Then, as well, I am the "appointed guide" to Avernus,' says Sappho with a delicious laugh. 'Will you be willing to descend there also?'

'With you as my guide ... yes,' answers Madeleine.

There follows one of *ces beaux silences*, more gallant than the most agreeable conversation: one of the silences during which the wings of Cupid can almost be heard fluttering. Why does the presence of that mignon god, all dimples and rose-buds, terrify mortals as well as delight them?

———

Thus did Madeleine's dreams quietly readjust themselves to their normal state and scornfully tremble away from reality.

PART II

'Cela t'amuse-t-il tant, me dit-il, d'édifier ainsi des systèmes?'

'Rien ne m'amuse plus qu'une éthique, répondis-je, et je m'y contente l'esprit. Je ne goûte pas une joie que je ne l'y veuille attachée.'

'Cela l'augmente-t-il?'

'Non, dis-je, cela me la légitime.'

Certes, il m'a plu souvent qu'une doctrine et même qu'un système complet de pensées ordonnées justifiât à moi-même mes actes; mais parfois je ne l'ai pu considérer que comme l'abri de ma sensualité.

ANDRÉ GIDE.

CHAPTER XII
THE FÊTE-DIEU

It was the Sunday of the octave of the *Fête-Dieu*—the Feast of *Corpus Christi*. God Himself had walked the streets like Agamemnon over purple draperies. The stench of the city had mingled with the perfume of a thousand lilies—to the Protestant mind, a symbol of the central doctrine of the day—Transubstantiation. Transubstantiation beaten out by the cold, throbbing logic of the Latin hymns of Saint Thomas Aquinas, and triumphantly confirmed at Bologna by the miraculous bleeding of the Host.

Seraphic logic and bleeding bread! A conjunction such as this hints at a secret vice of the cold and immaculate intellect. What if one came in a dark corner of one's dreams upon a celestial spirit feeding upon carrion?

Past gorgeous altars, past houses still hung with arras, the Troquevilles walked to Mass. From time to time they met processions of children apeing the solemn doings of Thursday, led by tiny, mock priests, shrilly chanting the office of the day. Other children passed in the scanty clothing of little Saint John, leading lambs on pink or blue ribbons. Everything sparkled in the May sunshine, and the air was full of the scent of flowers.

Et introibo ad altare Dei: ad Deum qui lætificat juventutem meam—very shortly they would be hearing these words in Church. They were solemn, sunny words well suited to the day, but, like the day, to Madeleine they seemed but a mockery. *Ad Deum qui lætificat juventutem meam*—To God who makes glad my youth! Where was the kind God of the Semi-Pelagians, and what joy did *she* have in her youth?

They walked in silence to their destination—the smug *bourgeois* Church Saint-André-des-Arts. Its atmosphere and furniture did not lend themselves to religious ecstasy. Among the congregation there was whispering and tittering and bows of recognition. The gallants were looking at the belles, and the belles were trying not to look at the gallants. From marble tombs smirked many a petrified magistrate, to whose vacuous pomposity the witty commemorative art of the day had added by a wise elimination of the third dimension, a flat, mocking, decorative charm.

Suddenly the frivolity vanished from the atmosphere. Monsieur Troqueville, who had been alternately yawning and spitting, pulled himself together and put on what Jacques called his 'Mass face'—one of critical solemnity which seemed to say: 'Here I am with a completely unbiassed mind, quite unprejudiced, and a fine judicial gift for sifting evidence. I am quite willing to believe that you have the power of turning bread into the

Body and Blood of Christ, but mind! no hocus-pocus, and not one tiny crumb left untransubstantiated!'

The clergy in the red vestments, symbolic in France of the Blessed Sacrament, preceded by solemn thurifer, marched in procession from the sacristy to the altar. And then began the Sacrifice of High Mass.

The *Introit* melted into the *Kyrie*, the *Kyrie* swelled into the *Gloria in excelsis*. The subdeacon sang the Epistle, the deacon sang the Gospel. The Gospel and Epistle solidified into the fine rigidity of the Creed.

Madeleine, quite unmoved by the solemn drama, was examining the creases in the neck of a fat merchant immediately in front of her. There were three real creases—the small half ones did not count—and as there were three lines in her Litany she might use them as a sort of Rosary. She felt that she must 'tell' the three creases before he turned his head.

'Blessed Virgin, Mother of Our Lord, give me the friendship of Mademoiselle de Scudéry. Guardian Angel that watchest over me, give me the friendship of Mademoiselle de Scudéry. Blessed Saint Magdalene, give me the friendship of Mademoiselle de Scudéry.'

Suddenly ... the sweet, nauseating smell of incense and the strange music of the Preface—an echo of the music of Paradise, so said the legend, caught in dreams by holy apostolic men.

Quia per incarnati Verbi mysterium nova inentis nostræ oculis lux tuæ claritatis infulsit: ut dum visibiliter Deum cognoscimus per hunc in INVISIBILIUM AMOREM RAPIAMUR.

Dozens of times before had Madeleine heard these terse Latin words, but to-day, for the first time, she felt their significance. 'Caught up to the love of invisible things'—*rapiamur*—a ghostly rape—the idea was beautiful and terrible. Suddenly a great longing swept over her for the still, significant life of the Spirit, for the shadowy lining of this bright, hard earth. Yet on earth itself strange lives had been led ... symbols, and bitter-sweet sacrifice, and little cells suddenly filled with the sound of great waters.

A ghostly rape ... she had a sudden vision of the nervous hands of the Almighty clutching tightly the yielding flesh of a thick, human body, as in a picture by the Flemish Rubens she had seen in the Luxembourg. Surely the body was that of the fat merchant with the wrinkled neck ... there ... sitting in front of her. Something is happening ... there are acolytes with lighted tapers ... a bell is ringing ... the central Mystery is being consummated. For one strange, poignant second Madeleine felt herself in a world of non-bulk and non-colour. She buried her face in her hands and, though her mind formed no articulate prayer, she worshipped the Unseen. Her mundane desires had, for the moment, dropped from her and their place was taken by her old ambition of one day being able to go up to the altar, strong in grace, a true penitent, to partake of the inestimable blessing of the Eucharist.

CHAPTER XIII
ROBERT PILOU'S SCREEN

When Mass was over, Madeleine walked home with her parents in absolute silence. She was terribly afraid of losing the flavour of her recent experience. She specially dreaded Jacques. He was such a scoffer; besides, at this moment, she felt a great distaste for the insincerity of her relationship with him. However, as it happened, he did not come in to dinner that day.

After dinner she went to her room and lay down on her bed, in the hopes of sleeping, and so guarding her religious emotion from the contamination of thoughts and desires—for, at the bottom of her heart, she knew quite well that her obsession was only dozing. Finally, she did fall asleep, and slept for some hours.

When she awoke, it was half-past four, and she realised with joy that she had nursed successfully the mystic atmosphere. She felt a need for space and fresh air, and hastily put on her pattens, mask, and cloak. As she came out of her room, her mother appeared from the parlour.

'Madeleine—dear life—whither in the name of madness, are you bound? You cannot be contemplating walking alone? Why, 'twill soon be dusk! Jacques should shortly return, and he'll accompany you!'

This was unbearable. In a perfect frenzy, lest the spell should be broken, Madeleine gathered up her petticoats and made a dash for the staircase.

'Madeleine! Madeleine! Is the child demented? Come back! I command you!'

'For God's sake, *let me be*!' screeched Madeleine furiously from half-way down the stairs. 'Curse her! With her shrill importunity she has shattered the serenity of my humour!' she muttered to herself, in the last stage of nervous irritation.

She had half a mind to go back and spend the rest of the afternoon in dinning into her mother that by her untimely interruption she had arrested a *coup de Grâce*, and come between her and her ultimate redemption. But pleasant though this would be, the soft sunshine of early June was more so, so she ran down the stairs and into the street.

At first she felt so irritated and ruffled that she feared the spell was broken for ever, but gradually it was renewed under the magical idleness of the Sunday afternoon. In a house opposite some one was playing a Saraband on the lute. From a neighbouring street came the voices and laughter of children—otherwise the whole neighbourhood seemed deserted.

Down the long rue des Augustins, that narrowed to a bright point towards the Seine, she wandered with wide, staring eyes, to meet something, she knew not what. Then up the quays she wandered, up and on, still in a trance.

Finally she took her stand on the Pont-Rouge, a little wooden bridge long since replaced. For some moments she gazed at the Seine urbanely flowing between the temperate tints of its banks, and flanked on its right by the long, gray gallery of the Louvre. Everything was shrouded in a delicate distance-lending haze; there was the Cité—miles and miles away it seemed—nuzzling into the water and dominated by the twin towers of Notre-Dame. They had caught the sun, and though unsubstantial, they still looked sturdy—like solid cubes of light. The uniform gray-greenness of everything—Seine and Louvre and Cité—and a quality in it all of decorative unreality, reminded Madeleine of a great, flat, gray-green picture by Mantegna of the death of Saint Sebastian, that she had seen in one of the Palaces.

The bell of Saint-Germain-des-Prés began to peal for Vespers. She started murmuring to herself the Vesper hymn—*Lucis Creator.*—

'Ne mens gravata crimine.

Vitæ sit exul munere,

Dum nil perenne cogitat,

Seseque culpis illigat.'

'Grant that the mind, borne down by the charge of guilt, be not an exile from the fulfilment of life, perennially pondering emptiness and binding itself by its transgressions.'

Yes, that was a prayer she had need of praying. 'An exile from the fulfilment of life'—that was what she had always feared to be. An exile in the provinces, far from the full stream of life—but what was Paris itself but a backwater, compared with the City of God? 'Perennially pondering emptiness'—yes, that was her soul's only exercise. She had long ceased to ponder grave and pregnant matters. The time had come to review once more her attitude to God and man.

She had come lately to look upon God as a Being with little sense of sin, who had a mild partiality for *attrition* in His creatures, but who never demanded *contrition*. And the compact into which she had entered with Him was this: she was to offer Him a little lip-service, perform daily some domestic duties and pretend to Jacques she was in love with him; in return for this He (aided by her dances) was to procure for her the entrée into the inner circle of the Précieuses, and the friendship of Mademoiselle de Scudéry!

And the tenets of Jansenism—it was a long time since she had boldly faced them. What were they?

Every man is a tainted creature, fallen into an incurable and permanent habit of sinning. His every action, his every thought—beginning from the puny egotism of his babyhood—is a loathsome sin in the eyes of God. The only remedy for the diseased will that prompts these sinful thoughts and actions is the sovereign, infallible grace that God sends on those whom He has decided in His secret councils to raise to a state of triumphant purity. And what does this Grace engender? An agony of repentance, a loathing of things visible, and a burning longing for things invisible—*in invisibilium amorem rapiamur*, yes, that is the sublime and frigid fate of the true penitent.

And she had actually deceived herself so far as to think that the Arch-Enemy of sin manifested His goodness like a weak, earthly father by gratifying one's worldly desires, one's 'concupiscence' which Jansenius calls the 'source of all the other vices'! No, His gifts to men were not these vain baubles, the heart's desires, but Grace, the Eucharist, His perpetual Presence on the Altar—gigantic, austere benefits befitting this solemn abstract universe, in which angels are helping men in the fight for their immortal souls.

Yes, this was the Catholic faith, this was the true and living God, to Whose throne she had dared to come with trivial requests and paltry bargainings.

She felt this evening an almost physical craving for perfect sincerity with herself, so without flinching she turned her scrutiny upon her love for Mademoiselle de Scudéry. There flashed into her mind the words of Jansenius upon the sin of Adam:—

'What could Adam love after God, away from whom he had fallen? What could so sublime a spirit love but the sublimest thing after God Himself, namely—*his own* spirit?... This love, through which he wished, somehow, to take joy in himself, in as much as he could no longer take joy in God, in itself did not long suffice. Soon he apprehended its indigence, and that in it he would never find happiness.

'Then, seeing that the way was barred that led back to God, the source of true felicity from which he had cut himself off, the want left in his nature precipitated him towards the creatures here below, and he wandered among them, hoping that *they* might satisfy the want. Thence come those bubbling desires, whose name is legion; those tight, cruel chains with which he is bound by the creatures he loves, that bondage, not only of himself but of all he imprisons by their love for him. Because, once again, in this love of his for all other things, it is above all *himself* that he holds dear. In all his frequent delights it is always—and this is a remnant of his ancient noble state—in *himself* that he professes to delight.'

How could she, knowing this passage, have deceived herself into imagining she could save her soul by love for a creature?

The words of Jansenius were confirmed by those of Saint Augustine:—

'I lived in adultery away from Thee.... For the friendship of this world is adultery against Thee,'

and her own conscience confirmed them both, for it whispered that her obsession for Mademoiselle de Scudéry was nothing but a subtle development of her *amour-propre*, and what was more, had swollen to such dimensions as completely to blot out God from her universe.

Well, she stood condemned in all her desires and in all her activities!

What was to be done? With regard to one matter at least her duty was clear. She must confess to Jacques that she had lied to him when she said she loved him.

And Mademoiselle de Scudéry ... would she be called upon to chase her from her heart? Oh, the cruelty of it! The horse-face and the plain gray gown ... the wonderful invention in *galanterie* made by herself and the Grecian Sappho ... the delicious 'light fire' of expectancy ... the desirability of being loved in return ... the deep, deep roots it had taken in her heart. To see the figure in gray serge growing smaller and smaller as earth receded from her, and as her new *amours*—the 'invisible things'—drew her up, and up with chill, shadowy arms—*she couldn't, she couldn't* face it!

In mental agony she leaned her elbows on the parapet of the bridge, and pressing her fingers against her eyes, she prayed passionately for guidance.

When she opened them, two gallants were passing.

'Have you heard the *mot* Ninon made to the Queen of Sweden?' one was asking.

'No, what was it?'

'Her Majesty asked her for a definition of the Précieuses, and Ninon said at once, "*Madame, les Précieuses sont les Jansénistes de l'amour!*" 'Twas prettily said, wasn't it?' They laughed, and were soon out of sight.

'Les Précieuses sont les Jansénistes de l'amour!' Madeleine laughed aloud, as there swept over her a flood of what she imagined to be divine illumination. Her prayer for guidance had been miraculously answered, and in a manner perfectly accordant with her own wishes. It was obviously a case of Robert Pilou's sacred screen. 'Profane history told by means of sacred prints becomes sacred history.' A Précieuse need only have a knack of sacramentalism to become in the same way a Jansenist, for there was a striking resemblance between the two creeds. In their demands on their followers they had the same superb disregard for human weakness, and in both this disregard was coupled with a firm belief in original sin (for the contempt and loathing with which the Précieuses regarded the manners of all those ignorant of their code sprang surely from a belief in 'original boorishness' which in their eyes was indistinguishable from 'original sin'), the only cure for which was their own particular form of grace. And the grace of the Précieuses, namely, *l'air galant*—that elusive social quality which through six or seven pages of *Le Grand Cyrus*, gracefully evades the definitions in which the agile authoress is striving to hold it, that quality without which the wittiest conversation is savourless, the most graceful compliment without fragrance, that quality which can be acquired by no amount of good-will or application, and which can be found in the muddiest poet and be lacking in the most elegant courtier—did it not offer the closest parallel to the mysterious grace of the Jansenists without which there was no salvation, and which was sometimes given in abundance to the greatest sinners and denied to the most virtuous citizens? And then—most striking analogy of all—the Précieuses' conception of the true lover possessed just those qualities demanded from us by Saint Paul and the Jansenists. What finer symbol, for instance, of the perfect Christian could be found than that of the hero of the *Astrée*, Céladon, the perfect lover?

Yes, in spite of Saint Augustine's condemnation of the men 'who blushed for a solecism,' she could sanctify her preciosity by making it the symbol of her spiritual development, and—oh, rapture—she could sanctify her obsession for Mademoiselle de Scudéry by making it definitely the symbol of her love for Christ, not merely a means of curing her *amour-propre*. Through *her*, she would learn to know Him. Had it not been said by Saint Augustine: '*My sin was just this, that I sought for pleasure, grandeur, vanity, not in Him, but in His creatures*,' by which he surely meant that the love of the creature for the creature was not in *itself* a sin, it only became so when it led to forgetting the Creator.

So, with singular rapidity this time, 'La folie de la Croix s'est atténuée.'

It was already twilight. In the Churches they would be celebrating Compline. The choir would be singing: '*Jube, Domine, benedicere,*' and the priest would answer: '*Noctem quietam et finem perfectum concedat nobis Dominus omnipotens.*'

The criers of wafers were beginning their nocturnal song: '*La joie! la joie! Voilà des oublies!*' It was time to go home; her mother would be anxious; she must try very hard not to be so inconsiderate.

It was quite dark when she reached the petite rue du Paon. She found Madame Troqueville almost frantic with anxiety, so she flung her arms round her neck and whispered her contrition for her present lateness and her former ill-humour. Madame Troqueville pressed her convulsively and whispered back that she was never ill-humoured, and even if she were, it was no matter. In the middle of this scene in came Berthe, nodding and becking. 'Ah! Mademoiselle is *câline* in her ways! She is skilled in wheedling her parents—a second Nausicaa!'

CHAPTER XIV
A DEMONSTRATION IN FAITH

The scruples with regard to having compromised with an uncompromising God which Madeleine entertained in spite of herself were silenced by the determination of settling things with Jacques. For a right action is a greater salve to conscience than a thousand good resolutions.

This determination gave her a double satisfaction, for she had realised that the relationship was also a sin against preciosity—and a very deadly sin to boot. For one thing, *les honnêtes femmes* must never love more than once, and then her shameful avowal that '*she loved him very much, and that he might take his fill of kissing,*' would surely cause the belles who staked their reputation on never permitting a gallant to succeed in expressing his sentiments and who were beginning to shudder at even the 'minor favours,' such as the acceptance of presents and the discreetest signs of the chastest complacency, to fall into a swoon seven fathoms deep of indignation, horror, and scorn.

The retraction should be made that very evening, she decided; it was to be her Bethel, a spiritual stone set up as a covenant between herself and God. But Jacques did not come back to supper that evening, so it happened that she celebrated her new *coup de grâce* in a vastly more agreeable manner.

After supper she had gone into her own room and had begun idly to turn over the pages of *Cyrus*, and, as always happened, it soon awoke in her an agonising sense of the author's charms, and a craving for closer communion with her than was afforded by the perusal of even these intimate pages. This closer communion could only be reached through a dance. In a second she was up and leaping:—

She has gone to a 'Samedi' where she finds a select circle of Sappho's friends ... then by a great effort of will she checks herself. Is she a Jansenist or is she not? And if she *is* a Jansenist, is this dancing reconcilable with her tenets? As a means of moulding the future it certainly is not, for the future has been decided once and for all in God's inscrutable councils. As a mere recreation, it is probably harmless. But is there no way of making it an integral part of her religious life? Yes, from the standpoint of Semi-Pelagianism it was a means of helping God to make the future, from the standpoint of Jansenism it can be *a demonstration in faith*, by which she tells God how safe her future is in His hands, and how certain she is of His goodness and mercy in the making of it.

Then, an extra sanctity can be given to its contents by the useful device of Robert Pilou's screen—let the talk be as witty and gallant as you please, as long as every conceit has a mystical second meaning.

This settled, once more she started her dance.

Madeleine has gone to a 'Samedi' at Mademoiselle de Scudéry's, where she finds a select circle of Sappho's friends.

The talk drifts to the writings of 'Callicrate,' as the late Monsieur Voiture was called.

'There is a certain verse of his from which an astute reader can deduce that he was not a Jansenist,' says Madeleine, with a deliciously roguish smile. 'Can any of the company quote this verse?'

A wave of amused interest passes over the room.

'I did not know that Callicrate was a theologian,' says Sappho.

'A theologian, yes, for he was an admirable professor of love's theory, but a real Christian, no, for he was but a feeble and faithless lover,' answers Madeleine, looking straight into Sappho's eyes. Sappho colours, and with a laugh which thrills Madeleine's ear, with a tiny note of nervousness says:—

'Well, Mademoiselle, prove your theory about Callicrate by quoting the verses you allude to, and if you cannot do so, we will exact a forfeit from you for being guilty of the crime of having aroused the delightful emotion of curiosity without the justification of being able to gratify it.' The company turn their smiling eyes on Madeleine, who proceeds to quote the following lines:—

'Ne laissez rien en vous capable de déplaire.

Faites-vous toute belle: et *tachez de parfaire*

L'ouvrage que les Dieux ont si fort avancé.'

'Now these lines allow great power to le libre arbitre, *and suppose a collaboration between the gods and mortals in the matter of the soul's redemption, which would, I am sure, bring a frown to the brows of* les Messieurs de Port-Royale.'

'Sappho, I think it is we that must pay forfeits to Mademoiselle, not she to us, for she has vindicated herself in the most spirituel *manner in the world,' says Cléodamas.*

'Let her lay a task on each of us that must be performed within five minutes,' suggests Philoxène.

'Mademoiselle, what labours of Hercules are you going to impose on us?' asks Sappho, smiling at Madeleine. Madeleine thinks for a moment and then says:—

'Each of you must compose a Proposition Galante *on the model of one of the Five.'*

The company is delighted with the idea, and Théodamas writes out the five original Propositions that the company may have their models before them, and proceeds to read them out:—

(1) *Some of God's commandments it is impossible for the Just to obey owing to the present state of their powers, in spite of the desire of doing so, and in spite of great efforts: and the Grace by which they might obey these commandments is lacking.*

(2) *That in the state of fallen nature, one never resists the interior grace.*

(3) *That to merit and demerit in the state of fallen nature, it is not necessary that man should have liberty opposed to necessity (to will), but that it suffices that he should have liberty opposed to constraint.*

(4) *That the Semi-Pelagians admitted the necessity of the inward grace preceding every action, even the inception of Faith, but that they were heretics in so far as they held that grace to be of such a nature that the will of man could either resist it or obey it.*

(5) *That it is a Semi-Pelagian error to say that the Founder of our faith died and shed His blood universally, for all men.*

They all take out their tablets and begin to write. At the end of five minutes Madeleine tells them to stop.

'I have taken the first as my model,' says Sappho, 'and indeed I have altered it only very slightly.' The company begs to hear it.

'No commandment of a lady is too difficult for an homme galant *to obey, for to him every lady is full of grace, and this grace inspires him with powers more than human.'*

Every one applauds, and expresses their appreciation of her wit.

'And now,' says Madeleine, 'that our appetite has been so deliciously whetted—if I may use the expression—by Sappho, have the rest of the company got their ragoûts *ready?'*

Doralise looks at Théodamas, and Théodamas at Philoxène, and they laugh.

'Mademoiselle, blindness is the penalty for looking on a goddess, and dumbness, I suppose, that of listening to two Muses. We are unable to pay our forfeits,' says Théodamas, with a rueful smile.

'Will not Mademoiselle rescue the Sorbonne galante *from ignominy, and herself supply the missing propositions?' says Sappho, throwing at Madeleine a glance, at once arch and challenging.*

'Yes! Yes!' cries the company, 'let the learned doctor herself compile the theology of Cupid!'

'When Sappho commands, even the doctors of the Sorbonne obey,' says Madeleine gallantly. 'Well, then, I will go on to the second proposition in which I will change nothing but one word. "That in the state of fallen nature, man never resists the external grace."' The company laughs delightedly.

'By the third I must admit to be vanquished,' she continues, 'the fourth is not unlike that of Sappho's! "That courtiers, although they admit the necessity of feminine grace preceding every movement of their passions, are heretics in so far that they hold the wishes of ladies to be of such a nature that the will of man can either, as it chooses, resist or obey them."'

'Delicious!' cries the company, 'that is furiously well expressed, and a well-merited condemnation of Condé and his petits-maîtres.'

'And now we come to the fifth, which calls for as much pruning as one of the famous Port-Royal pear-trees. "That it is an error of provincials and other barbarians to say that lovers burn with a universal flame, or that les honnêtes femmes give their favours to all men."' Loud applause follows.

'Mademoiselle,' says Théodamas, 'you have converted me to Jansenism.'

'Such a distinguished convert as the great Théodamas will certainly compensate the sect for all the bulls launched against it by the Holy Father,' says Madeleine gallantly.

'Well, I must admit that by one thing the Jansenists have certainly added to la douceur de la vie, and that is by what we may call their Miracle of the Graces,' says Sappho.

'What does Madame mean by "the Miracle of the Graces"?' asks Madeleine, smiling.

'I mean the multiplication of what till their day had been three Graces into at least four times that number. To have done so deserves, I think, to be called a miracle.'

'The most miraculous—if I may use the expression—of the miracles recorded in the Lives of the Saints has always seemed to me the Miracle of the Beautiful City,' says Madeleine innocently.

'What miracle is that? My memory fails me, if I may use the expression,' says Sappho, in a puzzled voice.

'Madame, I scarcely believe that a lady so widely and exquisitely informed as Sappho of Lesbos in both what pertains to mortals and in what pertains to gods, in short in Homer and in Hesiod, should never have heard of the "Miracle of the Beautiful City,"' says Madeleine, in mock surprise.

'Then Mademoiselle—as you say you can scarcely believe it—you show yourself to be a lady of but little faith!' says Sappho, her eye lighted by a delicious gleam of raillery.

'I must confess that the miracle Mademoiselle mentions has—if I may use the expression—escaped my memory too,' says Théodamas.

'And ours,' say Doralise and Philoxène.

'So this company of all companies has never heard of the Miracle of the Beautiful City!' cries Madeleine. 'Well, I will recount it to you.

'Once upon a time, in a far barbarian country, there lived a great saint. Everything about her was a miracle—her eyes, her hands, her figure, and her wit. One night an angel appeared to her and said: (I will not yet tell you the saint's name), "Take your lyre" (I forgot to mention that the saint's performance on this instrument was also a miracle, and a furiously agreeable one), "Take your lyre, and go and play upon it in the wilderness." And the saint obeyed the angel's command, though the wilderness was filled with lions and tigers and every other ferocious beast. But when the saint began to play they turned into ... doves and linnets.' A tiny smile of comprehension begins to play round the eyes of the company. Madeleine goes on, quite gravely:—

'But that was only a baby miracle beside that which followed. As the saint played, out of the earth began to spring golden palaces, surrounded by delicious gardens, towers of porphyry, magnificent temples, in short, all the agreeable monuments that go to the making of a great city, and of which, as a rule, Time is the only building contractor. But, in a few minutes, this great Saint built it merely by playing on her lyre. Madame, the city's name was Pretty Wit, and the Saint's name was ... can the company tell me?' and she looks roguishly round.

'It is a name of five letters, and its first letter is S and its last O,' says Théodamas, with a smile.

Madeleine flung herself breathless and exhausted on her bed.

Deep down her conscience was wondering if she had achieved a genuine reconciliation between Preciosity and Jansenism.

CHAPTER XV
MOLOCH

The period that ensued was one of great happiness for Madeleine. It was spent in floating on her own interpretation of the Jansenists' 'full sea of grace,' happy in the certainty, secure in the faith, that God in His own good time would grant her desires, and reverse the rôles of fugitive and pursuer. And being set free from the necessity of making her own future, *ipso facto* she was also released from the importunities of the gnat-like taboos and duties upon the doing or not doing of which had seemed to depend her future success.

She felt at peace with God and with man, and her family found her unusually gentle, calm, and sympathetic.

But Bethel was not yet raised. This was partly due to the inevitable torpor caused by an excess of faith. If it was God's will that she should have an explanation with Jacques, He would furnish the occasion and the words.

So the evenings slipped by, and Madeleine continued to receive Jacques's caresses with an automatic responsiveness.

Then, at a party at the Troguins, she met a benevolent though gouty old gentleman, in a black taffeta jerkin and black velvet breeches, and he was none other than Monsieur Conrart, perpetual secretary to the Academy, and self-constituted master of the ceremonies at the '*Samedis*' of Mademoiselle de Scudéry. Madeleine was introduced to him, and her demure attention to his discourse, her modest demeanour, and her discreet feminine intelligence pleased him extremely. She made no conscious effort to attract him, she just trusted God, and, to ring another change on her favourite *quolibet*, it was as if *la Grâce* confided to the Graces the secret of its own silent, automatic action. He grew very paternal, patted her on the knee with his fat, gouty hand, and focused his energies on the improvement of *her* mind instead of the collective mind of the company.

The end of it was that he promised to take her with him to the very next '*Samedi*.'

On the way home, she and Jacques went for a stroll in the Place Maubert, that favourite haunt of *petits-bourgeois*, where in pathetic finery they aired their puny pretensions to pass for *honnêtes gens*, or, more happily constituted, exercised their capacity for loud laughter and coarse wit, and the one privilege of their class, that of making love in public.

As a rule, Madeleine would rather have died than have been seen walking in the Place Maubert, but now, when her soul was floating on a sea of grace, so dazzlingly sunny, it mattered but little in which of the paths of earth her body chose to stray; however, this evening, her happiness was a little disturbed by an inward voice telling her that now was the time for enlightening Jacques with regard to her feelings towards him.

She looked at him; he was a lovable creature and she realised that she would sorely miss him. Then she remembered that on Saturday she was going to see Sappho, and in comparison with her the charm of pale, chestnut-haired young men lost all potency. She was going to see Sappho. God was very good!

They were threading their way between squares of box clipped in arabesque. It was sunset, and from a distant shrubbery there came the sounds of children at their play. The pungent smell of box, the voices of children playing at sunset; they brought to Madeleine a sudden whiff of the long, nameless nostalgia of childhood, a nostalgia for what? Perhaps for the *vitæ munus* (the fulfilment of life) of the Vesper hymn; well, on Saturday she would know the *vitæ munus*.

She seized Jacques's arm and, with shining eyes, cried out: 'Oh, God is exceeding merciful to His chosen! He keeps the promise in the Psalms, He "maketh glad our youth." When I think on His great goodness ... I want ... I want ... Oh, words fail me! How comes it, Jacques, you do not see His footsteps everywhere upon the earth?' She was trembling with exultation and her voice shook.

Jacques looked at her gently, and his face was troubled.

'One cannot reveal Grace to another by words and argument,' she went on, 'each must *feel* it in his own soul, but let it once be felt, then never more will one be obnoxious to doubts on ghostly matters, willy-nilly one will believe to all eternity!'

They found a quiet little seat beside a fountain and sat down. After a moment's silence Madeleine once more took up her *Te Deum*.

'Matter for thanksgiving is never wanting, as inch by inch the veil is lifted from the eyes of one's spirit to discover in time the whole fair prospect of God's most amiable Providence. Oh, Jacques, *why* are you blind?' His only answer was to kick the pebbles, his eyes fixed on the ground.

Then, in rather a constrained voice, he said: 'I would rather put it thus; matter for *pain* is never wanting to him who stares at the world with an honest and unblinking eye. What sees he? Pain—pain—and again pain. It is harsh and incredible to suppose that 'twould be countenanced by a *good* God. What say you, Chop, to pain?'

Madeleine was pat with her answers from Jansenism—the perfection of man's estate before the Fall, when there was granted him the culminating grace of free will, his misuse of it by his choice of sin, and its attendant, pain.

Jacques was silent for a moment, and then he said:—

'I can conceive of no scale of virtues wherein room is found for a lasting, durable, and unremitted anger, venting itself on the progeny of its enemy unto the tenth and twentieth-thousand generation. Yet, such an anger was cherished by your God, towards the children of Adam. Nor in any scale of virtues is there place for the pregnant fancy of an artificer, who having for his diversion moulded a puppet out of mud, to show, forsooth, the cunning of his hand, makes that same puppet sensible to pain and to affliction. Why, 'tis a subtle malice of which even the sponsors of Pandora were guiltless! Then his ignoble chicanery! With truly kingly magnanimity he cedes to the puppet the franchise of free will; but mark what follows! The puppet, guileless and trusting, proceeds to enjoy its freedom, when lo! down on its head descends the thunder-bolt, that it may know free will must not be exercised except in such manner as is accordant with the purposes of the giver. The pettifogging attorney!

'Yes, your God is bloodier than Moloch, more perfectly tyrant than Jove, more crafty and dishonest than Mercury.

'Have you read the fourth book of Virgil's *Æneid*? In it I read a tragedy more pungent than the cozenage of Dido—that of a race of mortals, quick in their apprehensions, tender in their affections, sensible to the dictates of conscience and of duty, who are governed by gods, ferocious and malign, as far beneath them in the scale of creation as are the roaring lions of the Libyan desert. And were I not possessed by the certainty that your faith is but a monstrous fiction, my wits would long ere now have left me in comparing the rare properties of good men with those of your low Hebrew idol.'

Madeleine looked at him curiously. This was surely a piece of prepared rhetoric, not a spontaneous outburst. So she was not the only person who in her imagination spouted eloquence to an admiring audience!

Although she had no arguments with which to meet his indictment, her faith, not a whit disturbed, continued comfortably purring in her heart. But as she did not wish to snub his outburst by silence—her mood was too benevolent—she said:—

'Do you hold, then, that there is no good power behind the little accidents of life?'

'The only good power lies in us ourselves, 'tis the Will that Descartes writes of—a magic sword like to the ones in *Amadis*, a delicate, sure weapon, not rusting in the armoury of a tyrannical god, but ready to the hand of every one of us to wield it when we choose. *Les hommes de volonté*—they form the true *noblesse d'épée*, and can snap their fingers at Hozier and his heraldries,' he paused, then said very gently, 'Chop, I sometimes fear that in your wild chase after winged horses you may be cozened out of graver and more enduring blessings, which, though they be not as rare and pretty as chimeras....'

'Because you choose to stick on them the name of chimeras,' Madeleine interrupted with some heat, 'it does not a whit alter their true nature. Though your mind may be too narrow to stable a winged horse, that is no hindrance to its finding free pasturage in the mind of God, of which the universe is the expression. And even if they should be empty cheats—which they are *not*— do you not hold the Duc de Liancourt was worthy of praise in that by a cunningly painted perspective he has given the aspect of a noble park watered by a fair river to his narrow garden in the Rue de Seine?'

'Why, if we be on the subject of painted perspectives,' said Jacques, 'it is reported that the late cardinal in his villa at Rueil had painted on a wall at the end of his *Citronière* the Arch of Constantine. 'Twas a life-size cheat and so cunning an imitation of nature was shown in the painting of sky and hills between the arches, that foolish birds, thinking to fly through have dashed themselves against the wall. Chop, it would vex me sorely to see you one of these birds!'

A frightened shadow came into Madeleine's eyes, and she furtively crossed herself. Then, once more, she smiled serenely.

For several moments they were silent, and then Jacques said hesitatingly:—

'Dear little Chop ... I would have you deal quite frankly with me, and tell me if you mean it when you say you love me. There are moments when a doubt ... I *must* know the truth, Chop!'

In an almost miraculous manner the way had been made easy for her confession, and ... she put her arms round his neck (in the Place Maubert you could do these things) and feverishly assured him that she loved him with all her heart.

CHAPTER XVI
A VISIT TO THE ABBAYE OF PORT-ROYAL

Madeleine's bitter self-reproaches for her own weakness were of no avail. She had to acknowledge once and for all that she had not the force to stand out against another personality and tell them in cold blood things they would not like. She could hedge and be lukewarm—as when Jacques wished to be formally affianced—but once she had got into a false position she could not, if the feelings of others were involved, extricate herself in a strong, straightforward way. Would God be angry that she had not set up the Bethel she had promised? No, because it was the true God she was worshipping now, not merely the projection of her own barbarous superstitions.

At any rate, to be on the safe side, she would go and visit Mère Agnès Arnauld at the Abbaye de Port-Royal (a thing she should have done long ago) for that would certainly please Him. So she wrote asking if she might come, and got back a cordial note, fixing Wednesday afternoon for the interview.

In spite of her exalted mood, she did not look forward to the meeting: 'I hate having my soul probed,' she told herself in angry anticipation. She could not have explained what hidden motive it was that forced her on Wednesday to make up her face with Talc, scent herself heavily with Ambre, and deck herself out in all her most worldly finery.

As it was a long walk to the Abbaye of Port-Royal—one had to traverse the whole of the Faubourg Saint-Jacques—Madame Troqueville insisted on Jacques accompanying her, and waiting for her, during the interview, at the abbaye gates.

They set out at about half-past two. Jacques seemed much tickled by the whole proceeding, and said that he longed for the cap of invisibility that, unseen, he might assist at the interview.

'You'll be a novice ere many months have passed!' he said, with a mischievous twinkle, 'what will you wager that you won't?'

'All in this world and the next,' Madeleine answered passionately.

'As you will, time will show,' and he nodded his head mysteriously.

'Jacques, do not be so fantastical. Why, in the name of madness, should I turn novice just because I visited a nun? Jacques, do you hear me? I bid you to retract your words!'

'And if I were to retract them, what would it boot you? They would still be true. You'll turn nun and never clap eyes again on old Dame Scudéry!' and he shrieked with glee. Madeleine paled under her rouge.

'So you would frustrate my hopes, and stick a curse on me?' she said in a voice trembling with fury. 'I'll have none of your escort, let my mother rail as she will, I'll not be seen with one of your make; what are you but my father's bawd? Seek him out and get you to your low revellings, I'll on my way alone!' and carrying her head very high, she strutted on by herself.

'Why, Chop, you have studied rhetoric in the Halles, the choiceness of your language would send old Scudéry gibbering back to her native Parnassus!' he called after her mockingly, then, suddenly conscience-stricken, he ran up to her and said, trying to take her hand: 'Why, Chop, 'tis foolishness to let raillery work on you so strangely! All said and done, what power have my light words to act upon your future? I am no prophet. But as you give such credence to my words why then I'll say with solemn emphasis that you will *never* be a novice, for no nuns would be so foolish as to let a whirlwind take the veil. No, you'll be cloistered all your days with Mademoiselle de Scudéry, and with no other living soul will you hold converse. Why, there's a pleasant, frigid, prophecy for you, are you content?'

Madeleine relented sufficiently to smile at him and let him take her hand, but she remained firm in her resolve to forgo his further escort, so with a shrug he left her, and went off on his own pursuits.

As Madeleine passed through the Porte Saint-Jacques, she seemed to leave behind her all the noisy operations of man and to enter the quiet domain of God and nature. On either side of her were orchards and monasteries in which, leisurely, slowly, souls and fruit were ripening. Over the fields of hay the passing wind left its pale foot-prints. Peace had returned to her soul.

Soon she was ringing the bell of the Abbaye of Port-Royal—that alembic of grace, for ever at its silent work of distilling from the warm passions of human souls, the icy draught of holiness—that mysterious depository of the victims of the Heavenly Rape.

She was shown into a waiting-room, bare and scrupulously clean. On the wall hung crayon sketches by Moustier of the various benefactors of the House. Madeleine gazed respectfully at this gallery of blonde ladies, simpering above their plump *décolletage*. They were inscribed with such distinguished names as Madame la Princesse de Guémené; Elizabeth de Choiseul-Praslin; Dame Anne Harault de Chéverni; Louise-Marie de Gonzagues de Clèves, Queen of Poland, who, the inscription said, had been a pupil of the House, and whom Madeleine knew to be an eminent Précieuse.

Some day would another drawing be added to the collection? A drawing wherein would be portrayed a plain, swarthy woman in classic drapery, whose lyre was supported by a young fair virgin gazing up at her, and underneath these words:—

Madeleine de Scudéry and Madeleine Troqueville, twin-stars of talent, piety, and love, who, in their declining years retreated to this House that they might sanctify the great love one bore the other, by the contemplation of the love of Jesus.

Madeleine's eyes filled with tears. Then a lay-sister came in and said she would conduct her to the *parloir*.

It was a great bare room, its only ornament a crucifix, and behind the grille there sat a motionless figure—the Mother Superior, Mère Agnès Arnauld. Her face, slightly tanned and covered with clear, fine wrinkles, seemed somehow to have been carved out of a very hard substance, and this, together with the austere setting of her white veil, gave her the look of one of the Holy Women in a picture by Mantegna. Her hazel eyes were clear and liquid and child-like.

When Madeleine reached the grille, she smiled charmingly, and said in a beautiful, caressing voice: 'Dear little sister, I have desired to see you this long time.'

Madeleine mumbled some inaudible reply. She tried to grasp the mystical fact that that face, these hands, that torso behind the grille had been built up tissue by tissue by the daily bread of the Eucharist into the actual flesh of God Himself. It seemed almost incredible!

Why was the woman staring at her so fixedly? She half expected her to break the silence with some reference to Mademoiselle de Scudéry, so certain was she that to these clear eyes her inmost thoughts lay naked to view.

At last, the beautiful voice began again: 'It would seem you have now taken up your abode in Paris. Do you like the city?'

'Exceeding well,' Madeleine murmured.

'Exceeding well—yes—exceeding well,' Mère Agnès repeated after her, with a vague smile.

Suddenly Madeleine realised that the intensity of her gaze was due to absent-mindedness, and that she stared at things without seeing them. All the same, she felt that if this pregnant silence were to continue much longer she would scream; she gave a nervous little giggle and began to fiddle with her hands.

'And what is your manner of passing the time? Have you visited any of the new buildings?'

The woman was evidently at a loss for something to say, why, in the name of madness, didn't she play her part and make inquiries about the state of her disciple's soul? Madeleine began to feel quite offended.

'Yes,' she answered, 'I have seen the Palais Mazarin and I have visited the Hôtel de Rambouillet.'

'Ah, yes, the Hôtel de Rambouillet. My cousins report it to be a very noble fabric. Some day when the family is in the country you may be able to see the apartments, which are adorned, I am told, in a most rare and costly manner.'

So she took it for granted that Madeleine had only seen the outside! It was annoying, but it was no use enlightening her, because, even if she listened, she would not be in the least impressed.

There was another pause, then Mère Agnès turned on her a quick, kind glance, and said:—

'Talk to me of yourself!'

'What manner of things shall I tell you?' Madeleine asked nervously.

'What of theology? Do you still fret yourself over seeming incongruities?' she asked with a little twinkle.

'No,' Madeleine answered with a blush, 'most of my doubts have been resolved.'

''Tis well, dear child, for abstracted speculation is but an oppilation to the free motion of the spirit. 'Tis but a faulty instrument, the intellect, even for the observing of the *works* of God, how little apt is it then, for the apprehension of God Himself? But the spirit is the sea of glass, wherein is imaged in lucid colours and untrembling outlines the Golden City where dwells the Lamb. Grace will be given to you, my child, to gaze into that sea where all is clear.'

She spoke in a soft, level, soothing voice. Her words were a confirmation of what Madeleine had tried to express to Jacques the other day in the garden of the Place Maubert, but suddenly—she could not have said why—she found herself echoing with much heat those very theories of his that had seemed so absurd to her then.

'But how comes it that God is good? He commands *us* to forgive, while He Himself has need of unceasing propitiation and the blood of His Son to forgive the Fall of Adam. And verily 'tis a cruel, barbarous, and most unworthy motion to "visit the sins of the fathers upon the children"; a *man* must put on something of a devil before he can act thus. He would seem to demand perfection in us while He Himself is moved by every passion,' and she looked at Mère Agnès half frightened, half defiant.

Mère Agnès, with knitted brows, remained silent for a moment. Then she said hesitatingly and as if thinking aloud:—

'The ways of God to man are, in truth, a great mystery. But I think we are too apt to forget the unity of the Trinity. Our Lord was made man partly to this end, that His Incarnation might be the instrument of our learning to know the Father through the Son, that the divine mercy and love, hitherto revealed but in speculative generals, might be turned into particulars proportioned to our finite understandings. Thus, if such mysteries as the Creation, the Preservation, nay, even the Redemption, be too abstracted, too speculative to be apprehended by our affections, then let us ponder the Miracle of the Loaves and Fishes, the tender words to the woman of Samaria, the command to "suffer the little children to come unto Him," for they are types of the other abstracted mercies, and teach us to acknowledge that God is of that nature, which knows no conjunctions but those of justice and mercy. Yes, my child, all your doubts find their resolution in the life of Jesus. I mind me when I was a girl, in the garden of the Palais, the *arborist du roy*— as he was called—grew certain rare flowers from the Orient to serve as patterns to the Queen and her ladies for their embroidery. But when it was determined to build the Place Dauphine the garden had to go, and with it these strange blossoms. But the Queen commanded the *arborist* to make her a book of coloured plates wherein should be preserved the form and colour of the Orient flowers. And this was done, so patterns were not wanting after all to the Queen and her ladies for their broidery. Thus, for a time 'our eyes did see, and our ears did hear, and our hands did handle' our divine Pattern and then He ascended into Heaven, but, in His great mercy He has left a book wherein in clear, enduring pigments are limned the pictures of His life, that we too might be furnished with patterns for our broidery. Read the Gospels, dear child, read them diligently, and, above all, hearken to them when they are read in the presence of the Host, for at such times the operation of their virtue is most sure.'

She paused, and then, as if following up some hidden line of thought, continued:—

'Sometimes it has seemed to me that even sin couches mercy. Grace has been instrumental to great sins blossoming into great virtues, and——'

'Thus, one might say, "Blessed are the proud, for they shall become meek; blessed are the concupiscent, for they shall become pure of heart,"' eagerly interposed Madeleine, her eyes bright with pleasure over the paradox.

'Perhaps,' said Mère Agnès, smiling a little. 'I am glad you are so well acquainted with the Sermon on the Mount. As I have said, there is no instrument apter to the acquiring of grace than a diligent reading of the Gospels; the late Bishop of Geneva was wont to insist on this with my sister and myself. But bear in mind the consent and union of design between the holy Life on earth and the divine existence in Eternity, if one is pricked out with love and justice, so also is the other. We should endeavour to read the Gospels with the apocalyptic eye of Saint John, for it was the peculiar virtue of this Evangelist that in the narration of particulars he never permitted the immersion of generals. The action of his Gospel is set in Eternity. I have ever held that Spanish Catholicism and the teaching of the Jesuit Fathers are wont to deal too narrowly with particulars, whereas our own great teachers—I speak in all veneration and humility—Doctor Jansen, nay, even our excellent and beloved Saint Cyran, in that their souls were like to huge Cherubim, stationary before the Throne of God, were apt to ignore the straitness of most mortal minds, and to demand that their disciples should reach with one leap of contemplation the very heart of eternity instead of leading them there by the gentle route of Jesus' diurnal acts on earth.'

She paused. Madeleine's cheeks were flushed, and her eyes bright. She had completely yielded to the charm of Mère Agnès's personality and to the hypnotic sway of the rich, recondite phraseology which the Arnaulds proudly called '*la langue de notre maison.*'

'By what sign can we recognise true grace?' she asked, after some moments of silence.

'I think its mark is an appetite of fire for the refection of spiritual things. Thus, if an angel appeared to you, bearing in one hand a cornucopia of earthly blessings, and in the other, holiness—not, mind, certain salvation, but just holiness—and bade you make your choice, without one moment of hesitation you would choose holiness. Which would *you* choose?' and she looked at Madeleine gently and rather whimsically.

'I would choose the cornucopia,' said Madeleine in a low voice.

There was a pause, and then with a very tender light in her eyes, Mère Agnès said: 'I wish you could become acquainted with one of our young sisters—Sœur Jacqueline de Sainte-Euphémie Pascal—but she is at Port-Royal des Champs. She was born with every grace of the understanding, and affections most sensible to earthly joys and vanities, but in her sacrifice she has been as unflinching as Abraham. Hers is a rare spirit.'

Madeleine felt a sudden wave of jealousy pass over her for this paragon.

'What is her age?' she asked resentfully.

'Sœur Jacqueline de Sainte-Euphémie? She must be in her twenty-eighth year, I should say. Courage, you have yet many years in which to overtake her,' and she looked at Madeleine with considerable amusement. With the intuitive insight, which from time to time flashed across her habitual abstractedness, she had divined the motive of Madeleine's question.

'When she was twelve years old,' she went on, 'she was smitten by the smallpox, which shore her of all her comeliness. On her recovery she wrote some little verses wherein she thanked God that He had spared her life and taken her beauty. Could *you* have done that? Alas, when I was young I came exceeding short of it in grace. I mind me, when I was some ten years old, being deeply incensed against God, in that He had not made me "Madame de France"! My soul was a veritable well of vanity and *amour-propre*.'

'So is mine!' cried Madeleine, with eager pride.

Again Mère Agnès looked much amused.

'My child, 'tis a strange cause for pride! And bear in mind, I am the *last* creature to take as your pattern. No one more grievously than I did ever fall away from the Grace of Baptism. Since when, notwithstanding all the privileges and opportunities of religion afforded by a cloistered life and the conversation of the greatest divines of our day, I have not weaned myself from the habit of sinning. But one thing I *have* attained by the instrument of Grace, and that is a "hunger and thirst after righteousness" that springs from the very depths of my soul. I tell you this, that you may be of good courage, for, believe me, my soul was of an exceeding froward and inductile complexion.'

'Did you always love Our Lord with a direct and particular love?' Madeleine asked.

'I cannot call to mind the time when I did not. Do you love Him thus?'

'No.'

'Well, so senseless and ungrateful is our natural state that even love for Christ, which would seem as natural and spontaneous a motion of our being as is a child's love of its mother, is absent from our hearts, before the operation of Grace. But, come, you are a Madeleine, are you not? A Madeleine who cannot love! The Church has ordained that all Christians should bear the name of a saint whom they should imitate in his or her particular virtue. And the virtue particular to Saint Madeleine was that she "loved much." Forget not your great patron saint in your devotions and she will intercede for you. And in truth when I was young, I was wont to struggle against my love for Him and tried to flee from Him with an eagerness as great as that with which I do now pursue Him. And I think, dear child, 'twill fall out thus with you.'

Madeleine was deeply moved. Mère Agnès's words, like the tales of a traveller, had stirred in her soul a *wanderlust*. It felt the lure of the Narrow Way, and was longing to set off on its pilgrimage. For the moment, she did not shrink from "the love of invisible things," but would actually have welcomed the ghostly, ravishing arms.

'Oh, tell me, tell me, what I can do to be holy?' she cried imploringly.

'You can do nothing, my child, but "watch and pray." It lies not in *us* to be holy. Except our soul be watered by Grace, it is as barren as the desert, but be of good cheer, for some day the "desert shall blossom like the rose." "Watch and pray" and *desire*, for sin is but the flagging of the desire for holiness. Grace will change your present fluctuating motions towards holiness into an adamant of desire that neither the tools of earth can break nor the chemistry of Hell resolve. Pray without ceasing for Grace, dear child, and I will pray for you too. And if, after a searching examination of your soul, you are sensible of being in the state necessary to the acceptance of the Blessed Sacrament, a mysterious help will be given you of which I cannot speak. Have courage, all things are possible to Grace.'

With tears in her eyes, Madeleine thanked her and bade her good-bye.

As she walked down the rue Saint-Jacques, the tall, delicately wrought gates of the Colleges were slowly clanging behind the little unwilling votaries of Philosophy and Grammar, but the other inhabitants of the neighbourhood were just beginning to enjoy themselves, and all was noise and colour. Old Latin songs, sung perhaps by Abelard and Thomas Aquinas, mingled with the latest ditty of the Pont-Neuf. Here, a half-tipsy theologian was expounding to a harlot the Jesuits' theory of 'Probabilism,' there a tiny page was wrestling with a brawny quean from the *Halles aux vins*. Bells were pealing from a score of churches; in a dozen different keys viols and lutes and guitars were playing sarabands; hawkers were crying their wares, valets were swearing; and there were scarlet cloaks and green jerkins and yellow hose. And all the time that quiet artist, the evening light of Paris, was softening the colours, flattening the architecture, and giving to the whole scene an aspect remote, classical, unreal.

Down the motley street marched Madeleine with unseeing eyes, a passionate prayer for grace walling up in her heart.

Then she thought of Mère Agnès herself. Her rôle of a wise teacher, exhorting young disciples from suave spiritual heights, seemed to her a particularly pleasant one. Though genuinely humble, she was *very* grown-up. How delightful to be able to smile in a tender amused way at the confessions of youth, and to call one "dear child" in a deep, soft voice, without being ridiculous!

Ere she had reached the Porte Saint-Jacques she was murmuring over some of Mère Agnès's words, but it was not Mère Agnès who was saying them, but she herself to Madame de Rambouillet's granddaughter when grown up. A tender smile hovered on her lips, her eyes alternately twinkled and filled with tears: 'Courage, dear child, I have experienced it all, I know, I know!'

CHAPTER XVII
'HYLAS, THE MOCKING SHEPHERD'

She reached home eager to tell them all about her visit.

Her father and Jacques were playing at spillikins and her mother was spinning.

'She is a marvellous personage,' she cried out, 'her sanctity is almost corporeal and subject to sense. And she has the most fragrant humility, she talked of herself as though there were no more froward and wicked creature on the earth than she!'

'Maybe there is not!' said Jacques, and Monsieur Troqueville chuckled delightedly. Madeleine flushed and her lips grew tight.

'Do not be foolish, Jacques. The whole world acknowledges her to be an exceeding pious and holy woman,' said Madame Troqueville, with a warning glance at Jacques, which seemed to say: 'In the name of Heaven, forbear! This new *vision* of the child's is tenfold less harmful and fantastical than the other.'

Madeleine watched Jacques grimacing triumphantly at her father as he deftly extricated spillikin after spillikin. He was entirely absorbed in the idiotic game. How could one be serious and holy with such a frivolous companion?

'Pray tell us more of Mère Agnès, my sweet. What were her opening words?' said Madame Troqueville, trying to win Madeleine back to good humour, but Madeleine's only answer was a cold shrug.

For one thing, without her permission they were playing with *her* spillikins. She had a good mind to snatch them away from them! And how dare Jacques be so at home in *her* house? He said he was in love with her, did he? Yet her entry into the room did not for one moment distract his attention from spillikins.

'Yes, tell us more of her Christian humility,' said Jacques, as he drew away the penultimate spillikin. 'I'll fleece you of two crowns for that,' he added in an aside to Monsieur Troqueville.

'They are all alike in that,' he went on, 'humility is part of their inheritance from the early Christians, who, being Jews and slaves and such vermin, had needs be humble except they wished to be crucified by the Romans for impudence. And though their creeping homilies have never ousted the fine old Roman virtue pride, yet pious Christians do still affect humility, and 'tis a stinking pander to——'

'Jacques, Jacques,' expostulated Madame Troqueville, and Monsieur Troqueville, shaking his head, and blowing out his cheeks, said severely:—

'Curb your tongue, my boy! You do but show your ignorance. Humility is a most excellent virtue, if it were not, then why was it preached by Our Lord? Resolve me in that!' and he glared triumphantly at Jacques.

'Why, uncle, when you consider the base origin of——'

'Jacques, I beseech you, no more!' interposed Madame Troqueville, very gently but very firmly, so Jacques finished his sentence in a comic grimace.

After a pause, he remarked, 'Chapuzeau retailed to me the other day a *naïveté* he had heard in a monk's Easter sermon. The monk had said that inasmuch as near all the most august events in the Scriptures had had a mountain for their setting, it followed that no one could lead a truly holy life in a valley, and from this premise he deduced——'

'In that *naïveté* there is a spice of truth,' Monsieur Troqueville cut in, in a serious, interested voice. 'I mind me, when I was a young man, I went to the Pyrenees, where my spirit was much vexed by the sense of my own sinfulness.'

'I' faith, it must have been but hypochondria, there can have been no true cause for remorse,' said Jacques innocently.

Monsieur Troqueville looked at him suspiciously, cleared his throat, and went on: 'I mind me, I would pass whole nights in tears and prayer, until at last there was revealed to me a strange and excellent truth, to wit, that the spirit is immune against the sins of the flesh. To apprehend this truth is a certain balm to the conscience, and, as I said, 'twas on a mountain that it was revealed to me,' and he looked round with solemn triumph.

Madame Troqueville and Madeleine exchanged glances of unutterable contempt and boredom, but Jacques wagged his head and said gravely that it was a mighty convenient truth.

'Ay, is it not? Is it not?' cried Monsieur Troqueville, his eyes almost starting out of his head with eagerness, triumph, and hope of further praise. 'Many a time and oft have I drawn comfort from it.'

'I have ever held you to be a Saint Augustin *manqué*, uncle. When you have leisure, you would do well to write your confessions—they would afford most excellent and edifying reading,' and Jacques's eyes as he said this were glittering slits of wickedness.

After supper the two, mumbling some excuse about an engagement to friends, put on their cloaks and went out, and Madeleine, wishing to be alone with her thoughts, went to her own room.

She recalled Mère Agnès's words, and, as they had lain an hour or so dormant in her mind, they came out tinted with the colour of her desires. Why, what was her exhortation to see behind the 'particulars' of the Gospels the 'generals' of Eternity, but a vindication of Madeleine's own method of sanctifying her love for Mademoiselle de Scudéry by regarding it as a symbol of her love of Christ? Yes, Mère Agnès had implicitly advised the making of a Robert Pilou screen. *Profane history told by means of sacred woodcuts becomes sacred history*, was, in Mère Agnès's words, to read history 'with the apocalyptic eye of Saint John,' it was to see 'generals' behind 'particulars.'

But supposing ... supposing the 'generals' should come crashing through the 'particulars,' like a river in spate that bursts its dam? And supposing God were to relieve her of her labour? In the beginning of time, He—the Dürer of the skies—on cubes of wood, hewn from the seven trees of Paradise, had cut in pitiless relief the story of the human soul. The human soul, pursuing a desire that ever evades its grasp, while behind it, swift, ineluctable, speed 'invisible things,' their hands stretched out to seize it by the hair.

What if from the design cut on these cubes he were to engrave the pictures of her life, that, gummed with holy resin on the screen of the heavens, they might show forth to men in 'particulars proportioned to their finite minds,' the 'generals' cut by the finger of God?

Mère Agnès had said: 'I was wont to struggle against my love for Him with an eagerness as great as that with which I do now pursue Him. And I think, dear child, 'twill fall out thus with you.' 'Who flees, she shall pursue; who spurns gifts, she shall offer them; who loves not, willy-nilly she shall love.' Was the Sapphic Ode an assurance, not that one day Mademoiselle de Scudéry would love her, but that she herself would one day love Christ? What if she had read the omens wrong, what if they all pointed to the Heavenly Rape? How could she ever have dreamed that grace would be the caterer for her earthly desires—Grace, the gadfly, goading the elect willy-nilly along the grim Roman road of redemption that, undeviating and ruthless, cuts through forests, pierces mountains, and never so much as skirts the happy meadows? That she herself was one of the elect, she was but too sure.

'*Sortir du siècle*'—where had she heard the expression? Oh, of course! It was in *La Fréquente Communion*, and was used for the embracing of the monastic life. The alternative offered to Gennadius had been to 'sortir du siècle ou de subir le joug de la pénitence publique.' Madeleine shuddered ... either, by dropping out of this witty, gallant century, to forgo the *vitæ munus* or else ... to suffer public humiliation ... could she bear another public humiliation such as the one at the Hôtel de Rambouillet? Her father had been humiliated before Ariane ... Jacques had been partly responsible.... *Hylas, hélas!* ... the Smithy of Vulcan ... was she going mad?

In the last few hours by some invisible cannon a breach had been made in her faith.

CHAPTER XVIII
A DISAPPOINTMENT

By Friday, Madeleine was in a fever of nervousness. In the space of twenty-four hours, she would know God's policy with regard to herself. Oh! could He not be made to realise that to deprive her of just this one thing she craved for would be a fatal mistake? Until she was *sure* of the love of Mademoiselle de Scudéry she had no energy or emotion to spare for other things. She reverted to her old litany:—'Blessed Virgin, Mother of our Lord, give me the friendship of Mademoiselle de Scudéry,' and so on, which she repeated dozens of times on end.

This time to-morrow it would have happened; she would know about it all. Oh, how could she escape from remembering this, and the impossibility of fitting a dream into time? Any agony would be better than this sitting gazing at the motionless curtain of twenty-four hours that lay between herself and her fate. Oh, for the old days at Lyons! Then, she had had the whole of Eternity in which to hope; now, she had only twenty-four hours, for in their hard little hands lay the whole of time; before and after lay Eternity.

Madame Troguin had looked in in the morning and chattered of the extravagance of the Précieuses of her quarter. One young lady, for instance, imagined herself madly enamoured of Céladon of the *Astrée*, and had been found in the attire of a shepherdess sitting by the Seine, and weeping bitterly.

'I am glad that our girls have some sense, are not you?' she had said to Madame Troqueville, who had replied with vehement loyalty to Madeleine, that she was indeed. 'They say that Mademoiselle de Scudéry—the writer of romances—is the fount of all these *visions*. She has no fortune whatever, I believe, albeit her influence is enormous both at the Court and in the Town.'

Any reference to Sappho's eminence had a way of setting Madeleine's longing madly ablaze. This remark rolled over and over in her mind, and it burnt more furiously every minute. She rushed to her room and groaned with longing, then fell on her knees and prayed piteously, passionately:—

'Give me the friendship of Mademoiselle de Scudéry. Give it me, dear Christ, take everything else, but *give me that*.' And indeed this longing had swallowed up all the others from which it had grown—desire for a famous *ruelle*, for a reputation for *esprit*, for the entrée to the fashionable world. She found herself (in imagination) drawing a picture to Sappho of the Indian Islands and begging her to fly there with her.

At last Saturday came, and with it, at about ten in the morning, a valet carrying a letter addressed to Madeleine in a small, meticulous writing. It ran thus:—

'MADEMOISELLE,—A malady so tedious and unpoetical, that had it not been given the entrée to the society of *les mots honnêtes* by being mentioned by several Latin poets, and having by its intrinsic nature a certain claim to royalty, for it shares with the Queen the power of granting "Le Tabouret"; a malady, I say, which were it not for these saving graces I would never dare to mention to one who like yourself embodies its two most powerful enemies—Youth and Beauty—has taken me prisoner. Mademoiselle's quick wit has already, doubtless, solved my little enigma and told herself with a tear, I trust, rather than a dimple, that the malady which has so cruelly engaged me to my chair is called—and it must indeed have been a stoic that thus named it!—La Goutte! Rarely has this unwelcome guest timed his visit with a more tantalising inopportuneness, or has shown himself more ungallant than to-day when he keeps a poor poet from the inspiration of beauty and beauty from its true mate, wit. But over one circumstance at least it bears no sway: that circumstance is that I remain, Mademoiselle, Your sincere and humble servitor,

'CONRART.'

In all this fustian Madeleine's 'quick wit' did not miss the fact that lay buried in it, hard and sharp, that she was not to be taken to Mademoiselle de Scudéry's that afternoon. She laughed. It had so palpably been all along the only possible climax. Of course. This moment had always been part of her sum of experience. All her life, her prayers, and placations had been but the remedies of a man with a mortal disease. As often in moments of intense suffering, she was struck by the strangeness of being contained by the four walls of a room, queer things were behind these walls, she felt, if she could only penetrate them.

Berthe ambled in under pretext of fetching something, looking *espiègle* and inquisitive.

'Good news, Mademoiselle?' she asked. But Madeleine growled at her like an angry animal, and with lips stretched from her teeth, driving her nails into her palms, she tore into her own room.

Once there, she burst into a passion of tears, banging her head against the wall and muttering, 'I hate God, I hate God!' So He considered, did He, that 'no one could resist the workings of the inward Grace'? Pish for the arrogant theory; *she* would disprove it, once and for all. Jacques was right. He was a wicked and a cruel God. All the Jansenist casuistry was incapable of saving Him from the diabolic injustice involved in the First Proposition:—

'Some of God's Commandments it is impossible for the just to fulfil.'

In plain words, the back is *not* made for the burden. Oh, the cold-blooded torturer! And the Jansenists with their intransigeant consistency, their contempt of compromise, were worthy of their terrible Master.

So, forsooth, He imagined that by plucking, feather by feather, the wings of her hopes, He could win her, naked and bleeding, to Him and His service? She would prove Him wrong, she would rescind His decrees and resolve the chain of predestination. No, *her* soul would never be 'tamed with frets and weariness,' *she* would never 'pursue, nor offer gifts,' and, willy-nilly, *she* would never love, from the design on His cubes of wood no print of *her* life would be taken.

And then the sting of the disappointment pricked her afresh, and again she burst into a passion of tears.

Pausing for breath, she caught sight of the Crucifix above her bed. A feeling of actual physical loathing seized her for her simpering Saviour, with His priggish apophthegms and His horrid Cross to which He took such a delight in nailing other people. She tore down the Crucifix, and made her fingers ache in her attempt to break it. And then, with an ingenuity which in ordinary circumstances she never applied to practical details, she broke it in the door.

A smothered laugh disclosed Berthe crouching by the wall, her face more than usually suggestive of a comic mask. Madeleine was seized by a momentary fear lest she should prove a spy of the sinister 'Compagnie du Saint-Sacrement'—that pack of spiritual bloodhounds that ran all heretics relentlessly to earth—and she remembered with a shudder the fate of Claude Petit and le Sieur d'Aubreville. But after all, *nothing* could hurt her now, so she flung the broken fragments in her face and '*tutoied*' her back to the kitchen.

She went and looked at her face in the glass. Her eyes were tired and swollen and heavy, and she noted with pleasure the tragic look in them. Then a sense of the catastrophe broke over her again in all its previous force and she flung herself upon her bed and once more sobbed and sobbed.

Madame Troqueville, when she came in laden with fish and vegetables from the Halles, was told by Berthe with mysterious winks that she had better go to Mademoiselle Madeleine. She was not in the least offended by Madeleine's unwonted treatment of her, and too profoundly cynical to be shocked by her sacrilege or impressed by her misery. With a chuckle for youth's intenseness she had shuffled silently back to her work.

Madame Troqueville flew to Madeleine. Her entry was Madeleine's cue for a fresh outburst. She would not be cheated of her due of crying and pity; she owed herself many, many more tears.

Madame Troqueville took her in her arms in an agony of anxiety. At first Madeleine kicked and screamed, irritated at the possibility of her mother trying to alleviate the facts. Then she yielded to the comfort of her presence and sobbed out that Conrart could not take her to Mademoiselle de Scudéry.

How gladly would Madame Troqueville have accepted this explanation at its face value! A disappointment about a party was such a poignant sorrow in youth and one to which all young people were subject. But although she welcomed hungrily any sign of normality in her child, deep down she knew that *this* grief was not normal.

'But, my angel,' she began gently, 'Monsieur Conrart will take you some other time.'

'But I can't wait!' Madeleine screamed angrily; 'all my hopes are utterly miscarried.'

Madame Troqueville smiled, and stroked her hair.

''Tis foolish to rouse one's spleen, and waste one's strength over trifles, for 'twill not make nor mend them, and it works sadly on your health.'

Madeleine had been waiting for this. She ground her teeth and gave a series of short, sharp screams of tearless rage.

'For my sake, my angel, for my sake, forbear!' implored her mother.

'I shall scream and scream all my life,' she hissed. ''Tis my concern and no one else's. Ba-ah, ou-ow,' and it ended off in a series of shrill, nervous, persistent 'ee's.'

Madame Troqueville sighed wearily, and sat silent for some minutes.

There was a lull in the sobbing, and then Madame Troqueville began, very gently, 'Dear, dear child, if you could but learn the great art of *indifference*. I know that....'

But Madeleine interrupted with a shrill scream of despair.

'Hush, dear one, hush! Oh, my pretty one, if I could but make life for you, but 'tis not in my power. All I can do is to love you. But if only you would believe me ... hush! my sweet, let me say my say ... if *only* you would believe me, to cultivate indifference is the one means of handselling life.'

'But I *can't*.'

'Try, my dearest heart, try. My dear, I have but little to give you *in any way*, for I cannot help you with religion, in that—you may think this strange, and it may be wicked—I have always had but little faith in these matters; and I am not wise nor learned, so I cannot help you with the balm of Philosophy, which they say is most powerful to heal, but one thing I have learned and that is to be supremely indifferent—in *most* matters. Oh, dear treasure....'

'But I *want*, I *want*, I *want* things!' cried Madeleine.

Madame Troqueville smiled sadly, and for some moments sat in silence, stroking Madeleine's hair, then she began tentatively,—

'At times I feel ... that *"petite-oie,"* as you called it, frightened me, my sweet. It caused me to wonder if you were not apt to throw away matters of moment for foolish trifles. Do you remember how you pleased old Madame Pilou by telling her that she was not like the dog in the fable, that lost its bone by trying to get its reflection, well....'

'I said it because I thought it would please her, one must needs talk in a homely, rustic fashion to such people. Oh, let me be! let me be!' To have her own words used against her was more than she could bear; besides, her mother had suggested, by the way she had spoken, that there was more behind this storm than mere childish disappointment at the postponement of a party, and Madeleine shrank from her obsession being known. I think she feared that it was, perhaps, rather ridiculous.

Madame Troqueville gazed at her anxiously for some minutes, and then said,—

'I wonder if *Sirop de Roses* is a strong enough purge for you. Perhaps you need another course of steel in wine; and I have heard this new remedy they call "Orviétan" is an excellent infusion, I saw some in the rue Dauphine at the Sign of the Sun. I will send Berthe at once to get you some.'

CHAPTER XIX
THE PLEASURES OF DESPAIR

The disappointment had indeed been a shattering blow, and its effects lasted much longer than the failure at the Hôtel de Rambouillet. For then her vanity or, which is the same thing, her instinct of self-preservation, had not allowed her to acknowledge that she had been a social failure. But this disappointment was a hard fact against whose fabric saving fancy beat its wings in vain. Sometimes she would play with the thought of suicide, but would shrink back from it as the final blow to all her hopes. For, supposing she should wake up in the other world, and find the old longing gnawing still, like Céladon, when he wakes up in the Palace of Galathée? She would picture herself floating invisible round Mademoiselle de Scudéry, unable to leave any footprint on her consciousness, and although this had a certain resemblance to her present state, as long as they were both in this world, there must always be a little hope. And then, supposing that the first knowledge that flashed on her keener, freer senses when she had died was that if only she had persevered a year longer, perhaps only a month longer, the friendship of Mademoiselle de Scudéry would have been hers! She took some comfort from the clammy horror of the thought. For, after all, as long as she was alive there must always be left a few grains of hope ... while *she* was alive ... but what if one night she should be wakened by the ringing of a bell in the street, and running to the window see by the uncertain light of the lantern he held in one hand, a *macabre* figure, looking like one of the Kings in the pack of cards with which Death plays against Life for mortal men, the stiff folds of his old-world garment embroidered with skulls and tears and cross-bones! And what would he be singing as he rang his bell?:—

'Priez Dieu pour l'âme de la Demoiselle de Scudéry qui vient de trépasser.'

Vient de trépasser! Lying stiff and cold and lonely, and Madeleine had never been able to tell her that she loved her.

Good God! There were awful possibilities!

She was haunted, too, by the fear that God had *not* deserted her, but had resolved in His implacable way that willy-nilly she must needs eventually receive His bitter gift of Salvation. That, struggle though she would, she would be slowly, grimly weaned from all that was sweet and desirable, and then in the twinkling of an eye caught up 'to the love of Invisible Things.' 'One cannot resist the inward Grace;' well, she, at least, would put up a good fight.

Then a wave of intense self-pity would break over her that the all-powerful God, who by raising His hand could cause the rivers to flow backwards to their sources, the sun to drop into the sea, when she approached Him with her prayer for the friendship of a poverty-stricken authoress—a prayer so paltry that it could be granted by an almost unconscious tremble of His will, by an effort scarcely strong enough to cause an Autumn leaf to fall—that this God should send her away empty-handed and heart-broken.

Yes, it was but a small thing she wanted, but how passionately, intensely she wanted it.

If things had gone as she had hoped, she would by now be known all over the town as the incomparable Sappho's most intimate friend. In the morning she would go to her *ruelle* and they would discuss the lights and shades of their friendship; in the afternoon she would drive with her in le Cours la Reine, where all could note the happy intimacy between them; in the evening Sappho would read her what she had written that day, and to each, life would grow daily richer and sweeter. But actually she had been half a year in Paris and she and Sappho had not yet exchanged a word. No, the trials of Céladon and Phaon and other heroes of romance could not be compared to this, for they from the first possessed the *estime* of their ladies, and so what mattered the plots of rivals or temporary separations? What mattered even misunderstandings and quarrels? When one of the lovers in *Cyrus* is asked if there is something amiss between him and his mistress, he answers sadly:—

'Je ne pense pas Madame que j'y sois jamais assez bien pour y pouvoir être mal.'

and that was her case—the hardest case of all. In the old sanguine days at Lyons, when the one obstacle seemed to be that of space, what would she have said if she had been told how far away she would still be from her desire after half a year in Paris?

One day, when wandering unhappily about the Île Notre-Dame, with eyes blind to the sobriety and majestic sweep of life that even the ignoble crowd of litigants and hawkers was unable to arrest in that island that is at once so central and so remote, she had met Marguerite Troguin walking with her tire-woman and a girl friend. She had come up to Madeleine and had told her with a giggle that they had secretly been buying books at the Galerie du Palais. 'They are stowed away in there,' she whispered, pointing to the large market-basket carried by the tire-woman, 'Sercy's *Miscellany of Verse*, and the *Voyage à la Lune*, and the *Royaume de Coquetterie*; if my mother got wind of it she'd burn the books and send me to bed,' at which the friend giggled and the tire-woman smiled discreetly.

'They told us at Quinet's that the first volume of a new romance by Mademoiselle de Scudéry is shortly to appear. Oh, the pleasure I take in *Cyrus*, 'tis the prettiest romance ever written!' Marguerite cried rapturously. 'I have heard it said that Sappho in the Sixth volume is a portrait of herself, I wonder if 'tis true.'

'It is, indeed, and an excellent portrait at that, save that the original is ten times wittier and more *galante*,' Madeleine found herself answering with an important air, touched with condescension.

'Are you acquainted with her?' the two girls asked in awed voices.

'Why, yes, I am well acquainted with her, she has asked me to attend her *Samedis*.'

And afterwards she realised with a certain grim humour that could she have heard this conversation when she was at Lyons she would have concluded that all had gone as she had hoped.

During this time she did not dance, because that would be a confession that hope was not dead. That it should be dead she was firmly resolved, seeing that, although genuinely miserable, she took a pleasure in nursing this misery as carefully as she had nursed the atmosphere of her second *coup de grâce*. By doing so, she felt that she was hurting something or some one—what or who she could not have said—but something outside herself; and the feeling gave her pleasure. All through this terrible time she would follow her mother about like a whimpering dog, determined that she should be spared none of her misery, and Madame Troqueville's patience and sympathy were unfailing.

Jacques, too, rose to the occasion. He lost for the time all his mocking ways, nor would he try to cheer her up with talk of 'some other Saturday,' knowing that it would only sting her into a fresh paroxysm of despair, but would sit and hold her hand and curse the cruelty of disappointment. Monsieur Troqueville also realised the gravity of the situation. On the rare occasions when the fact that some one was unhappy penetrated through his egotism, he was genuinely distressed. He would bring her little presents—a Portuguese orange, or some Savoy biscuits, or a new print—and would repeat over and over again: ''Tis a melancholy business! A melancholy business!' One day, however, he added gloomily: ''Tis the cruellest fate, for these high circles would have been the fit province for Madeleine and for me,' at which Madeleine screamed out in a perfect frenzy: 'There's *no* similarity between him and me! *none!* NONE! NONE!' and poor Monsieur Troqueville was hustled out of the room, while Jacques and her mother assured her that she was not in the least like her father.

Monsieur Troqueville seemed very happy about something at that time. Berthe told Madeleine that she had found hidden in a chest, a *galant* of ribbons, a pair of gay garters, an embroidered handkerchief, and a cravat.

'He is wont to peer at them when Madame's back is turned, and, to speak truth, he seems as proud of them as Mademoiselle was of the bravery she bought at the Fair!' and she went on to say that by successful eavesdropping she had discovered that he had won them as a wager.

'It seems that contrary to the expectations of his comrades he has taken the fancy of a pretty maid! He! He! Monsieur's a rare scoundrel!' but Madeleine seemed to take no interest in the matter.

The only thing in which she found a certain relief was in listening to Berthe's tales about her home. Berthe could talk by the hour about the sayings and doings of her young brothers and sisters, to whom she was passionately devoted. And Madeleine could listen for hours, for Berthe was so remote from her emotionally that she felt no compulsion to din her with her own misery, and she felt no rights on her sympathy, as she did on her mother's, whom she was determined should not be spared a crumb of her own anguish. In her childhood, her imagination had been fascinated by an object in the house of an old lady they had known. It was a small box, in which was a tiny grotto, made of moss and shells and little porcelain flowers, out of which peeped a variegated porcelain fauna—tiny foxes and squirrels and geese, and blue and green birds; beside a glass Jordan, on which floated little boats, stood a Christ and Saint John the Baptist, and over their heads there hung from a wire a white porcelain dove. To many children smallness is a quality filled with romance, and Madeleine used to crave to walk into this miniature world and sail away, away, away, down the glass river to find the tiny cities that she felt sure lay hidden beyond the grotto; in Berthe's stories she felt a similar charm and lure.

She would tell how her little brother Albert, when minding the sheep of a stern uncle, fell asleep one hot summer afternoon, and on waking up found that two of the lambs were missing.

'Then, poor, pretty man, he fell to crying bitterly, for any loss to his pocket my uncle takes but ill, when lo! on a sudden, there stood before him a damsel of heroic stature, fair as the *fleurs de lys* on a royal banner, in antic tire and her hair clipped short like a lad's, and quoth she, smiling: "Petit paysan, voilà tes agneaux!" and laying the two lost lambs by his side, she vanished. And in telling what had befallen him he called her just "the good Shepherdess," but the *curé* said she could be no other than Jeanne, la Pucelle, plying, as in the days before she took to arms, the business of a shepherdess.'

Then she would tell of the little, far-away inn kept by her father, with its changing, motley company; of the rustic mirth on the *Nuit des Rois*; of games of Colin-maillard in the garret sweet with the smell of apples; of winter nights round the fire when tales were told of the Fairy Magloire, brewer of love-potions; of the *sotret*, the fairy barber of Lorraine, who curled the hair of maidens for wakes and marriages, or (if the *curé* happened to drop in) more guileless legends of the pretty prowess of the *petit Jésus*.

Madeleine saw it all as if through the wrong end of a telescope—tiny and far-away.

CHAPTER XX
FRESH HOPE

One afternoon Madame Troqueville called Madeleine in an eager voice. Madeleine listlessly came to her.

'I have a piece of news for you,' she said, looking at her with smiling eyes.

'What is it?... Doubtless some one has invited us to a Comedy,' she said wearily.

'No! I came back by the Île and there I chanced on Monsieur Conrart walking with a friend'—Madeleine went deadly white—'And I went up and accosted him. He has such a good-natured look! I told him how grievously chagrined you had been when his project came to naught of driving you to wait upon Mademoiselle de Scudéry, indeed I told him it had worked on you so powerfully you had fallen ill.'

'You didn't! Oh! Oh! Oh! 'Tis not possible you told him that!' wailed Madeleine, her eyes suddenly filling with tears.

'But come, my dear heart, where was the harm?' Madeleine covered her face with her hands and writhed in nervous agony, giving little short, sharp moans.

'Oh! Oh! I would liefer have *died*.'

'Come, my heart, don't be so fantastical, he was so concerned about it, and you haven't yet heard the pleasantest part of my news!'

'What?' asked Madeleine breathlessly, while wild hopes darted through her mind, such as Mademoiselle de Scudéry having confessed a secret passion for her to Conrart.

'This Saturday, he is coming in his coach to fetch you to wait on her!'

Madeleine received the news with a welter of different emotions— wriggling self-consciousness, mortification at the thought of Conrart knowing, and perhaps telling Mademoiselle de Scudéry, how much she cared, excitement bubbling up through apprehension, premature shyness, and a little regret for having to discard her misery, to which she had become thoroughly accustomed. She trembled with excitement, but did not speak.

'Are you pleased?' her mother asked, taking her hands. She felt rather proud of herself, for she disliked taking the field even more than Madeleine did, and she had had to admonish herself sharply before making up her mind to cross the road and throw herself on Conrart's mercy.

'Oh! yes ... yes ... I think I am,' and Madeleine laughed nervously. Then she kissed her mother and ran away. In a few minutes she came back looking as if she wanted to say something.

'What's amiss, my dear life?' Madeleine drew a hissing breath through her teeth and shut her eyes, blushing crimson.

'Er ... did ... er ... did he seem to find it odd, what you told him about my falling ill, and all that?'

'Dearest heart, here is no matter for concern. You see I was constrained to make mention of your health that it should so work on his pity that he should feel constrained to acquit himself towards you and——'

'Yes, but what did you say?'

'I said *naught*, my dear, that in any way he could take ill. I did but acquaint him with the eagerness with which you had awaited the visit and with the bitterness of your chagrin when you heard it was not to be.'

'But I thought you said that you'd said somewhat concerning—er—my making myself ill?'

'Well, and what if I did? You little goose, you——'

'Yes, but what did you say?'

'How can I recall my precise words? But I give you my word they were such that none could take amiss.'

'Oh! But *what* did you say?' Madeleine's face was all screwed up with nerves, and she twisted her fingers.

'Oh! Madeleine, dear!' sighed her mother wearily. 'What a pother about nothing! I said that chagrin had made you quite ill, and he was moved to compassion. Was there aught amiss in that?'

'Oh, no, doubtless not. But ... er ... I hope he won't acquaint Mademoiselle de Scudéry with the extent of my chagrin!'

'Well, and what if he did? She would in all likelihood be greatly flattered!'

'Oh! Oh! Oh! Oh! do you think he will? I'd *kill* myself if I thought he had!'

Madame Troqueville gave up trying to reduce Madeleine's emotions to reason, and said soothingly, 'I'm certain, my dearest, he'll do nothing of the kind, I dare swear it has already escaped his memory.' And Madeleine was comforted.

She ran into her own room, her emotions all in a whirl, and flung herself on her bed.

Then she sprang up, and, after all these leaden-footed weeks, she was again dancing.

PART III

Ainsi de ce désir que le primitif croyait être une des forces de l'univers et d'où il fit sortir tout son panthéon, le musulman a fait Allâh, l'être parfait auquel il s'abandonne. De même que le primitif logeait dans la cuiller promenée processionnellement son désir de voir l'eau abreuver la terre, ainsi le musulman croit qu'Allâh réalise la perfection en dehors de lui. Sous une forme plus abstraite l'argument ontologique de Descartes conclura de l'idée du parfait à son existence, sans s'apercevoir qu'il y a là, non pas un raisonnement, un argument, mais une imagination. Et cependant, à bien entendre les paroles des grands croyants, c'est en eux qu'ils portent ce dieu: il n'est que la conscience de l'effort continuel qui est en nous. La grâce du Janséniste n'est autre que cet effort intérieur.'

DOUTTÉ—*Magie et Religion.*

CHAPTER XXI
'WHAT IS CARTESIANISM?'

With the return of hope quite involuntarily Madeleine began once more to pray. But to whom was she praying? Surely not to the hard, remote God of the Jansenists, for that, she knew by bitter experience, would avail her nothing. Jansenism led straight to the 'Heavenly Rape'; of that she was convinced. If, as in spite of herself she could not doubt, there was only one God, and He such a Being as the Jansenists presented Him, then she must not pray, for prayers only served to remind Him of her existence, and that He should completely forget her was her only hope of escape from the 'ravishing arms.'

But ghostly weapons she *must* have with which to fight for success on Saturday. If not prayers, then something she could *do*; if not the belief in a Divine Ally, then some theory of the universe which justified her in hoping. For in Madeleine there was this much of rationalism—perverted and scholastic though it might be—that for her most fantastic superstitions she always felt the need of a semi-philosophical basis.

Suddenly she remembered Jacques's words in the Place Maubert: ''Tis the will that Descartes writes of—a magic sword like to the ones in *Amadis*.' To will, was not that the same as to desire? Mère Agnès had insisted on the importance of desiring. She had talked about the *adamant of desire that neither the tools of earth can break nor the chemistry of Hell resolve*. Hours of anguish could testify to that adamant being hers, but what if the adamant were a talisman, and that in its possession lay the certainty of success? She must find out about Cartesianism.

She ran into the parlour.

'Jacques, I would fain learn something of Descartes,' she cried.

'Descartes? Oh, he's the rarest creature! 'Tis reported he never ceases from sniffling in his nose, and like Allah, he sits clad in a dressing-gown and makes the world.'

Monsieur Troqueville cocked an eye full of intelligent interest and said, in his prim company voice: 'In good earnest, is that so?' But Madeleine gave one of Jacques's ringlets a sharp tweak, and asked indignantly what he meant by 'dressing-gowns and Allah.'

'Why, Allah is the Turk's God,' then, seeing that Monsieur Troqueville with pursed-up lips was frowning and shaking his head with the air of a judge listening to an over-specious counsel, he added,—

'Well, uncle, do you lean to a contrary opinion?'

'All the world is aware that Mohammed is the Turk's God—*Mohammed*. But you have ever held opinions eccentric to those of all staid and learned doctors!'

'Uncle, I would have you know that *Allah* is the Turk's God.'

'Mohammed!'

'Allah, I say, and as there is good ground for holding that he is ever clad in a Turkish dressing-gown, thus....'

'They dub their God Mohammed,' roared Monsieur Troqueville, purple in the face.

'Mohammed or Allah, 'tis of little moment which. But I would fain learn something of Descartes' philosophy,' said Madeleine wearily.

'Well,' began Jacques, delighted to hold forth, ''Tis comprised in the axiom, *cogito, ergo sum*—I think, therefore I am—whence he deduces....'

'Yes, but is it not he who holds that by due exercise of the will one can compass what one chooses?' broke in Madeleine, to the evident delight of Monsieur Troqueville, for he shot a triumphant glance at Jacques which seemed to say, 'she had you there!'

Jacques gave her a strange little look. 'I fear not,' he answered dryly; 'the Will is not the bountiful beneficent Venus of the Sapphic Ode.' Madeleine's face fell.

''Tis the opinion he holds with regard to the power exercised by the will over the passions that you had in mind,' he went on. 'He holds the will to be the passions' lawful king, and though at times 'tis but an English king pining in banishment, by rallying its forces it can decapitate *"mee lord protectour"* and re-ascend in triumph the steps of its ancient throne. This done, 'tis no longer an English king but an Emperor of Muscovy—so complete and absolute is its sway over the passions.

'Ainsi de vos désirs toujours reine absolue

De la plus forte ardeur vous portez vos esprits

Jusqu'à l'indifférence, et peut-être au mépris,

Et votre fermeté fait succéder sans peine

La faveur au dédain, et l'amour à la haine.

'There is a pretty dissertation for you, adorned with a most apt quotation from Corneille. Why, I could make my fortune in the Ruelles as a Professor of *philosophie pour les dames*!' he cried with an affectionate little *moue* at Madeleine, restored to complete good humour by the sound of his own voice. But Madeleine looked vexed, and Monsieur Troqueville, his eyes starting from his head with triumph, spluttered out, ''Twas from *Polyeucte*, those lines you quoted, and how does Pauline answer them?

'Ma raison, il est vrai, dompte mes sentiments;

Mais, quelque authorité que sur eux elle ait prise,

Elle n'y règne pas, elle les tyrannise,

Et quoique le dehors soit sans émotion,

Le dedans n'est que trouble et que sédition.

'So you see, my young gallant, I know my Corneille as well as you do!' and he rubbed his hands in glee. '"Le dedans n'est que trouble et que sédition," how would your old Descartes answer that? 'Tis better surely to yield to every Passion like a gentleman, than to have a long solemn face and a score of devils fighting in your heart like a knavish Huguenot ... *hein*, Jacques? *hein?*' (It was not that Monsieur Troqueville felt any special dislike to the tenets of Cartesianism in themselves, he merely wished to prove that Jacques had been talking rubbish.)

'Well, uncle, there is no need to be so splenetic, 'tis not my philosophy; 'tis that of Descartes, and though doubtless——'

But Madeleine interrupted a discussion that threatened to wander far away from the one aspect of the question in which she was interested.

'If I take your meaning, Descartes doesn't teach one how to compass what one wishes, he only teaches us how to be virtuous?'

Monsieur Troqueville gave a sudden wild tavern guffaw, and rubbing his hands delightedly, cried, 'Pitiful dull reading, Jacques, *hein?*'

'You took his book for a manual of love-potions, did you?' Jacques said in a low voice, with a hard, mocking glint in his eyes.

He had divined her thought, and Madeleine blushed. Then his face softened, and he said gently,—

'I will get you his works, nor will it be out of your gain to read them diligently.'

CHAPTER XXII
BEES-WAX

As he had promised, Jacques brought her the works of Descartes, and she turned eagerly to their pages. Here, surely, she would find food sweeter to her palate than the bitter catechu of Jansenism which she had spewed from her mouth with scorn and loathing.

But to her intense annoyance, she found the third maxim in the *Discourse on Method* to be as follows:—

My third maxim was ever to endeavour to conquer myself rather than fortune, and to change my own desires rather than the order of the universe. In short, to grow familiar with the doctrine that 'tis but over our own thoughts we hold complete and absolute sway. Thus, if after all our efforts we fail in matters external to us, it behoofs us to acknowledge that those things wherein we fail belong, for us at least, to the domain of the impossible.

Here was a doctrine as uncompromising with regard to individual desires as Jansenism itself.

Oh, those treacherous twists in every creed and every adventure which were always suddenly bringing her shivering to the edge of the world of reality, face to face with its weary outstretched horizons, its cruelly clear outlines, and its three-dimensional, vivid, ruthless population. Well, even Descartes was aware that it was not a pleasant place, for did he not say in the *Six Meditations*:—

But the Reason is that my Mind loves to wander, and suffers not itself to be bounded within the strict limits of Truth.

But were these limits fixed for ever: were we absolutely powerless to widen them?

A few lines down the page she came on the famous wax metaphor:—

Let us choose for example this piece of Beeswax: it was lately taken from the comb; it has not yet lost all the taste of the honey; it retains something of the smell of the flowers from whence 'twas gathered, its colour, shape, and bigness are manifest; 'tis hard, 'tis cold, 'tis easily felt, and if you will knock it with your finger, 'twill make a noise. In fine, it hath all things requisite to the most perfect notion of a Body.

But behold whilst I am speaking, 'tis put to the fire, its taste is purged away, the smell is vanished, the colour is changed, the shape is altered, its bulk is increased, it becomes soft, 'tis hot, it can scarce be felt, and now (though you can strike it) it makes no noise. Does it yet continue the same wax? Surely it does: this all confess, no one denies it, no one doubts it. What therefore was there in it that was so evidently known? Surely none of those things which I perceive by my senses; for what I smelt, tasted, have seen, felt, or heard, are all vanished, and yet the wax remains. Perhaps 'twas this only that I now think on, to wit, that the wax itself was not that taste of honey, that smell of flowers, that whiteness, that shape, or that sound, but it was a body which a while before appeared to me so and so modified, but now otherwise.

She was illuminated by a sudden idea—startling yet comforting. In *itself* her bugbear, the world of reality, was an innocuous body without form, sound, or colour. Once before she had felt it as it really is—cold and nil— when at the *Fête-Dieu* the bell at the most solemn moment of the Mass had rung her into 'a world of non-bulk and non-colour.'

Yes, the jarring sounds and crude colours which had so shocked and frightened her were but delusions caused by the lying 'animal-spirits' of man. The true contrast was not between the actual world and her own world of dreams, not between the design cut by God's finger upon cubes of wood and her own frail desires, but between the still whiteness of reality and the crude and garish pattern of cross purposes thrown athwart it by the contrary wills of men.

Well, not only was Jansenism distasteful, but it was also untrue, and here was a grave doctor's confirmation of the magical powers of her adamant of desire.

The pattern of cross-purposes was but a delusion, and therefore not to be feared. The only reality being a soft *maniable* Body, why should she not turn potter instead of engraver and by the plastic force of her own will give the wax what form she chose?

Through her dancing she would exercise her will and dance into the wax the fragrance of flowers, the honey of love, the Attic shape she longed for.

Madeleine is following Théodamas (Conrart) into Sappho's reception-room. A dispute is raging as to whether Descartes was justified in regarding

Love as *soulageant pour l'estomac.* They turn to Madeleine and ask for her opinion: she smiles and says,—

'Twould provide the Faculty with an interesting *thèse du Cardinal*, but 'tis a problem that I, at least, am not fitted to tackle, in that I have never tasted the gastric lenitive in question.'

'If the question can be discussed by none but those experienced in love,' cries Sappho, 'then are we all reduced to silence, for which of us will own to such a disgraceful experience?'

The company laughs. 'But at least,' cries Théodamas, 'we can all of us in this room confess to a wide experience in the discreet passion of Esteem, although the spiritual atoms of which it is formed are too subtle, its motions too delicate to produce any effect on so gross an organ as the one in question.'

'Do you consider that the heart is the seat of esteem, or is esteem too refined to associate with the Passion considered as the chief denizen of that organ from time immemorial?' asks Doralise.

'The words "time immemorial" shows an ignorance which in a lady as full of agreeable information as yourself, has something indescribably piquant and charming,' says Aristée, with a delicious mixture of the gallant and the pedant. 'For 'tis well known,' he continues, 'that the Ancients held the liver to be the seat of the passion in question.'

'Well, then,' cries Madeleine gaily, 'these pagans were, I fear, more evangelical in their philosophy than we, if they made love and its close attendant, Hope, dwell together in ... *le foie*! But,' she continues, when the company had laughed at her sally, 'I hear that this same Descartes has stirred up by his writings a serious revolt in our members, what one might call an organic Fronde.'

'Pray act as our *Muse Historique* and recount us this *historiette*,' cries Sappho gaily.

'Would it be an affront to the dignity of Clio to ask her to cite her authorities?' asks Aristée.

'My authority,' answers Madeleine, 'is the organ whom Descartes has chiefly offended, and the prime mover of the revolt—my heart! For you must know that the ungallant philosopher in his treatise on the Passions sides neither with the Ancients nor the Moderns with regard to the seat of the Tender Passion.'

'To the Place de Grèves with the Atheist and Libertine!' cries the company in chorus.

'And who has this impious man dared to substitute for our old sovereign?' asks Théodamas.

'Why, a miserable pretender of as base an origin and as high pretensions as Zaga-Christ, the so-called King of Ethiopia, in fact, an ignoble little tube called the Conarium.'

'Base usurper!' cries all the company save Sappho, who says demurely,—

'I must own to considering it a matter rather for rejoicing than commiseration that so noble an organ as the heart should at last be free from a grievous miasma that has gone a long way to bringing its reputation into ill-odour. I regard Descartes not as the Heart's enemy but rather as its benefactor, as the venerable Teiresias who comes at the call of the noble Œdipus, desirous of discovering wherein lies the cause of his country's suffering. Teiresias tells him that the cause is none other than the monarch's favourite page, a pretty boy called Love. Whereupon the magnanimous Œdipus, attached though he is to this boy by all the tenderest bonds of love and affection, wreathes him in garlands and pelts him with rose-buds across the border. Then once more peace and plenty return to that fair kingdom, and *les honnêtes gens* are no longer ashamed of calling themselves subjects of its King.'

As she finishes this speech, Sappho's eye catches that of Madeleine, and they smile at each other.

'Why, Madame,' cries Théodamas, laughing, 'the inhabitant of so mean an alley as that in which Descartes has established Love, must needs, to earn his bread, stoop to the meanest offices, therefore we may consider that Descartes was in the right when he laid down that one of the functions of Love is to *soulager l'estomac*.'

CHAPTER XXIII
MADEMOISELLE DE SCUDÉRY'S SATURDAY

For the next few days Madeleine danced and desired and repeated mechanically to herself: 'I *will* get the love of Mademoiselle de Scudéry,' feeling, the while, that the facets of the adamant were pressing deep, deep into the wax of reality.

Then Saturday came, and Monsieur Conrart arrived in his old-fashioned coach punctually at 12.30. She took her place by his side and they began to roll towards the Seine.

'I trust Acanthe will be worshipping at Sappho's shrine to-day. His presence is apt to act as a spark setting ablaze the whole fabric of Sappho's wit and wisdom,' said Conrart in the tone of proud proprietorship he always used when speaking of Mademoiselle de Scudéry. Who was Acanthe? Madeleine felt a sudden pang of jealousy, and her high confidence seemed suddenly to shrink and shrivel up as it always did at any reminder that Mademoiselle de Scudéry had an existence of her own, independent of that phantom existence of hers in Madeleine's imaginings. She felt sick with apprehension.

As they passed from the rue de la Mortellerie into the fine sweep of the rue Sainte-Antoine the need for sympathy became peremptory. Conrart had been giving her a dissertation on the resemblance between modern Paris and ancient Rome, she had worn a look of demure attention, though her thoughts were all to the four winds. There was a pause, and she, to break the way for her question, said with an admirable pretence of half-dazzled glimpses into long vistas of thought: 'How furiously interesting. Yes—in truth—there is a great resemblance,' followed by a pause, as if her eyes were held spellbound by the vistas, while Conrart rubbed his hands in mild triumph. Then, with a sudden quick turn, as if the thought had just come to her,—

'I must confess to a sudden access of bashfulness; the company will all be strange to me.'

Conrart smiled good-naturedly.

'Oh, 'twill pass, I dare swear, as soon as you have seen Sappho. There is an indescribable mixture of gentleness and raillery in her manners that banishes bashfulness for ever from her *ruelle.*'

'Well, I must confess I did not find it so, to say truth she didn't charm me; her ugliness frightened me, and I thought her manners as harsh as her voice,' Madeleine found herself saying. Conrart opened his small innocent eyes as wide as they would go.

'Tut-tut, what blasphemy, and I thought you were a candidate for admission to our agreeable city!' he said in mild surprise. 'But here we are!'

They had pulled up before a small narrow house of gray stone. Madeleine tried to grasp the fact in all its thrillingness that she was entering the door of Mademoiselle de Scudéry's house, but somehow or other she could not manage it.

'I expect they will be in the garden,' said Conrart. 'Courage!' he added over his shoulder, with a kind twinkle. In another moment Madeleine was stepping into a tiny, pleasant garden, shadowed by a fine gnarled pear-tree in late blossom, to the left was seen the vast, cool boscage of the Templars' gardens, and in front there stretched to the horizon miles of fields and orchards.

The little garden seemed filled with people all chattering at once, and among them Madeleine recognised, to her horror, the fine figure of Madame Cornuel. Then the bony form of Mademoiselle de Scudéry, clad in gray linen, detached itself from the group and walked towards them. She showed her long teeth in a welcoming smile. Mignonne, her famous dove, was perched on her shoulder.

'This is delicious, Cléodomas,' she barked at Conrart, and then gave her hand with quite a kind smile to Madeleine. 'Mignonne affirms that all Dodona has been dumb since its prophet has been indisposed. Didn't you, my sweeting?' and she chirped grotesquely at the bird.

'Jésus!' groaned Madeleine to herself. 'A child last time and now a bird!'

'Mignonne's humble feathered admirer at Athis sends respectfully *tender* warblings!' Conrart answered, with an emphasis on 'tender,' as he took Mademoiselle de Scudéry's hand, still looking, in spite of himself, ridiculously paternal.

In the meantime the rest of the company had gathered round them. A distinguished-looking man, not in his first youth, and one of the few of the gentlemen wearing a plumed hat and a sword, said in a slow, rather mincing voice,—

'But what of *indisposed*, Monsieur? Is it not a word of the last deliciousness? I vow, sir, if I might be called *indisposed*, I would be willing to undergo all the sufferings of Job—in fact, even of Benserade's *Job*——'

'Chevalier, you are cruel! Leave the poor patriarch to enjoy the prosperity and *regard* that the Scriptures assure us were in his old age once more his portion!' answered Mademoiselle de Scudéry, and the company laughed and cried 'Bravo!' This sally Madeleine understood, as accounts had reached Lyons of the Fronde within the Fronde—the half-jesting quarrel as to the respective merits of Voiture's sonnet to *Uranie* and Benserade's to *Job*—which had divided literary Paris into two camps, and she knew that Mademoiselle de Scudéry had been a partisan of Job. However, she was much too self-conscious to join in the laughter, her instinct was to try to go one better. She thought of 'But Benserade's Job isn't old yet!'—when she was shy she was apt to be seized by a sort of wooden literalness—but the next minute was grateful to her bashfulness for having saved her from such bathos.

'But really, Madame, *indisposed* is ravishing; is it your own?' persisted the gentleman they called Chevalier.

'Well, Chevalier, and what if it is? A person who has invented as many delightful words as you have yourself shows that his obligingness is stronger than his sincerity if he flatters so highly my poor little offspring!' Madeleine gave a quick glance at the Chevalier. Could it be that this was the famous Chevalier de Méré, the fashionable professor of *l'air galant*, through whose urbane academy had passed all the most gallant ladies of the Court and the Town? It seemed impossible.

All this time a long shabby citizen in a dirty jabot had been trying in vain to catch Mademoiselle de Scudéry's eye. Now he burst out with,—

'A propos of *words*—er—of *words*,' and he spat excitedly—on Madame Cornuel's silk petticoat. She smiled with one corner of her mouth, raised her eyebrows, then pulling a leaf, gingerly rubbed the spot, and flung it away with a little *moue* of disgust. The shabby citizen, quite unconscious of this by-play, which was giving exquisite pleasure to the rest of the company, went on: 'What do you think then of my word affreux—aff-reux—a-f-f-r-e-u-x? It seems to me not unsuccessful—*hein*—*hein*?'

'Affreux?' repeated an extremely elegant young man, with a look of mock bewilderment.

'Affreux! What can it possibly mean, Monsieur Chapelain?'

'But, Monsieur, it tells us itself that it is a lineal descendant of the *affres* so famous in the reign of Corneille the Great, a descendant who has emigrated to the kingdom of adjectives. It is ravishing, Monsieur; I hope it may be granted eternal fiefs in our language!' said Mademoiselle de Scudéry courteously to poor Chapelain, who had begun to look rather discomfited. Madeleine realised with a pang that Mademoiselle de Scudéry had quite as much invention as she had herself, for the friend of her dreams had *just* enough wit to admire Madeleine's.

'Affreux—it is——' cried Conrart, seeking a predicate that would adequately express his admiration.

'Affreux,' finished the elegant young man with a malicious smile. Mademoiselle de Scudéry frowned at him and suggested their moving into the house. Godeau (for he was also there) stroked the wings of Mignonne and murmured that she had confessed to him a longing to peck an olive branch. Godeau had not recognised Madeleine, and she realised that he was the sort of person who never would.

They moved towards the house. Through a little passage they went into the Salle. The walls were covered with samplers that displayed Mademoiselle de Scudéry's skill in needlework and love of adages. The coverlet of the bed was also her handiwork, the design being, somewhat unsuitably, considering the lady's virtue and personal appearance, a scene from the *amours* of Venus and Adonis. There were also some Moustier crayon sketches, and portraits in enamel by Petitot of her friends, and—by far the most valuable object in the room—a miniature of Madame de Longueville surrounded by diamonds. Madeleine looked at them with jealous eyes; why was not *her* portrait among them?

Poor Chapelain was still looking gloomy and offended, so when they had taken their seats, Mademoiselle de Scudéry, with a malicious glance at the others, asked him if he would not recite some lines from *La Pucelle*. The elegant young man, who was sitting at the feet of Mademoiselle Legendre closed his eyes, and taking out an exquisite handkerchief trimmed with *Point du Gênes* with gold tassels in the form of acorns, used it as a fan. Madame Cornuel smiled enigmatically.

'Yes, Monsieur, pray give us that great pleasure!' cried Conrart warmly. Chapelain cleared his throat, spat into the fireplace and said,—

'It may be I had best begin once more from the beginning, as I cannot flatter myself that Mademoiselle has kept the thread of my argument in her head.' 'Like the thread of Ariadne, it leads to a hybrid monster!' said the elegant young man, *sotto voce*.

In spite of Mademoiselle de Scudéry's assurances that she remembered the argument perfectly, Chapelain began to declaim with pompous emphasis,—

Je chante la Pucelle, et la sainte Vaillance

Qui dans le point fatal, où perissait la France,

Ranimant de son Roi la mourante Vertu,

Releva son État, sous l'Anglais abbatu.'

On he went till he came to the couplet—

'Magnanime Henri, glorieux Longueville,

Des errantes Vertus, et le Temple, et l'asile—'

Here Madame Cornuel interrupted with a gesture of apology—"'L'asile des *errantes* vertus,'" she repeated meditatively. 'Am I to understand that *Messieurs les Académiciens* have decided that *vertu* is feminine?' Chapelain made an awkward bow.

'That goes without saying, Madame; we are not entirely ungallant; *les Vertus et les dames sont synonymes!*' 'Bravo!' cried the Chevalier. But Madame Cornuel said thoughtfully,—

'Poor Monsieur de Longueville, he is then an *hôpital pour les femmes perdues*; who is the Abbess: Madame his wife or—Madame de Montblazon?' Every one laughed, including Mademoiselle de Scudéry, and Madeleine feverishly tried to repeat her formula ten times before they stopped. Chapelain stared, reddened, and began with ill-concealed anger to assure Madame Cornuel that 'erring' was only the secondary meaning of the word; its primary meaning was 'wandering,' and thus he had used it, and in spite of all the entreaties of Mademoiselle de Scudéry, Conrart, and the Chevalier, he could not be persuaded to resume his recitation.

Then for a time the conversation broke up into groups, Mademoiselle de Scudéry devoting herself to Chapelain, and Madeleine found herself between Godeau and the Chevalier, who spoke to each other across her.

'What of Madame de la Suze?' asked Godeau. The Chevalier smiled and shrugged.

'As dangerous an incendiarist as ever,' he answered. 'A hundred Troys burn with her flame.'

'What a splendid movement her jealousy used to have; it was a superb passion to watch at play!'

'Ah! but it is killing her, if another poet's poems are praised, it means the vapours for a week.'

'She must sorely resent, then, the present fecundity of Mnemosyne.'

'Yes, for the most part, a *galant homme* must needs speak of the Muses to a poetess as ten, but to her we must speak as if there were but one!'

Godeau laughed.

'But what ravishingly languishing eyes!' the Chevalier went on rapturously.

'And what a mouth! there is something in its curves at once voluptuous and chaste; oh, it is indescribable; it is like the mouth of a Nymph!' cried the little prelate with very unecclesiastical fervour.

'You think it chaste? Hum,' said the Chevalier dryly. 'Her *chastity*, I should say, belongs to the band of Chapelain's *"vertus errantes."*' Godeau gave a noncommittal, ecclesiastical smile. 'I was speaking of her *mouth*,' he answered.

'Ah! what the Church calls a "lip-virtue." I see.'

Godeau gave another smile, this time a rather more laïcal one.

'And what of the charming Marquise, dear Madame de Sévigné?' Godeau went on. The Chevalier flung up his hands in mute admiration.

'There surely is the *asile des vertus humaines!*' cried Godeau. 'Ah, well, they both deserve an equal degree of admiration, but which of the two ladies do we *like* best?' They both chuckled knowingly.

'Yes, *Dieu peut devenir homme mais l'homme ne doit pas se faire Dieu,*' went on Godeau, according to the fashion among worldly priests of reminding the company of their calling, even at the risk of profanity. Then Madeleine said in a voice shaking with nervousness,—

'Don't you think that parallel portraits, in the manner of Plutarch, might be drawn of these two ladies?'

There was rather a startled look on Godeau's ridiculous, naughty little face. He had forgotten that this young lady had been listening to their conversation, and it seemed to him as unsuitable that strange and obscure young ladies should listen to fashionable bishops talking to their intimates, as it was for mortals to watch Diana bathing. But the Chevalier looked at her with interest; she had, the moment he had seen her, entered into his consciousness, but he had mentally laid her aside until he had finished with his old friend Godeau.

'There are the seeds in that of a successful *Galanterie*, Mademoiselle,' he said. 'Why has it never occurred to us before to write *parallel* portraits? We are fortunate in having for *le Plutarque de nos jours* a charming young vestal of Hebe instead of an aged priest of Apollo!' and he bowed gallantly to Madeleine.

Oh, the relief to be recognised as a *person* at last, and by the Chevalier de Méré, too, for Madeleine was sure it was he.

'Monsieur du Raincy,' he cried to the elegant young man who was still at Mademoiselle Legendre's feet and gazing up into her eyes. 'We think parallel portraits of Madame de Sévigné and Madame de La Suze would be *du dernier galant*, will you be *le Plutarque galant?*'

'Why not share the task with the Abbé Ménage? Let him do Mme. de Sévigné, and you, the other!' said Godeau with a meaning smile. Du Raincy looked pleased and self-conscious. He took out of his pocket a tiny, exquisitely chased gold mirror, examined himself in it, put it back, looked up. 'Well, if it is I that point the contrasts,' he said, 'it might be called "the Metamorphosis of Madame La Marquise de Sévigné into a *Mouche*," for she will be but a *mouche* to the other.'

'Monsieur Ménage might have something to say to that,' smiled the Chevalier.

Poor Madeleine had been trying hard to show by modest smiles of ownership that the idea was hers: she could have cried with vexation. ''Twas my conceit!' she said, but it was in a small voice, and no one heard it.

'What delicious topic enthralls you, Chevalier?' cried out Mademoiselle de Scudéry in her rasping voice, feeling that she had done her duty by Chapelain for the present. The Chevalier answered with his well-preserved smile,—

'Mademoiselle, you need not ask, the only topic that is not profane in the rue de Beauce—the heavenly twins, Beauty and Wit.' Madeleine blushed crimson at the mention of beauty, in anticipation of Mademoiselle de Scudéry's embarrassment; it was quite unnecessary, Sappho's characteristic was false vanity rather than false modesty. She gave a gracious equine smile, and said that these were subjects upon which no one spoke better than the Chevalier.

'Mademoiselle, do you consider that most men, like Phaon in your *Cyrus*, prefer a *belle stupide*—before they have met Sappho, I need not add—to a *belle spirituelle?*' asked Conrart. Mademoiselle de Scudéry cleared her throat and all agog to be dissertating, began in her favourite manner: 'Beauty is without doubt a flame, and a flame always burns—without being a philosopher I think I may assert that,' and she smiled at Chapelain.

'But all flame is grateful—if I may use the expression—for fuel, and wit certainly makes it burn brighter. But seeing that all persons have not sufficient generosity, and *élan galant* to yearn for martyrdom, they naturally shun anything which will make their flame burn more fiercely; not that they prefer a slow death, but rather having but a paltry spirit they hope, though they would not own it, that their flame may die before they do themselves. Then we must remember that the road to Amour very often starts from the town of Amour-Propre and wit is apt to put that city to the sword, while female stupidity, like a bountiful Ceres, fertilises the soil from her over-flowing Cornucopia. On the other hand, *les honnêtes gens* start off on the perilous journey from the much more glorious city of Esteem, and are guided on their way by the star of Wit.'

Every one had listened in admiring attention, except Madeleine, who, through the perverseness of her self-consciousness, had given every sign of being extremely bored.

'I hear a rumour—it was one of the linnets in your garden that told me—that shortly a lady will make her début at Quinets' in whom wit and beauty so abound that all the *femmes galantes* will have to pocket their pride and come to borrow from her store,' said the Chevalier. Conrart looked important. 'I am already in love to the verge of madness with Clélie,' he said; 'is it an indiscretion to have told her name?' he added, to Mademoiselle de Scudéry.

'The Chevalier de Méré would tell you that it is indiscreet to the verge of crime to mention the name of one's flame,' she answered with a smile, but she did not look ill-pleased. So Clélie was to be the name of the next book! Madeleine for some reason was so embarrassed and self-conscious at the knowledge that she did not know what to do with herself.

'I picture her dark, with hazel eyes and——' began Mademoiselle Legendre.

'And I guess that she is young,' said Madame Cornuel, with a twinkle. Du Raincy sighed sentimentally.

'Well, Monsieur, tell us what is *la Jeunesse*?' said Godeau.

'La Jeunesse?' he cried. 'La Jeunesse est belle; la Jeunesse est fraîche; la Jeunesse est amoureuse,' he cried, rolling his eyes.

'But she rarely enters the *Royaume du Tendre*,' said a little man as hideous as an ape—terribly pitted by smallpox—whom they called Pellisson, with a look at Mademoiselle de Scudéry. That lady smiled back enigmatically, and Madeleine found herself pitying him from the bottom of her heart for having no hope of ever getting there himself. There was a lull, and then people began to get up and move away. The Chevalier came up to Madeleine and sat down by her. He twisted his moustache, settled his jabot, and set to.

'Mademoiselle, I tremble for your Fate!' Madeleine went white and repeated her formula.

'Why do you say that?' she asked, not able to keep the anxiety out of her voice, for she feared an omen in the words.

'To a lady who has shown herself the mistress of so many *belles connaissances*, I need not ask if she knows the words of the Roman Homer: *Spretæ injuria formæ*?' Madeleine stared at his smiling, enigmatical face, could it be that he had guessed her secret, and by some occult power knew her future?

'I am to seek as to your meaning,' she said, flushing and trembling.

'*Jésus!*' said the Chevalier to himself, 'I had forgotten the prudery of the provinces; can it be she has never before been accosted by a *galant homme?*'

'*Pray* make your meaning clear!' cried Madeleine.

'Ah! not such a prude after all!' thought the Chevalier. 'Why, Mademoiselle, we are told that excessive strength or virtue in a mortal arouses in the gods what we may call *la passion galante*, to wit, jealousy, from which we may safely deduce that excessive beauty in a lady arouses the same passion in the goddesses.'

'Oh, *that's* your meaning!' cried Madeleine, so relieved that she quite forgot what was expected of her in the *escrime galante*.

'In truth, this *naïveté* is not without charm!' thought the Chevalier, taking her relief for pleasure at the compliment.

'But what mischief could they work me—the goddesses, I mean?' she asked, her nerves once more agog.

'The goddesses are ladies, and therefore Mademoiselle must know better than I.'

'But have you a foreboding that they may wreak some vengeance on me?'

The poor Chevalier felt quite puzzled: this must be a *visionnaire*. 'So great a crime of beauty would doubtless need a great punishment,' he said with a bow. Madeleine felt tempted to rush into the nearest hospital, catch smallpox, and thus remove all cause for divine jealousy. The baffled Chevalier muttered something about a reunion at the Princesse de Guémené and made his departure, yet, in spite of the strangeness of Madeleine's behaviour, she had attracted him.

Most of the guests had already left, but Conrart, Chapelain, Pellisson, and a Mademoiselle Boquet—a plain, dowdy little *bourgeoise*—were still there, talking to Mademoiselle de Scudéry. The Chevalier's departure had left Madeleine by herself, so Conrart called out to her,—

'A lady who has just been gallantised by the Chevalier de Méré' (so it *was* he!) 'will carry the memory of perfection and must needs be a redoubtable critic in manners; Sappho, may she come and sit on this *pliant* near me?' Madeleine tried to look bored, succeeded, and looked *gauche* into the bargain. Conrart patted her knee with his swollen, gouty hand, and said to Mademoiselle de Scudéry: 'This young lady feels a bashfulness which, I think, does her credit, at meeting La Reine de Tendre, Princesse d'Estime, Dame de Reconnaissance, Inclination, et Terrains Adjacents.' The great lady smiled and answered that if her 'style' included Ogress of Alarmingness, she would cease to lay claim to it. Here was Madeleine's chance. Mademoiselle de Scudéry was smiling kindly at her and giving her a conversational opening. All she did was to mutter her formula and look with stony indifference in the opposite direction. Mademoiselle de Scudéry raised her eyebrows a little and forthwith Madeleine was excluded from the conversation.

Shortly afterwards Conrart asked Madeleine if she was ready to go, and they rose. A wave of inexpressible bitterness and self-reproach broke over Madeleine as Mademoiselle de Scudéry took her hand absently and bade her good-bye. Her new god in a dressing-gown had loyally done his part, but she, like a fool, had spoiled it all. And yet, she felt if she had it all over again, she would be seized by the same demon of perversity, that again all her instincts would hide her real feelings under a wall of shields. And Conrart, what would he think of her? However, he seemed to think nothing in particular. He was evidently trying to find out what Madeleine's impressions of the company had been, and when she, anxious to make atonement, praised them enthusiastically, he chuckled with pleasure, as if her praise enhanced his own self-importance. 'But the rest of us are but feeble luminaries compared to Sappho—*the most remarkable woman of the century*—she was in excellent vein on Beauty and Wit.' It was on the tip of Madeleine's tongue to say 'A trifle pedantic!' but she checked herself in time. 'She always does me the honour of spending part of July and August at my little country house. It is delicious to be her companion in the country, the comparisons she draws between life and nature are most instructive, as well as infinitely gallant. And like all *les honnêtes gens* she is as ready to learn as to instruct; on a fine night we sometimes take a stroll after supper, and I give the company a little dissertation on the stars, for though she knows a thousand agreeable things, she is not a philosopher,' he added complacently.

'Ah, but, Monsieur, a grain of philosophy outweighs an ounce of agreeable knowledge; there is a solidity about your mind; I always picture the great Aristotle with your face!' Madeleine's voice was naturally of a very earnest timbre, and this, helped by her lack of humour and a halting way of speaking which suggested sincerity, made people swallow any outrageous compliment she chose to pay them. Conrart beamed and actually blushed, though he *was* perpetual and honorary secretary of the Academy, and Madeleine but an unknown young girl!

'Aristotle was a very great man, Mademoiselle,' he said modestly. Madeleine smiled. 'There have been great men *since* Agamemnon,' she said. Really this was a *very* nice girl!

'Mademoiselle, I would like you to see my little *campagne*——' he began.

'That would be furiously agreeable, but I fear I could not come till the end of July,' said Madeleine with unwonted presence of mind.

'Dear, dear, that is a long while hence, but I hope we shall see you then.'

'You are vastly kind, Monsieur; when shall I come?' Madeleine asked firmly.

'Well—er—let me see—are you free to come on the first day of August?'

'Entirely, I thank you,' cried Madeleine eagerly. 'Oh! with what pleasant expectancy I shall await it!—and you must *promise* to give me a lesson about the stars.' The beaming old gentleman promised with alacrity, and made a note of the date in his tablets.

At that moment, Madeleine caught sight of Jacques, strolling along the Quay, and suddenly filled with a dread of finding herself alone with herself, she told Conrart that she saw her cousin, and would like to join him.

CHAPTER XXIV
SELF-IMPOSED SLAVERY

'I knew you would have to pass this way, and I have been waiting for you this half-hour,' said Jacques. 'Well, how went the encounter?' That Madeleine was not in despair was clear from the fact that she was willing to talk about it.

'Oh! Jacques, I cannot say. Mademoiselle de Scudéry was entertaining the whole company with discourse, but when she did address a word to me I was awkward and bashful—and—and—not over civil. Do you think she will hate me?' She waited anxiously for his answer.

'Awkward, bashful, and not over civil!' laughed Jacques. 'What did you do uncivil? Did you put out your tongue and hiccough in her face? *Oh*, that you had! Or did you deliberately undress and then dance about naked? I would that people were more inclined to such pleasant antics!'

'In good earnest I did *not*,' said Madeleine severely. 'But I feigned not to be interested when she talked, and averted my eyes from her as if the sight of her worked on my stomach. Oh! what *will* she think of me?'

'Well, I don't know, Chop,' Jacques said dubiously; 'it seems you used arts to show yourself in such colours as 'twould be hard to like!'

'Do people never take likings to bashful, surly people?' she persisted.

'I fear me they are apt to prefer smooth-spoken, courtly ones,' he answered with a smile. 'But, take heart, Chop, you will meet with her again, doubtless, when you must compel yourself to civility and to the uttering of such *galanterie* as the occasion furnishes, and then the issue cannot choose but be successful. Descartes holds admiration to be the mother of the other passions; an you arouse admiration the others will follow of their own accord.'

''Tis easy to talk!' wailed Madeleine, 'but her visible presence works so strangely upon me as to put me out of all my precepts, and I am driven to unseemly stammering or to uncivil silence.'

'*Lingua sed torpet, tenuis sub artus Flamma demanat*, etcetera. Have you been studying that most witty anatomy of the lover in the volume of Catullus that I lent you?' asked Jacques, rather mockingly.

'Yes,' said Madeleine, blushing. Then, after a pause,—

'It seems that ... er ... er ... my father ... that this Ariane ... that, in short, he has prospered in his suit of late?'

'Has he? I am exceeding glad to hear it,' said Jacques dryly. Then, looking at her with his little inscrutable smile, he added: 'You show a most becoming filial interest in your father's *roman*; 'tis as if you held its issue to be tied up in some strange knot with the issue of your own.'

How sinister he was looking! Madeleine stared at him with eyes of terror. She tried to speak but no sound would come from her lips.

Suddenly his expression became once more kind and human.

'Why, Chop,' he cried, 'there are no bounds set to your credulity! I verily believe your understanding would be abhorrent of no fable or fiction, let them be as monstrous as they will. In good earnest you are in sore need of a dose of old Descartes!'

'But, Jacques, I have of late been diligently studying him and yet it has availed me nothing. My will has lost naught of its obliquity.'

'How did you endeavour to straighten it ... *hein?*' Jacques asked very gently.

Madeleine hung her head and then confessed her theory about the Wax, and how she had tried upon reality the plastic force of her will.

Jacques threw out his hands in despair.

'Oh, Chop!' he cried, 'it is a sin to turn to such maniac uses the cleanest, sweetest good sense that ever man has penned! That passage about the wax is but a *figure*! The only way to compass what we wish is to exercise our will first on our own passions until they will take what ply we choose, and then to exercise it on the passions of others. Success *lies in you* but is not to be compassed by vain, foolish rites after the manner of the heathen and the Christians. Why, you have made yourself a slave, bound with the fetters of affrighting fancies that do but confound the senses and scatter the understanding. The will is the only talisman. Exercise yourself in the right using of it against your next meeting with Mademoiselle de Scudéry, then when that meeting comes, at one word from you the bashful humours—docile now—will cower behind your spleen, and the mercurial ones will go dancing through your blood up to your brain, whence they will let fall a torrent of conceits like sugar-plums raining from the Palais Mazarin, and thus in Mademoiselle de Scudéry you will arouse the mother of the passions—Admiration.'

They both laughed, and arm in arm—Madeleine with a serene look in her eyes—made their way to the petite rue du Paon.

CHAPTER XXV
THE SYMMETRY OF THE COMIC MUSE

July came, making the perfume of the meadows more fragrant, the stench of the Paris streets more foul.

Madeleine had adopted Jacques's rationalism, and, having discarded all supernatural aids, was applying her energies to the quelling of her 'passions.'

It stood to reason that *l'amitié tendre* could only spring from the seeds of Admiration. It behoved her, then, to make herself worthy of Admiration. The surest way of achieving this was to perfect herself in the *air galant*, and she had the great good fortune to procure the assistance of one of the most eminent professors of this difficult art. For the Chevalier de Méré wrote an elaborate Epistle asking her to grant him the privilege of waiting on her, which she answered in what she considered a masterpiece of elegant discretion, consisting of pages of obscure preciosity ending in the pleasant sting of a little piquant 'yes.'

He became an almost daily visitor, and, unfailingly suave and fluent, he would give her dissertations on life and manners, filled with that tame, *fade* common sense which had recently come to be regarded as the last word in culture.

She was highly flattered by his attentions, naturally enough, for he was considered to have exquisite taste in ladies and had put the final polish on many an eminent Précieuse. Under his tuition she hoped to be, by the time of her visit to Conrart, a past-mistress in the art of pleasing, and to have her 'passions' in such complete control as to be quite safe from an attack of bashfulness.

A July of quiet progress—then August and Mademoiselle de Scudéry! She awaited the issue of this next meeting with quiet confidence. There is a comfortable solidity about four weeks, like that of a square arm-chair in which one can sit at one's ease, planning and dreaming. If Madeleine had been gifted with clarity of vision she would have realised that, for her, true happiness was to be found nowhere but in that comfortable, sedentary posture. Only those very dear to the gods can distinguish between what they really want and what they think they want.

Berthe was full of sly hints with regard to the Chevalier, and his visits elicited from her many an aphorism on the tender passion. She had evidently given to him the rôle formerly played by Jacques in her version of Madeleine's *roman*.

And what of Jacques? He was naturally very jealous of the Chevalier and very angry with Madeleine.

He was now rarely at home in the evenings. Monsieur Troqueville, who, during the first week of July, was forced to keep his room by a severe attack of gout, seemed strangely uneasy.

Suddenly Jacques ceased coming home even to sleep, and at the mention of his name Monsieur Troqueville would be threatened by a fit of apoplexy.

When alone with Madeleine he was full of vague threats and warnings such as: 'When I get hold of that rascally cousin of yours, I would see him that dares prevent me strangling him!' 'Have a care lest that scoundrel Jacques stick a disgrace upon you, as he has done to me!' 'If you'll be ruled by me you'll have none of that fellow! 'Tis a most malicious and treacherous villain!'

A sinister fear began to stir in Madeleine's heart.

After a week's absence, Jacques appeared at supper, dishevelled and debonair, with rather a wicked gleam in his narrow eyes. The atmosphere during the meal was tense with suppressed emotion, and it was evident that Monsieur Troqueville was thirsting for his blood.

Supper over, Madeleine made a sign to Jacques to follow her.

'Well?' she asked him, once they were in her own room.

'Well?' he answered, smiling enigmatically.

'You have been about some mischief—I know it well. Recount me the whole business without delay.'

'Some mischief? 'Tis merely that I have been driving the playwright's trade and writing a little comedy, on life instead of on foolscap.'

'I do not take your meaning.'

'No? Have you ever remarked that Symmetry is the prettiest attribute of the Comic Muse? Here is my cast—two Belles and one Gallant. Belle I. loathes the Gallant like the seven deadly sins, while he most piteously burns with her flame, and has been hoodwinked by his own vanity and the persuasions of a friend that she burns as piteously with his. Now, mark the inverted symmetry—the Gallant loathes Belle II., while she burns with his flame and is persuaded that he does with hers. Why, the three are as prettily interrelated as a group of porcelain figures! I am of opinion that Comedy is naught but Life viewed geometrically.'

'You talk in riddles, Jacques, and I am entirely without clue to your meaning—save that it is some foolishness,' cried Madeleine with intense irritation. Jacques's only answer was an inscrutable smile.

'Read me your riddle without delay, or you'll have me stark mad with your nonsense!' she cried with tears of suspense and impatience in her eyes.

So Jacques told her how after his first rebuff Monsieur Troqueville had for a time ceased to pester Ariane with his addresses, and had found balm for his hurt vanity in pretending to his tavern companions that his success with Ariane had been complete, and that he held her heart in the hollow of his hand. He had almost come to believe this himself, when one evening his friends in the tavern, who had of course never believed his story, had insisted on seeing Ariane in the flesh. It was in vain that Monsieur Troqueville had furiously reiterated that 'the lady being no common bawd, but exceeding dainty of her favours, would never stoop to such low company as theirs.' The company was obdurate, reiterating that unless they saw her with their own eyes they would hold his '*Chimène*' to be but a '*chimère*,' and that like Troy in Euripides' fable, it was but for a phantom lady that he burned. Finally, Monsieur Troqueville, goaded beyond all endurance, vowed that the lady would be with them ere an hour was passed. The company agreed that if he did not keep his word he would have to stand drinks all round and kiss their grim Huguenot hostess, while if Ariane appeared within an hour they would give him as brave a *petite-oie* as their joint purses could afford. (At the words '*petite-oie*' Madeleine went pale.) Once outside the tavern Monsieur Troqueville gave way to despair, and Jacques was so sorry for him that although he felt certain the business would end in ridicule for them both, he rushed to Ariane's house to see if he could move her to pity. Fortunately he found her alone and bored—and took her fancy. To cut a long story short, before the hour was up, amid the cheers of the revellers and the Biblical denunciations of the hostess, Ariane made her epiphany at the tavern and saved Monsieur Troqueville's face. After that Jacques went often to see Ariane, and delivered the love-letters he carried from Monsieur Troqueville, not to her but to her ancient duenna, in whose withered bosom he had easily kindled a flame for his uncle. Finally, having promised him a meeting with his lady, he had thrown him into the arms of the duenna.

When Jacques had finished his story, Madeleine, who had gazed at him with a growing horror in her eyes, said slowly,—

'To speak truth, you seem to me compact of cruelty.' At once he looked penitent. 'No, Chop, 'tis not my only humour. One does not hold Boisrobert and the other writers of Comedy to be cruel in that they devise droll situations for their characters.'

'That is another matter.'

'Well, maybe you are in the right. 'Twas a scurvy trick I played him, and I am ashamed. Are you grievously wroth with me, Chop?'

'I can hardly say,' she answered and, her eyes wandering restlessly over the room, she twisted her hands in a way she had when her nerves were taut. 'There are times when I am wont to wonder ... if haply I do not somewhat resemble my father,' she added with a queer little laugh.

The idea seemed to tickle Jacques. She looked at him angrily.

'You hold then that there is truth in what I say?' and try as she would she could not get him to say that there was not.

CHAPTER XXVI
BERTHE'S STORY

Madeleine was feeling restless, so she asked Berthe to come and sit by her bed and talk to her.

'Tell me a story,' she commanded, and Berthe delightedly launched forth on her favourite theme, that of Madeleine's resemblance to her youngest brother.

'Oh, he often comes to me and says, "Tell me a story, Berthe," like that, "tell me a story, Berthe," and I'll say, "Do you think I have nothing better to do, sir, than tell you stories. Off you go and dig cabbages;" and he'll say, with a bow, "Dig them yourself, Madame"—oh, he's *malin*, ever pat with an answer; he is like Monsieur Jacques in that way. One day——'

'Please tell me a story,' Madeleine persisted. 'Tell me the one about Nausicaa.'

'Ah! that was the one that came back to me when Mademoiselle turned with such zeal to housewifery!' and she chuckled delightedly.

'Tell it to me!'

'Well, it was a pretty tale my grandmother used to tell; she heard it from *her* grandmother, who had been tire-woman to a great lady in the reign of good King Francis.'

'Begin the tale,' commanded Madeleine firmly.

'Oh, Mademoiselle will have her own way—just like Albert,' winked Berthe, and began,—

'Once upon a time, hundreds of years ago, there lived a rich farmer near Marseilles. My grandmother was wont to say he was a king, but that cannot have been, for, as you will see, his daughter did use to do her own washing. Mademoiselle hates housework, doesn't she? *I* can see you are ill-pleased when Madame talks of a *ménage* of your own——'

'*Go on*,' said Madeleine. Berthe cackled, 'Just like Albert!' she exclaimed.

'Well, this farmer had an only daughter, who was very beautiful; she had an odd name: it was Nausicaa. She was *rêveuse*, like Mademoiselle and me, and used to love to lie in her father's orchard reading romances or looking out over the sea, which lay below. She did not care for the sons of the farmers round that came wooing her with presents of lambs and apples or with strings of beads which they bought from sailors at the harbour; they seemed to her clumsy with their foolish grins and their great hands, for Nausicaa was exceeding nice,' and Berthe winked meaningly. 'And there were merchants, too, with long beards and grave faces, and gold chains, who sought her hand, but she was aware that they looked on her as nothing better than the rare birds their ships brought them from the Indies. Well, one night, Our Lady appeared to her in a dream and said: "Lève-toi, petite paresseuse, les jeunes demoiselles doivent s'occuper du mariage et de leur ménage." And she bade Nausicaa go to the river, and wash all her linen, for if a Prince came he would be ill-pleased to find her foul. And Nausicaa woke up feeling very strange and as if fair wondrous things were coming to meet her. 'Tis a fancy that seizes us all at times, and much good it does us!' And Berthe gave her long, soft chuckle, while Madeleine scowled at her.

'As soon as she was dressed, Nausicaa ran into the fields to find her father, and she put her arms round his neck and hid her face on his shoulder and said, laughing,—

"'Father, I am fain you should lend me a cart and four mules for to-day," and her brothers, who were standing near, laughed and asked who was waiting for her at the other end. And Nausicaa tossed her head and said she did but want to wash her linen in the river. And her father pinched her ear and kissed her and said that he would order four of his best mules to be harnessed. And when her mother heard of her project she clapped her hands with joy and winked at the old nurse, for she divined the thought in Nausicaa's mind, and the poor soul was exceeding glad.'

'Go on,' Madeleine commanded feverishly, forestalling a personal deviation.

'Well, the mother filled a big hamper full of the delicate fare that Nausicaa liked best—*pain d'épice*, and quince jam and preserved fruits and a fine fat capon, and bade four or five of the dairymaids go with her and help her with her washing, and Nausicaa filled a great basket with her linen, and they all climbed into the cart, and Nausicaa took the reins and flicked the whip, and the mules trotted off. When they got to the river they rolled up their sleeves and set to, and they laughed and talked over their work, for Nausicaa was not proud. And when all the linen was washed and laid out on the grass to dry they sat down and ate their dinner and talked, and Nausicaa sang them songs, for she had brought her lute with her. And then they played at *Colin-Maillard* and at ball, and then they danced a *Branle*, and poor grannie used always to say that they were as lovely as the angels dancing in Paradise. Every one, of course, was comely long ago'—and Berthe interrupted her narration to chuckle.

'Grannie used always to go on like this: "They laughed and played as maidens will when they are among themselves, but they little knew what was watching them from behind a bush of great blue flowers," and we used to say, with our eyes as round as buttons—"Was it a bear, grannie?" "No." "Was it a *lutin*, then?" And we were grievously disappointed when she would say, "No, it was a man!" Well, it was a great Roman lord called Ulysse who had fought with Charlemagne at the Siege of Troy, and when he started on his voyage home, Saint Nicholas, the sailors' saint, who did not love him, pestered him with storms and shipwrecks and monstrous fish so that the years passed and he got no nearer home. And all the time he kept on praying to Our Lady to give him a safe and speedy return, and at last she heard his prayer, and when Saint Nicholas had once again wrecked his ship she rescued him from the sea and walked over the waves with him in her arms as if he were a little child till she reached the river near Marseilles, and then she laid him among the rushes by its banks, and there he slept. And when he woke up she worked a miracle so that the wrinkles and travel-stains and sunburn dropped away from him, and his rags she changed into a big hat with fine plumes, and a jerkin of Isabelle satin, and a cloak lined with crimson plush, and breeches covered with ribbons, so that he was once more the fine young gallant that had years ago started for the wars. And she told him to step out from behind the bush and accost Nausicaa. Oh, believe me, he knew what to say, for he was as *malin* as a fox! He made as fine a bow as you could see and told Nausicaa that she must be a king's daughter. And her heart was fluttering like a bird—poor, pretty soul!—as she remembered her dream. Not that she had need to call it to mind, for, as Mademoiselle doubtless will understand, she had thought of nothing else all day!' Madeleine looked suspiciously at the comic mask, but Berthe went on,—

'And then my lord Reynard tells of his misfortunes, and the hours he had spent struggling in the cold sea, and of his hunger, and of how his ship was lost, and he longing for his own country, "until I saw Mademoiselle," with another bow, so that tears came to the eyes of Nausicaa and her maids, and shyly kind, she asked him if he would be pleased to take shelter under her father's roof, which, as you will believe, was just what he had been waiting for! And her parents welcomed the handsome stranger kindly, the father as man to man, the mother a little shyly, for she saw that he was a great lord, though he did not tell his name, and she feared that he might think poorly of their state. All the same, her mind was busy weaving fantasies, and when she told them to her husband he mocked her for a vain and foolish woman, but for all that, he looked troubled and not well pleased. Nausicaa did not tell her parents of her dream, but that evening when her old nurse was combing her hair—my grannie used to say it was a comb made of pink coral—she asked her whether she thought that dreams might be taken as omens, and the old woman, who from the question divined the truth, brought out a dozen cases of dreams coming true.'

'Does it end happily?' Madeleine interrupted feverishly.

'Mademoiselle will see,' chuckled Berthe, her expression inexpressibly sly.

'Don't look so strangely, Berthe, you frighten me!' cried Madeleine. She was in a state of great nervous excitement.

'But, Mademoiselle, it is only a tale—it is *just* like Albert, he will sometimes cry his eyes out over a sad tale. I remember one evening at the Fête des Rois, the Curé——'

'Go on with the story,' cried Madeleine.

'Where was I? Oh, yes.... Well, Ulysse stayed with them some days, and he would borrow a blue smock from one of Nausicaa's brothers and help to bring in the hay, and in the evening tell them stories of strange countries or play to them on the lute. And he would wander with Nausicaa in the orchard, and though his talk was pretty and full of *fleurettes*, he never spoke of love. Well, one evening a Troubadour—Mademoiselle knows what that is?'

'Of course!'

'Came to the door and they asked him in, and after supper he sang them songs all about the Siege of Troy and the hardships undergone by Charlemagne and his knights when they fought there for *la belle Hélène*, and as he listened Ulysse could not keep from weeping, and they watched him, wondering. And when the song was finished they were all silent. And then Ulysse spoke up, saying he would no longer keep his name from them— "and, indeed," he added proudly, "it is not a name that need make its bearer blush, for," said he, "I am the lord Ulysse!" At that they all exclaimed with wonder, and Nausicaa turned as white as death, but Ulysse did not look at her. Then he told them of all the troubles sent him by Saint Nicholas and how fain he was to get to his own country and to his lady who was waiting for him in a high tower, but that he had no ship. Then Nausicaa's father clapped him on the shoulder, although he was such a great lord, and told him that he had some ships of his own to carry his corn to barren countries like England, and that he should have one to take him home. Then he filled up their glasses with good red Beaume and drank to his safe arrival, but Nausicaa said never a word and left the room. And next morning she was there, standing by a pillar of the door to bid him godspeed, smiling bravely, for though she was but a farmer's daughter she had a *noble fierté*. But after he had gone she could do nothing but weep, and pray to the Virgin to send her comfort. And some tell that in time she forgot the lord Ulysse and the grievous sorrow he had brought on her, and wedded with a neighbouring farmer and gat him fair children.

'But others tell that the poor soul could not rid herself of the burden of her grief, but did use to pass the nights in weeping and the days in roaming, wan and cheerless, by the sea-waves or through the meadows. And one eve as she wandered thus through a field of corn, it chanced that one of God's angels was flying overhead, and he saw the damsel, and his strange bloodless heart was filled with love and pity of her, and he swooped down on her and caught her up to Paradise.

' ... There is Madame calling me!' and Berthe hurried from the room.

Madeleine lay quite still on her bed, with a frightened shadow in her eyes. Ever since Jacques's dissertation on the Symmetry of the Comic Muse, terror had been howling outside the doors of her soul, but now it had boldly entered and taken possession.

CHAPTER XXVII
THE CHRISTIAN VENUS

The sane and steady procedure of the last few weeks—to prepare for the arousing of Admiration in Mademoiselle de Scudéry by a course in the art of pleasing—now seemed to Madeleine inadequate and frigid. She felt she could no longer cope with life without supernatural aid.

Once more her imagination began to pullulate with tiny nervous fears.

There would be onions for dinner—a vegetable that she detested. She would feel that unless she succeeded in gulping down her portion before her father gave another hiccough, she would never gain the friendship of Mademoiselle de Scudéry. She would wake up in the middle of the night with the conviction that unless, standing on one leg, she straightway repeated '*cogito, ergo sum*' fifteen times, Conrart would be seized by another attack of gout which would postpone her visit.

But these little fears—it would be tedious to enumerate them all—found their source in one great fear, to wit *lest the Sapphic Ode and the adventures of Nausicaa formed one story.*

The Ode tells how Venus appeared to Sappho and promised her rare things; but were these promises fulfilled? The Ode does not tell us, but we know that Sappho leapt from a cliff into the cold sea. The Virgin appears to Nausicaa, and although her promises are not as explicit as those of Venus, they are every whit as enticing, and what do they lead to? To a maiden disillusioned, deserted, and heart-broken, finding her final consolation in the cold and ravishing embraces of an Angel.

She, too, by omens and signs had been promised rare things; she had abandoned God, but had she ceased to believe in His potency? She remembered the impression left on Jacques by the fourth book of the *Eneid*, and Descartes' discarded hypothesis of an evil god, *le grand trompeur*—the 'great cheat,' he had called Him. Perhaps He had sent the Virgin to Nausicaa, Dame Venus to Sappho, and to herself a constellation of auspicious stars, to cozen them with fair promises that He might have the joy of breaking them—and their hearts as well.

One evening when her nerves were nearly cracking under the strain of this idea, she went to the kitchen to seek out Berthe.

'Berthe,' she said, 'when you do strangely desire a thing shall come to pass, what means do you affect to compass it?'

Berthe gave her a sly look and answered: 'I burn a candle to my patron saint, Mademoiselle.'

'And is the candle efficacious to the granting of your prayers?'

'As to their granting, it hangs upon the humour of Saint Berthe.'

'Do you know of any charm that will so work upon her as to change her humour from a splenetic to a kindly one?'

'There is but two charms, Mademoiselle, that will surely work upon the humours of the great—be they in Paradise or on the earth—they be flattery and presents. Albeit, I am a good Catholic, I hold my own opinions on certain matters, and I cannot doubt that once the Saints are safe in Paradise they turn exceeding grasping, crafty, and malicious. Like financiers, they are glutted on the farthings of the poor—a pack of Montaurons!'

'And in what manner does one flatter them?'

'Why, by novenas and candles and prostrating oneself before their images. As for me, except I have a prayer I strangely desire should be granted, I do never affect to kneel at Mass, I do but bend forward in my seat. In Lorraine we hold all this bowing and scraping as naught but Spanish tomfoolery! You'd seek long before you found one of *us* putting ourselves to any discomfort for the Saints, except it did profit us to do so!' and for at least a minute she chuckled and winked.

Well, here was a strange confirmation of her theory—a wicked hierarchy could only culminate in a wicked god. Yes, but such ignoble Saints would surely not be incorruptible. Might not timely bribes change their malicious designs? Also, it was just possible that Nausicaa and Sappho had neglected the rites and sacrifices without which no compact is valid between a god and a mortal. But could she not learn from their sad example? *Her* story was still in the making, by timely rites she might bring it to a happy issue.

With a sudden flash of illumination she felt she had discovered the secret of her failure. It was due to her neglect of her own patron saint, Saint Magdalene, who was as well the patron saint of Madeleine de Scudéry, a mystic link between their two souls, without which they could never be united.

Forget not your great patron saint in your devotions. It was her particular virtue that she greatly loved, had been the words of Mère Agnès. *She greatly loved*—why, it was all as clear as day; was she not the holy courtesan, and as such had she not taken over the functions of the pagan Venus, she who had appeared to Sappho? As the Christian Venus, charm and beauty and wit and *l'air galant*, and all the qualities that inspire Admiration must be in her gift, and Madeleine had neglected her! It was little wonder she had failed. Why, at the very beginning of her campaign against *amour-propre* she should have invoked her aid—'the saint who so greatly loved.'

Thus, link by link, was forged a formidable chain of evidence proving the paramount importance of the cult of Saint Magdalene.

What could she do to propitiate her? The twenty-second of July was her Feast, just a few days before the visit to Conrart. That was surely a good omen. She made a rapid calculation and found that it would fall on a Sunday, what if ... she shuddered, for something suddenly whispered to her soul a sinister suggestion.

That afternoon the Chevalier de Méré came to wait on her, and in the course of his elegantly didactic monologue, Madeleine inadvertently dropped her handkerchief: he sprang to pick it up, and as he presented it to her apostrophised it with a languorous sigh,—

'Ah, little cambric flower, it would not have taken a seer to foretell that happiness as exquisite as yours should precede a fall!'

Then, according to his custom of following up a concrete compliment by a dissertation on the theory of *Galanterie* he launched into an historical survey of the use to which the *Muse Galante* had made, in countless admirable sonnets, of the enviable intimacy existing between their fair wearer and such insensible objects as a handkerchief or a glove.

'But these days,' he continued, 'the envy of a poet *à la mode* is not so much aroused by gloves of *frangipane* and handkerchiefs of Venetian lace, in that a franchise far greater than *they* have ever enjoyed has been granted by all the Belles of the Court and Town to ignoble squares of the roughest cloth— truly evangelical, these Belles have exalted the poor and meek and——'

'I don't take your meaning, pray explain,' Madeleine cut in.

'Why, dear Rhodanthos, have you never heard of Mère Madeleine de Saint-Joseph of the Carmelites?'

'That I have, many a time.'

'Well, as you know, in her life time she worked miracles beyond the dreams of Faith itself, and at her death, as in the case of the founder of her Order, the great Elias, her virtue was transmitted to her cloak, or rather to her habit, portions of which fortunate garment are worn by all the *belles dévotes* next ... er ... their ... er next ... er ... their sk ... next their secret garden of lilies, with, I am told, the most extravagant results; it is her portion of the miraculous habit that has turned Madame de Longueville into a penitent, for example, but its effects are sometimes of a more profane nature, namely— breathe it low—success in the tender passion!' Madeleine's eyes grew round.

'Yes, 'tis a veritable cestus of Venus, which, I need hardly remind a lady of such elegant learning as Mademoiselle, was borrowed by Juno when anxious to rekindle the legitimate passion in the bosom of Jove. And speaking of Juno I remember——'

But Madeleine had no more attention to bestow on the urbane flow of the Chevalier's conversation. She was ablaze with excitement and hope ... Mère *Madeleine* de Saint-Joseph, the mystical name again! And the cestus of Venus ... it was surely a message sent from Saint Magdalene herself. The Chevalier had said that these relics had usurped the rôle previously played in the world of fashion by lace handkerchiefs and gloves of *frangipane*, in short of the feminine *petite-oie*. Thus, by obtaining a relic, she would kill two birds with one stone; she would absorb the virtue of Saint Magdalene and at the same time destroy for ever the bad magic of that *petite-oie* of bad omen which she had bought at the Foire St. Germain. The very next day she would go to the Carmelites, and perhaps, *perhaps*, if they had not long ago been all distributed, procure a piece of the magical habit. At any rate she would consolidate her cult for Saint Magdalene by burning some candles in the wonderful chapel set up in her honour in the Church of the Carmelites.

CHAPTER XXVIII
THE ASCENT OF MOUNT CARMEL

Many strange legends had gone to weave round the Convent of the Carmelites—so long the centre of fashionable Catholicism—an atmosphere of romantic mystery.

Tradition taught that the order had been founded on the summit of Mount Carmel by Elias himself. Its earliest members were the mysterious Essenes, but they were converted to Christianity by Saint Peter's Pentecostal sermon, and built on the mountain a chapel to the Blessed Virgin Mary, she herself becoming a member of their order. Her example was followed by the Twelve Apostles, and any association with that mysterious company of sinister semi-plastic beings, menacing sinners with their symbolic keys and crosses, had filled Madeleine since her childhood with a nameless terror.

The Essenes and the Apostles! The Carmelites thus preserved the Mysteries of both the Old and the New Testaments.

Madeleine, as she stood at the door of their Convent, too awe-struck to enter, felt herself on the confines of the Holy Land—that land half geographical, half Apocalyptical, where the Unseen was always bursting through the ramparts of nature's laws; where Transfigurations and Assumptions were daily events, and Assumptions not only of people but of cities. Had not Jerusalem, with all its towers and palm-trees and gardens and temples, been lifted up by the lever of God's finger right through the Empyrean, and landed intact and all burning with gold in the very centre of the Seventh Heaven?

Summoning up all her courage she passed into the court. It was quite empty, and over its dignified proportions there did indeed seem to lie the shadow of the silent awful Denizen of 'high places.' Dare she cross it? Once more she pulled herself together and made her way into the Church.

It was a gorgeous place, supported by great pillars of marble and bronze and hung with large, sombre pictures by Guido and Philippe de Champagne, while out of the darkness gleamed the 'Arche d'Alliance' with its huge sun studded with jewels.

The atmosphere though impressive was familiar—merely Catholicism in its most luxuriant form, and Madeleine took heart. She set out in quest of the Magdalene's Chapel. Here and there a nun was kneeling, but she was the only stranger.

Yes, it was but meet that here—the grave of sweet Mademoiselle de Vigean's love for the great Condé and of many another romantic tragedy— the Magdalene should be specially honoured.

The Chapel was small and rich, its door of fretted iron-work made it look not unlike a great lady's *alcove*. It was filled with pictures by Le Brun and his pupils of scenes from the life of the Saint. There she was in a dark grove, with tears of penitence streaming from the whites of large upturned eyes. And there she was again, beneath the Cross, and there watching at the Tomb, but always torn by the same intensity of pseudo emotion, for Le Brun and Guido foreshadowed in their pictures that quality of poignant, artificial anguish which a few years later was to move all sensibilities in the tragedies of Racine.

Madeleine was much moved by the Magdalene's anguish, and hesitated to obtrude her own request. But her throbbing desire won the day, and remembering what Berthe had said about flattery she knelt before the largest picture and began by praising the Magdalene's beauty and piety and high place in Paradise, and then with humble importunity implored the friendship of her namesake.

When she opened her eyes, there was the Magdalene as absorbed as before in the intensity of her own emotion. Le Brun's dramatic chiaroscuro brings little comfort to suppliants—the eternal impassivity of the Buddha is far less discouraging than an eternal emotion in which we have no part.

Madeleine felt the chill of repulse. Perhaps in Paradise as on earth the Saints were sensible to nothing but the cycle of the sacred Story, and knew no emotions but passionate grief at the Crucifixion, ecstasy at the Resurrection, awe at the Ascension, and child-like joy as the Birth comes round again.

'I am scorned in both the worldly and the sacred alcoves,' she told herself bitterly, nevertheless, she determined to continue her attentions.

She bought three fine candles and added them to those already burning on the Magdalen's altar. What did the Saint do with the candles? Perhaps at night when no one was looking she melted them down, then added them to the wax of reality and moulded, moulded, moulded. Once more Madeleine fell on her knees, and there welled from her heart a passion of supplication.

Sainte Madeleine, the patron saint of all Madeleines ... of Madeleine Troqueville and of Madeleine de Scudéry ... the saint who had loved so much herself ... the successor of she whom Jacques had called 'the beneficent and bountiful Venus' ... surely, surely she would grant her request.

'Deathless Saint Magdalen of the damasked throne,' she muttered, 'friend of Jesus, weaver of wiles, vex not my soul with frets and weariness but hearken to my prayer. Who flees, may she pursue; who spurns gifts may she offer them; who loves not, willy-nilly may she love. Broider my speech with the quaint flowers of Paradise, on thine own loom weave me wiles and graces to the ensnaring of my love. Up the path of Admiration lead Sappho to my desire.'

She felt a touch on her shoulder, and, looking round, saw a lay-sister, in the brown habit of the Carmelites. Her twinkling black eyes reminded Madeleine of another pair of eyes, but whose she could not remember.

'I ask pardon, Madame,' the sister said in a low voice, 'but we hold ourselves the hostesses, as it were, of all wanderers on Carmel. Is there aught that I can do for you?'

Madeleine's heart began to beat wildly; the suddenness with which an opportunity had been given her for procuring her wish seemed to her of the nature of a miracle. Through her perennial grief at the old, old story, the Magdalene must have heard her prayer. A certainty was born in on her that her desire would be granted. She and the other Madeleine would one day visit the Chapel together, and side by side set up rows and rows of wax candles in gratitude for the perfection of their friendship.

'Oh, sister, I am much beholden to you,' she stammered. The nun led the way out of the Church into the great garden that marched with that of the Luxembourg and rivalled it in magnificence. She sat down by a statue of the Virgin, enamelled in gold and azure.

Madeleine thought with contemptuous pity of the comparatively meagre dimensions and furnishing of Port-Royal, and triumphed to think how far she had wandered from Jansenism.

'You have the air of one in trouble,' said the nun kindly. Her breath smelt of onions, and somehow or other this broke the spell of the situation for Madeleine. It was a touch of realism not suited to a mystical messenger.

'I perceive graven on your countenance the lines of sorrow, my child,' she went on, 'but to everything exists its holy pattern, and these lines can also be regarded as a blessing, when we call to mind the holy stigmata.' She gabbled off this speech as though it had been part of the patter of a quack.

'Yes, I am exceeding unhappy,' said Madeleine; 'at least I am oppressed by fears as to the issue of certain matters,' she corrected herself, for 'unhappy' seemed a word of ill-omen.

'Poor child!' said the Sister, 'but who knows but that oil and balm of comfort may not pour on you from Mount Carmel?'

'Oh, do you think it may?' Madeleine cried eagerly.

''Tis a strange thing, but many go away from here comforted. It is richly blessed.'

'I wonder,' Madeleine began hesitatingly. 'I fear 'tis asking too much—but if I could but have a relic of the blessed Mère Madeleine de Saint-Joseph! The world reports her relics more potent than any other Saint's.' (In spite of the efforts of many great French ladies, Mère Madeleine de Saint-Joseph had *not* been canonised. Madeleine knew this, but she thought she would please the Carmelite by ignoring it.)

At Madeleine's words the little nun wriggled her body into a succession of Gallic contortions, in which eyebrows and hands played a large part, expressive of surprise, horror, and complete inability to grant such an outrageous request. But Madeleine pleaded hard, and after a dissertation on the extraordinary virtue of the habit, and a repeated reiteration that there were only one or two scraps of it left, the Carmelite finally promised that one of these scraps should be Madeleine's.

She went into the Convent and came back with a tiny piece of frayed cloth, and muttering a prayer she fixed it inside Madeleine's bodice.

Madeleine was almost too grateful to say 'thank you.'

'All the greatest ladies of the Court and the Town are wont to wear a portion of the sacred habit,' the nun continued complacently. Madeleine found herself wondering quite seriously if the mère Madeleine de Saint-Joseph had been a *Gargamelle* in proportions.

'To speak truth, it must have been a huge and capacious garment!' she said in all good faith. The nun gave her a quick look out of her shrewd little eyes, but ignored the remark.

'And now Mademoiselle will give us a contribution for our Order, will she not?' she said insinuatingly. Madeleine was much taken aback. She blushed and said,—

'Oh, in earnest ... 'tis accordant with my wishes ... but ... er ... how much?'

'Do but consult your own heart, and it will go hard but we shall be satisfied. I have given you what to the eyes of the flesh appears but a sorry scrap of poor rough fustian, but to the eyes of the spirit it has the lustre of velvet, and there is not a Duchess but would be proud to wear it!'

Why, of course, her eyes were like those of the mercer at the Fair who had sold her the '*petite-oie*'!

However, one acquires merit by giving to holy Houses ... and also, Mademoiselle has procured something priceless beyond rubies. Madeleine offered a gold louis, and the nun was profuse in her thanks. They parted at the great gates, the nun full of assurances as to the efficacy of the amulet, Madeleine of grateful thanks.

It had been a strange adventure, and she left the Sacred Mountain with conflicting emotions.

CHAPTER XXIX
THE BODY OF THE DRAGON

If you remember, when Madeleine had realised that the feast of Saint Magdalene was approaching, an idea had flashed into her head which she had not then dared to entertain. But it had slowly crept back and now had established itself as a fixed purpose. It was this—on the feast of Saint Magdalene to communicate, *without having first received Absolution*. She felt that it would please the potent Saint that she should commit a deadly sin in her honour. Also, it would mean a complete and final rupture with Jansenism. And with one stroke she would annihilate her Salvation—that predestined ghostly certainty to the fulfilment of which the Celestial Powers seemed bent on sacrificing all her worldly hopes and happiness. Yes, she would now be able to walk in security along the familiar paths of life, unhaunted by the fear of the sudden whirr of wings and then—the rape to the love of invisible things.

So on Sunday, the twenty-second of July, she partook of the Blessed Sacrament. Arnauld had written in the 'Fréquente Communion': *'therefore as the true penitent eats the body of Jesus Christ, so the sinner eats the body of the Dragon.'*

Well, and so she was eating the body of the Dragon! The knowledge gave her a strange sense of exaltation and an awful peace.

CHAPTER XXX
A JAR

It was the day before the meeting. Early next morning the Chevalier de Méré was to call for her in his coach and drive her out to Conrart's house. He was also taking that tiresome little Mademoiselle Boquet. That was a pity, but she was particularly pleased that the Chevalier himself was to be there, he always brought out her most brilliant qualities.

She was absolutely certain of success ... the real world seemed to have become the dream world ... she felt as if she had been turned into a creature of some light, unsubstantial substance living in an airless crystal ball.

That afternoon, being Thursday and a holiday, she went an excursion with Jacques to Chaillot, a little village up the Seine. She walked in a happy trance, and the fifteenth century Church, ornate and frivolous, dotted with its black Minims—'*les bons hommes de Chaillot*'—and the coach of the exiled Queen-Mother of England's gaily rattling down the cobbled street, seemed to her—safe inside her crystal ball—pretty and unreal and far-away, like Berthe's stories of Lorraine.

Then they wandered into a little copse behind the village and lay there in the fantastic green shade, and Madeleine stroked and petted Jacques and laughed away his jealousy about the Chevalier, and promised that next week she would go with him to the notary and plight her troth.

Then they got up and she took his arm; on her face was a rapt smile, for she was dreaming particularly pleasant things about herself and Sappho.

Suddenly Jacques's foot caught in a hidden root ... down he came, dragging Madeleine after him ... smash went the crystal ball, and once more she saw the world bright and hard and menacing and felt around her the rough, shrewd winds.

So Jacques had made her fall—just when she was having such pleasant dreams of Sappho!

Hylas, hélas! Timeo Danaos et dona ferentes. Birds thinking to fly through have dashed themselves against the wall. 'Tis as though the issue of his roman were tied in a strange knot with that of yours. I have been writing a little comedy on life instead of on foolscap. In the smithy of Vulcan are being forged weapons which will not tarry to smash your fragile world into a thousand fragments ... weapons? Perhaps one of them was 'the scimitar of the Comic Muse' (or was it the 'symmetry'? It did not really matter which.)

Who was the mercer at the Fair? He had the same eyes as the nun at the Carmelites.... Her father, too, had a *petite-oie* ... he had put his faith in bravery.

Perhaps Venus-Magdalen and the Comic Muse were one ... and their servant was Hylas the mocking shepherd. *The wooden cubes on which God's finger had cut a design ... generals and particulars. Have a care lest that scoundrel Jacques stick a disgrace upon you, as he has done to me! A comedy written upon life instead of upon foolscap.*

In morbid moments she had often heard a whisper to which she had never permitted herself to listen. She heard the whisper now, louder and more insistent than ever before. To-day she could not choose but listen to it.

Her 'roman' had to follow the pattern of her father's. Her father's 'roman,' as slowly it unfolded, was nothing but a magical pre-doing of her own future, more potent than her dances. And God had deputed the making of it to—Jacques. He was the playwright, or the engraver, or the moulder of wax—it mattered little in what medium he wrought his sinister art.

There was still time to act. 'She would *do*, she would *do*, she would *do*.' Action is the only relief for a hag-ridden brain. An action that was ruthless and final—that would break his power and rid her of him for ever. That action should be consummated.

All the while that this train of fears and memories had been coursing through her brain, she had chattered to Jacques with hectic gaiety.

When they got home she ran to the kitchen to find Berthe.

'Berthe, were you ever of opinion I would wed with Monsieur Jacques?'

Berthe leered and winked. 'Well, Mademoiselle,' she said, 'Love is one thing—marriage is another. Monsieur Jacques could not give Mademoiselle a coach and a fine *hôtel* in the Rue de Richelieu. I understand Mademoiselle exceeding well, in that we are not unlike in some matters,' and she gave her grotesque grin. 'As for me, I would never wed with a man except he could raise me to a better condition than mine own—else what would it profit one? But if some plump little tradesman were to come along——'

'But did you hold that I would wed with Monsieur Jacques?' Madeleine persisted.

'Well, if Mademoiselle *did* wed with him, she would doubtless be setting too low a price on herself, though he is a fine young gentleman and *malin comme un singe*; he is like Albert, nothing escapes him.'

'Do you think the Saints like us to use each other unkindly?'

Berthe laughed enigmatically, 'I think 'tis a matter of indifference to them, so long as they get the *sous*.'

'But don't you think it might accord well with their humour if they are as wicked as you say they are?'

Part of the truth suddenly flashed on Berthe, and she winked and chuckled violently. 'Oh, Mademoiselle is sly!' she cried admiringly. 'I think it would please them not a little were Mademoiselle to jilt a poor man that she might wed with a rich one, for then there would be gold for them instead of copper!'

And Madeleine, having forced her oracle into giving her a more or less satisfactory answer, fled from the room in dread of Berthe mentioning the name of the Chevalier de Méré and thereby spoiling the oracular answer.

She called Jacques to her room at once, and found herself—she who had such a horror of hurting the feelings of her neighbours that she would let a thief cut her purse-strings rather than that he should know that she knew he was a thief—telling him without a tremor that his personality was obnoxious to her, his addresses still more so, and that she wanted to end their relationship once and for all. Jacques listened in perfect silence. At her first words he had gone white and then flushed the angry red of wounded vanity, and then once more had turned white. When she had finished, he said in a voice of icy coldness,—

'Mademoiselle, you have an admirable clearness of exposition; rest assured I shall not again annoy you with my addresses—or my presence,' and with his head very high he left the room.

CHAPTER XXXI
THE END OF THE 'ROMAN'

Madeleine listened to Jacques's light footsteps going down the long flight of stairs, and knew that he had gone for ever. With this knowledge came a sense of peace she had not known for days, and one of sacramental purity, such as must have filled the souls of pious Athenians when at the Thargelia the *Pharmakoi* were expelled from the city.

Yes, just in time she had discovered the true moral of the Sapphic Ode and the story of Nausicaa, to wit, that the gods will break their promises if man fails to perform the necessary rites and ceremonies. Ritually, her affairs were in exquisite order. By her sacrilegious Communion (she still shuddered at the thought of it) she had consolidated her cult for the powerful Saint Magdalene, and at the same time cut out of her heart the brand of God, by which in the fullness of time the ravishing Angel would have discovered his victim. And, finally, by her dismissal of Jacques, she had rid herself of a most malign miasma. The wax of reality lay before her, smooth and white and ready for her moulding. All she had to do now was to sparkle, and, automatically, she would arouse the passion of Admiration.

Suddenly she remembered another loose thread that needed to be gathered up. The *roman* of her dances had not been brought to a climax.

An unwritten law of the style gallant makes the action of a *roman* automatically cease after a declaration of love. Nothing can happen afterwards. What if she should force time to its fullness and make a declaration? It would be burning her boats, it would be staking all her happiness on this last meeting, for if it were a failure hope would be dead. For, owing to her strange confusion of the happenings of her dances with those of real life, the *roman* of the one having been completed, its magical virtue all used up, its colophon reached, she felt that the *roman* of the other would also have reached its colophon, that nothing more could happen. But for great issues she must take great risks ... *dansons!*

Sappho and Madeleine are reclining on a bank, the colour and design of which rival all the carpets in the bazaars of Bagdad. There is no third person to mar their ravishing solitude à deux. *Madeleine is saying,—*

'I must confess, Madame, that your delicious writings have made me a heretic.'

Sappho laughs gaily. 'Then I tremble for your fate, for heretics are burned.'

'In that case I am indeed a heretic, for a flame has long burned me,' says Madeleine boldly. But Sappho possesses in a high degree the art of hearing only what she chooses, and she says, a trifle coldly,—

'If my writings have made you a heretic, they must themselves be heretical. Do they contain Five Propositions worthy of papal condemnation?'

'Madame, you are resolved to misunderstand me. They have made me a heretic in regard to the verdict of posterity as to the merits of the ancients, for since I have steeped myself, if I may use the expression, in your incomparable style I have become as deaf as Odysseus to the siren songs of Greece and Rome.'

'That is indeed heresy,' cries Sappho with a smile that shows she is not ill-pleased. 'I fear it will be visited by excommunication by the whole College of Muses.'

'The only punishment of heresy—you have yourself said so—is ... flame,' says Madeleine, gazing straight into the eyes of Sappho. This time she is almost certain she can perceive a blush on that admirable person's cheek—almost certain, for the expression of such delicate things as the Passions of Sappho must need itself be very delicate. Descartes has said that a blush proceeds from one of two passions—love or hate. En voilà un problème galant!

'To justify my heresy, permit me, Madame, to recall to your mind a poem by your namesake, the Grecian Sappho,—

'That man seems to me greater than the gods who doth sit facing thee and sees thee and hears thy delicate laughter. When this befalls me my senses clean depart ... all is void ... my tongue cleaves to the roof of my mouth, drop by drop flame steals down my slender veins ... there is a singing in mine ears ... my eyes are covered with a twin night.

She pauses, but Sappho laughs—perhaps not quite naturally—and cries,—

'Mademoiselle, your heresy still stands unjustified!'

'Why, Madame, how could any one of taste take pleasure in verse so devoid of wit, of grace, of galanterie ... so bare, so barbarous, after they have been initiated into the Parnassian Mysteries of your incomparable verse and prose? Why, what I have quoted is the language of lexicographers and philosophers, not the divine cadences of a poet. Put in metre Descartes' description of the signs by which the movements of the Passions may be detected, namely,—

"The chief signs by which the Passions show themselves are the motions of the eyes and the face, changes of colour, trembling, languor, faintness, laughter, tears, moans, and sighs," and you will have a poem every whit as graceful and well-turned!

The poem of Sappho I. is a "small thing" ... but if it had proceeded from the delicious pen of Sappho II. it would have been a "rose"!'

'And how should I have effected this miracle?' asks Sappho with a smile.

'I think, Madame, you would have used that excellent device of the Muse Galante which I will call that of Eros Masqué.'

'Eros Masqué? Is he unseen then as well as unseeing?'

'On his first visit, frequently, Madame. And this droll fact—that lovers pierced by as many of his arrows as Saint Sebastian by those of the Jews are wont to ignore the instrument by which they have got their wounds—has been put to pretty use by many poètes galants. For example, an amorous maiden or swain doth describe divers well-known effects of the tender passion, and then asks with a delicious naïveté, "Can it be Love?" And this simple little question, if inserted between each of the symptoms enumerated by Sappho, would go far to giving her poem the esprit it so sadly lacks. But, Madame, far the most ravishing of all the poems of Eros Masqué are your own incomparable verses in the sixth volume of "Cyrus":—

'Ma peine est grande, et mon plaisir extrême,

Je ne dors point la nuit, je rêve tout le jour;

Je ne sais pas encore si j'aime,

Mais cela ressemble a l'amour.

'Voyant Phaon mon âme est satisfaite,

Et ne le voyant point, la peine est dans mon cœur

J'ignore encore ma defaite

Mais peut-être est-il mon vainqueur?

'Tout ce qu'il dit me semble plein de charmes!

Tout ce qu'il ne dit pas, n'en peut avoir pour moi,

Mon cœur as-tu mis bas les armes?

Je n'en sais rien, mais je le crois.

'Do not these verses when placed by the side of those of the Grecian Sappho justify for ever my heresy?'

'I should be guilty myself of the heresy of self-complacency were I to subscribe your justification,' cries Sappho with a delicious air of raillery.

'Madame, the device of Eros Masqué serves another purpose besides that of charming the fancy by its grace and drollery.... It makes Confession innocent, for although that Sacrament is detested by Précieuses as fiercely as by Protestants, the most precise and prudish of Précieuses could scarce take umbrage at a Confession expressed by a string of naïve questions.'

'There, Madame, you show a deplorable ignorance of the geography of the heart of at least one Précieuse. I can picture myself white with indignation on receiving the Socratic Confession you describe,' says Sappho, but the ice of her accents thaws into two delicious little dimples.

'"Mais votre fermeté tient un peu du barbare," to quote the great Corneille,' cries Madeleine with a smile. 'You called it a Socratic Confession, alluding I presume to the fact that it was cast in the form of questions, but a Socratic Confession, if my professors have not misled me, is very close to a Platonic one. Can you picture yourself white with rage at receiving a Platonic Confession?'

'Before I can answer that question you must describe to me a Platonic Confession,' says Sappho demurely.

'Tis the confession of a sentiment the purity and discreetness of which makes it the only tribute worthy to be laid at the feet of a Précieuse. Starting from what Descartes holds to be the coldest of the Passions, that of Admiration, it takes its demure way down the slope of Inclination straight into the twilight grove of l'Amitié Tendre—

'Auprès de cette Grote sombre

Oh l'on respire un air si doux;

L'onde lutte avec les cailloux,

Et la lumière avec l'ombre.

'Dans ce Bois, ni dans ces montagnes

Jamais chasseur ne vint encore:

Si quelqu'un y sonne du Cor

C'est Diane avec ses compagnes.

These delicious verses of the gentle Tristan might have been a description of the land of l'Amitié Tendre, so charmed is its atmosphere, so deep its green shadows, so heavy its brooding peace. For all round it is traced a magic circle across which nothing discordant or vulgar can venture.... Without, moan the Passions like wild beasts enchained, the thunder booms, the lightning flashes, and there is a heap as high as a mountain of barbed arrows shot by Love, all of which have fallen short of that magic circle.

'Happy they who have crossed it!

'Madame, I called the Grecian Sappho a barbarian.... Barbarian or no she discovered hundreds of years ago the charm by which the magic circle can be crossed ... the charm is simple when you know it; it is merely this ... take another maiden with you. It has never been crossed by man and maid, for in sight of the country's cool trees and with the murmur of its fountains in their ear they have been snatched from behind by one of the enchained passions, or grievously wounded by one of the whizzing arrows ... Madame, shall we try the virtue of the Grecian Sappho's charm?'

And Sappho murmurs 'yes.'

So Madeleine put her fate 'to the touch, to win or lose it all,' and there was something exhilarating in the thought that retreat now was impossible.

CHAPTER XXXII
'UN CADEAU'

The next morning—the morning of *the* day—Madeleine woke up with the same feeling of purification; she seemed to be holding the day's culmination in her hands, and it was made of solid white marble, that cooled her palms as she held it.

Berthe, with mysterious winks, brought her a sealed letter. It was from Jacques:—

'DEAR CHOP,—I am moving to the lodgings of a friend for a few days, and then I go off to join the Army in Spain. Take no blame to yourself for this, for I have always desired strangely to travel and have my share in manly adventures, and would, 'tis likely, have gone anyhow. I would never have made a good Procureur. I have written to Aunt Marie to acquaint her with my sudden decision, in such manner that she cannot suspect what has really taken place.

'Oh, dear! I had meant to rail against you and I think this is nothing toward it! 'Tis a strange and provoking thing that one cannot—try as one will—be moved by *real* anger towards those one cares about! Not that I have any real cause to be angry upon your score—bear in mind, Chop, that I know this full well—but in spite of this I would dearly like to be!

'JACQUES.'

As she read it, she realised that she had made a big sacrifice. Surely it would be rewarded!

She dressed in a sort of trance. Her excitement was so overwhelming, so vibrantly acute, that she was almost unconscious.

Then the Chevalier, with little Mademoiselle Boquet, drove up to the door, and Madeleine got in, smiling vaguely in reply to the Chevalier's compliments, and they drove off, her mother and Berthe standing waving at the door. On rolled the *carrosse* past La Porte Sainte-Antoine, through which were pouring carts full of vegetables and fruit for the Halles, and out into the white road beyond; and on rolled the smooth cadences of the Chevalier's voice—'To my mind the highest proof that one is possessed of wit and that one knows how to wield it, is to lead a well-ordered life and to behave always in society in a seemly fashion. And to do that consists in all circumstances following the most *honnête* line and that which seems most in keeping with the condition of life to which one belongs. Some rôles in life are more advantageous than others; it is Fortune that casts them and we cannot choose the one we wish; but whatever that rôle may be, one is a good actor if one plays it well ...' and so on. Fortunately, sympathetic monosyllables were all that the Chevalier demanded from his audience, and these he got from Mademoiselle Boquet and Madeleine.

And so the journey went on, and at last they were drawing up before a small, comfortable white house with neatly-clipped hedges, shrubberies, and the play of a sedate fountain. Madame Conrart, kind and flustered, was at the door to meet them, and led them into a large room in which Conrart in an arm-chair and Mademoiselle de Scudéry busy with her embroidery in another arm-chair sat chatting together. Conrart's greeting to Madeleine was kindness itself, and Mademoiselle de Scudéry also said something polite and friendly. She pretended not to hear her, and moved towards Madame Conrart, for as soon as her eyes had caught sight of Sappho, she had been seized by the same terrible self-consciousness, the same feeling of 'nothing matters so long as I am seen and heard as little as may be.'

Then came some twenty minutes of respite, for Mademoiselle Boquet with her budget of news of the Court and the Town acted as a rampart between Madeleine and Mademoiselle de Scudéry. But at dinner-time her terror once more returned, for general conversation was expected at meals. 'Simple country fare,' said Conrart modestly, but although the dishes were not numerous, and consisted mainly of home-reared poultry, there were forced peaches and grapes and the table was fragrant with flowers.

'Flora and Pomona joining hands have never had a fairer temple than this table,' said the Chevalier, and all the company, save Madeleine, added their tribute to their host's bounty. But Madeleine sat awkward and tongue-tied, too nervous to eat. The precious moments of her last chance were slipping by; even if she thought of a thousand witty things she would not be able to say them, for her tongue felt swollen and impotent. Descartes on the Will was just an old pedant, talking of what he did not understand.

At last dinner was over, and Conrart suggested they should go for a little walk in the grounds. He offered his arm to Mademoiselle de Scudéry, the Chevalier followed with Madame Conrart, so Madeleine and Mademoiselle Boquet found themselves partners. But even then Madeleine was at first unable to break the spell of heavy silence hanging over her. 'Blessed Saint Magdalene, help me! help me! help me!' she muttered, and then reminded herself that being neither half-witted nor dumb, it did not demand any gigantic effort of will to *force* herself to behave like an *honnête femme* ... and to-day it was a matter of life or death.

She felt like a naked, shivering creature, standing at the top of a gigantic rock, and miles below her lay an icy black pool, but she must take the plunge; and she did.

She began to reinforce her self-confidence by being affected and pretentious with Mademoiselle Boquet, but the little lady's gentle reserve made her vaguely uncomfortable. She was evidently one of those annoying little nonentities with strong likes and dislikes, and a whole bundle of sharp little judgments of their own, who are always vaguely irritating to their more triumphant sisters. Then she tried hard to realise *emotionally* that the gray female back in front of her belonged to Mademoiselle de Scudéry—to the *Reine de Tendre*; to Sappho—but somehow her imagination was inadequate. The focus of all her tenderness was not this complacent lady, but the Sappho of her dances.

As, for example, I find in myself two divers Ideas of the Sun, one as received by my senses by which it appears to me very small, another as taken from the arguments of Astronomers by which 'tis rendered something bigger than the Globe of the Earth. Certainly both of these cannot be like that sun which is without me, and my reason persuades that that Idea is most unlike the Sun, which seems to proceed immediately from itself.

She remembered these words of Descartes' Third Meditation ... two suns and two Sapphos, and the one perceived by the senses, not the real one ... and yet, and yet she could *never* be satisfied with merely the Sappho of the dances, even though metaphysically she were more real than the other. Her happiness depended in merging the two Sapphos into one ... she must remember, reality is colourless and silent and malleable ... a white, still Sappho like the Grecian statues in the Louvre ... to the Sappho of her dances she gave what qualities she chose, so could she to the Sappho who was walking a few paces in front of her ... forward la Madeleine! Then the Chevalier came and walked on her other side. She told herself that this was a good opportunity of working herself into a vivacious mood, which would bridge over the next awful chasm. So she burst into hectic persiflage, and to Hell with Mademoiselle Boquet's little enigmatical smile!

They were walking in a little wood. Suddenly from somewhere among the trees came the sound of violins. A *cadeau* for one of the ladies! Madeleine felt that she would die with embarrassment if it were not for her—yes, *die*—humiliated for ever in the eyes of Mademoiselle de Scudéry, in relationship to whom she always pictured herself as a triumphant beauty, with every inch of the stage to herself.

There was a little buzz of expectation among the ladies, and Madame Conrart, looking flustered and pleased, said: 'I am sure it is none of our doing.' Madeleine stretched her lips in a forced smile, in a fever of anxiety.

Then suddenly they came to an open clearing in the wood, and there was a table heaped with preserved fruits and jams and sweetmeats and liqueurs, all of them rose-coloured. The napkins were of rose-coloured silk and folded into the shape of hearts, the knives were tiny darts of silver. Behind stood the four fiddlers scratching away merrily at a *pot pourré* of airs from the latest *ballet de cour*. The ladies gave little 'ohs!' of delight, and Conrart looked pleased and important, but that did not mean anything, for he was continually taking a possessive pride in matters in which he had had no finger. The Chevalier looked enigmatic. Conrart turned to him with a knowing look and said,—

'Chevalier, you are a professor of the *philosophie de galanterie*, can you tell us whether rose pink is the colour of *Estime* or of *le Tendre*?'

'Descartes is dumb on the relation of colours to the Passions, so it is not for me to decide,' the Chevalier answered calmly, 'all *I* know is that the Grecian rose was pink.' Madeleine's heart gave a bound of triumph.

The fiddles started a languorous saraband, and from the trees a shower of artificial rose-petals fell on the ladies. Mademoiselle de Scudéry looked very gracious.

'Our unknown benefactor has a very fragrant invention,' she said in a tone which seemed to Madeleine to intimate that *she* was the queen of the occasion. Vain, foolish, ugly creature, how dare she think so, when she, Madeleine, was there! Had she not heard what the Chevalier had said about the 'Grecian rose'?—(though why she should know that the Chevalier called Madeleine 'Rhodanthos,' I fail to perceive!)—she would put her in her place. She gave a little affected laugh, and, looking straight at the Chevalier, she said,—

'It is furiously gallant. I thank you a thousand times.'

The Chevalier looked nonplussed, and stammered out that 'Cupid must have known that a bevy of Belles had planned to visit that wood.'

Madeleine had committed the unpardonable crime—she had openly acknowledged a *cadeau*, whereas *Galanterie* demanded that the particular lady it was intended to honour should be veiled in a piquant mystery. Why, it was enough to send all the ladies of *Cyrus* shuddering back for ever to their Persian seraglios! But she had as well broken the spell of silence woven by Mademoiselle de Scudéry's presence. That lady exchanged a little look with Mademoiselle Boquet which somehow glinted right off from Madeleine's shining new armour. She gulped off a liqueur and gave herself tooth and nail to the business of shining. She began to flirt outrageously with the Chevalier, and though he quite enjoyed it, the *pédagogue galant* in him made a mental note to give Madeleine a hint that this excessive *galanterie* smacked of the previous reign, while the present fashion was a witty prudishness. Certainly, Mademoiselle de Scudéry was not looking impressed, but, somehow, Madeleine did not care; the one thing that mattered was that she should be brilliantly in the foreground, and be very witty, and then Mademoiselle de Scudéry *must* admire her.

Mademoiselle de Scudéry soon started a quiet little chat with Conrart, which caused Madeleine's vivacity to flag; how could she sparkle when her sun was hidden?

'Yes, *la belle Indienne* would doubtless have found her native America less barbarous than the *milieu* in which she has been placed by an exceeding ironical fortune,' Mademoiselle de Scudéry was saying. Madeleine, deeply read in *La Gazette Burlesque*, knew that she was speaking of the beautiful and ultra-refined Madame Scarron, forced to be hostess of the most licentious *salon* in Paris.

''Tis my opinion she falls far short of Monsieur Scarron in learning, wit, and galanterie!' burst in Madeleine. She did not think so really; it was just a desire to make herself felt. Mademoiselle de Scudéry raised her eyebrows.

'Is Mademoiselle acquainted with Madame Scarron?' she inquired in a voice that implied she was certain that she was not. In ordinary circumstances, such a snub, even from some one for whose good opinion she did not care a rap, would have reduced her to complete silence, but to-day she seemed to have risen invulnerable from the Styx.

'No, I haven't been presented to her—although I have seen her,' she said.

'And yet you speak of her as though you had much frequented her? You put me in mind, Mademoiselle, of the troupe of players in my brother's comedy who called themselves *Comédiens du Roi*, although they had played before His Majesty but once,' said Mademoiselle de Scudéry coldly.

'In earnest, I have no wish to pass as Madame Scarron's comedian. Rumour has it she was born in a prison,' Madeleine rejoined insolently. 'Moreover, I gather from her friends, the only merit in her prudishness is that it acts as a foil to her husband's wit.'

Mademoiselle de Scudéry merely raised her eyebrows, and Conrart, attempting to make things more comfortable, said with a good-natured smile,—

'Ah! Sappho, the young people have their own ideas about things, I dare swear, and take pleasure in the *genre burlesque*!'

(Jacques would have smiled to hear Madeleine turned into the champion of the burlesque!) 'Well, all said, the burlesque, were it to go to our friend Ménage (whom one might call the Hozier[4] of literary forms) might get a fine family tree for itself, going back to the Grecian Aristophanes—is that not so, Chevalier?' went on Conrart. The Chevalier smiled non-committally.

'No, no,' interrupted Madeleine; 'certainly not Aristophanes. I should say that the Grecian Anthology is the founder of the family; a highly respectable ancestor, though *de robe* rather than *d'épée*, for I am told Alexandrian Greek is not as noble as that of Athens. It contains several epigrams, quite in the manner of Saint-Amant.' She was quoting Jacques, from whom, without knowing a word of Greek, she had gleaned certain facts about Greek construction and literature.

Though Conrart never tried to conceal his ignorance of Greek, he could scarcely relish a reminder of it, while to be flatly contradicted by a fair damsel was not in his Chinese picture of Ladies and Sages. Mademoiselle de Scudéry came to his rescue,—

'For myself, I have always held that all an *honnête homme* need know is Italian and Spanish'—(here she smiled at Conrart, who was noted for his finished knowledge of these two tongues)—'the nature of the passions, *l'usage de monde*, and above all, Mythology, but that can be studied in a translation quite as well as in the original Greek or Latin. This is the *necessary* knowledge for an *honnête homme*, but as the word *honnête* covers a quantity of agreeable qualities, such as a swift imagination, an exquisite judgment, an excellent memory, and a lively humour naturally inclined to learning about everything it sees that is curious and that it hears mentioned as worthy of praise, the possessor of these qualities will naturally add a further store of agreeable information to the accomplishments I have already mentioned. These accomplishments are necessary also to an *honnête femme*, but as well as being able to *speak* Italian and Spanish, she must be able to *write* her native French; I must confess that the orthography of various distinguished ladies of my acquaintance is barely decent! As well as knowing the nature and movements of the Passions she must know the causes and effects of maladies, and a quantity of receipts for the making of medicaments and perfumes and cordials ... in fact of both useful and gallant distillations, as necessity or pleasure may demand. As well as being versed in Mythology, that is to say, in the *amours* and exploits of ancient gods and heroes, she must know what I will call the modern Mythology, that is to say the doings of her King and the *historiettes* of the various Belles and Gallants of the Court and Town.'

All the company had sat in rapt attention during this discourse, except Madeleine, who had fidgeted and wriggled and several times had attempted to break in with some remark of her own. Now she took advantage of the slight pause that followed to cry out aggressively: 'Italian and Spanish *may* be the language of *les honnêtes gens*, but Greek is certainly that of *les gens gallants*, if only for this reason, that it alone possesses the lover's Mood.' Madeleine waited to be asked what that was, and the faithful Chevalier came to her rescue.

'And what may the lover's mood be, Mademoiselle?' he asked with a smile.

'What they call the Optative—the Mood of wishing,' said Madeleine. The Chevalier clapped delightedly, and Conrart, now quite restored to good humour, also congratulated her on the sally; but Mademoiselle de Scudéry looked supremely bored.

The violins started a light, melancholy dance, and from behind the trees ran a troop of little girls, dressed as nymphs, and presented to each of the ladies a bouquet, showing in its arrangement the inimitable touch of the famous florist, La Cardeau. Madeleine's was the biggest. Then they got up and moved on to a little Italian grotto, where they seated themselves on the grass, Madame Conrart insisting that her husband should sit on a cloak she had been carting about with her for the purpose all the afternoon. He grumbled a little, but sat down on it all the same.

'And now will the wise Agilaste make music for us?' he asked. All looked invitingly towards Mademoiselle Boquet. She expressed hesitation at performing in a garden where such formidable rivals were to be found as Conrart's famous linnets, but she finally yielded to persuasion, and taking her lute, began to play. It was exquisite. First she played some airs by Couperin, then some pavanes by a young Italian, as yet known only to the elect and quite daring in his modernity, by name Lulli, and last a frail, poignant melody of the time of Henri IV., in which, as in the little poem of the same period praised by Alceste, '*la passion parlait toute pure.*'

Madame Conrart listened with more emotion than any of them, beating time with her foot, her eyes filling with tears. When Mademoiselle Boquet laid down her lute, she drew a deep sigh. 'Ah! Now that's what *I* call agreeable!' Conrart frowned at her severely, but Mademoiselle de Scudéry and the Chevalier were evidently much amused. The poor lady, realising that she had made a *faux pas*, looked very unhappy.

'Oh! I did not mean to say ... I am sure ... I hope you will understand!' she said to the company, but looking at Conrart the while.

'We will understand, and indeed we would be very dull if we failed to, that you are ever the kindest and most hospitable of hostesses,' said Mademoiselle de Scudéry. Madame Conrart looked relieved and said,—

'I am sure you are very obliging, Mademoiselle.' Then she turned to Madeleine, 'And you, Mademoiselle, do you sing or play?' Madeleine said in a superior tone that she did not, and the Chevalier, invariably adequate, said: 'Mademoiselle is a *merciful* Siren.'

And so the afternoon passed, until it was time to take their leave. The Conrarts were very kind and friendly and hoped Madeleine would come again, but Mademoiselle de Scudéry had so many messages to send by Mademoiselle Boquet to friends in Paris, that she forgot even to say good-bye to her.

On the drive home the Chevalier and Mademoiselle Boquet had a learned discussion about music, and Madeleine sat silent and wide-eyed. It was eight o'clock when they reached the petite rue du Paon. Madeleine rushed in to her mother, who was waiting for her, and launched into a long excited account of the day's doings, which fulfilled the same psychological need that a dance would have done, and then she went to her room, for her mother wished to discuss the violent decision come to so suddenly by Jacques.

She went straight to bed and fell asleep to the cry of the *Oublieux*—'La joie! la joie! Voilà des oublies!'

CHAPTER XXXIII
FACE TO FACE WITH FACTS

She awoke next morning to the sense that she must make up her account. How exactly did things stand? She certainly had been neither *gauche* nor silent the day before. Saint Magdalene had done all she had asked of her, but by so doing had she played her some hideous trick?

She had had absolute faith in Descartes' doctrine that love proceeds from admiration, and that admiration is caused by anything rare and extraordinary. She *was* rare, she *was* extraordinary, but had she aroused admiration? And even if she had, could it not be the forerunner of hate as well as of love?

Alas! how much easier would be self-knowledge, and hence, if the Greeks were right, how much easier too would be virtue, if the actions of our passions were as consistent, the laws that govern them as mechanical, as they appear in Descartes' Treatise. Moreover, how much easier would be happiness if, docile and catholic like birds and flowers, we were never visited by these swift, exclusive passions, which are so rarely reciprocal.

No, if Mademoiselle de Scudéry did not feel for her *d'un aveugle penchant le charme imperceptible*, the Cestus of Venus itself would be of no avail. Even if she had not cut herself off from the relief of her dances by bringing them to a climax beyond which their virtue could not function, this had been, even for their opiate, too stern and dolorous a fact.

Circumstances had forced her bang up against reality this time. She must find out, once and for all, how matters stood, that is to say, if she had aroused the emotion of admiration. She must have her own suspicions allayed—or confirmed. The only way this could be done, was to go to the Chevalier's house and ask him. The spoken word carried for her always a strange finality. Suspense would be unbearable; she must go *now*.

She dressed hurriedly, slipped on her mask and cloak, and stole into the street. The strange antiphony of the hawkers rang through the morning, and there echoed after her as she ran the well-known cry: *Vous désirez quelque ch-o-o-se?* This cry in the morning, and in the evening that of the *Oublieux.—La joie! la joie! Voilà des oublies!* ... Did one answer the other in some strange way, these morning and evening cries? It could be turned into a dialogue between Fate and a mortal, thus:—

Fate: Vous désirez quelque cho-o-o-se?

Mortal: La joie! la joie!

Fate: Voilà—*l'oubli*.

On she ran, careless of the surprise of the passers-by, over the Pont-Neuf, already busy, and driving its motley trade, then along the Quais on the other side, past the Louvre, and up the Rue de Richelieu, where the Chevalier lived. She had naturally never been to his rooms, but she knew where they were. She slipped in at the main doorway and up the long stairs, her heart beating somewhere up in her throat. She knew he lived on the second landing. She knocked many times before the door was opened by a lackey in a night-cap. He gaped when he first saw her, and then grinned broadly.

'Mademoiselle must see Monsieur? Monsieur is abed, but Mademoiselle doubtless will not mind that!'

'Tell Monsieur that Mademoiselle Troqueville *must* see him on urgent business,' Madeleine said severely.

The lackey grinned again, and led her through a great bare room, surrounded by carved wooden chests, in which, doubtless, the Chevalier kept his innumerable suits of clothes. They served also as beds, chairs, and tables to the Chevalier's army of lackeys and pages, for some were lying full length on them snoring lustily, and others, more matinal, were sitting on them cross-legged, and, wrapped in rugs, were playing at that solace of the vulgar— Lasquinet. Madeleine felt a sudden longing to be one of them, happy, lewd, soulless creatures!

She was shown into an elegant little waiting-room, full of small inlaid tables and exquisite porcelain. The walls were hung with crayon sketches, and large canvasses of well-known ladies by Mignard and Beaubrun. Some of them were in allegorical postures—there was the celebrated Précieuse, Madame de Buisson, holding a lyre and standing before a table covered with books and astronomical instruments ... she was probably meant to represent a Muse ... she was leering horribly ... was it the Comic Muse?

It must have been for about a quarter of an hour that Madeleine waited, sitting rigid and expressionless.

At last the Chevalier arrived, fresh from his valet's hands, in a gorgeous Chinese dressing-gown, scented and combed. He held out both his hands to her and his eyes were sparkling, to Madeleine it seemed with a sinister light, and she found herself wondering, as she marked the dressing-gown, if he were Descartes. Anything was possible in this Goblin-world.

She suddenly realised that she must find the 'urgent business' that had wrenched the Chevalier from his morning sleep. She could not very well blurt put 'Did Mademoiselle de Scudéry like me?' but what *could* she say?

'Dear Rhodanthos, I cursed my valet for not being winged when I heard it was you, and—as you see—my impatience was too great for a jerkin! What brings you at this hour? That you should turn to me in your trouble, if trouble it is, is a prettier compliment than all *les fleurettes* of all the polite Anthologies. What has metamorphosed the Grecian rose into a French lily?'

Madeleine blushed, and stammered out that she did not know. Then the Chevalier took matters into his own hands. This behaviour might smack of the reign of Louis XIII., but it was very delicious for all that.

He took her in his arms. Madeleine lay there impassive. After all, it saved her the trouble of finding a reason; for the one thing that was left in this emotional ruin was the old shrinking from people knowing how much it mattered. But as to what he might think of her present behaviour, 'twas a matter of no moment whatever. She held him at arm's length from her for a minute.

'Tell me,' she said archly, 'did you find yesterday a pleasant diversion?' His cheeks were flushed, and there was the dull drunken look in his eyes which is one of the ways passion expresses itself in middle-aged men. 'Come back to me!' he muttered thickly, without answering her question.

'First tell me if you found it diverting!' she cried gaily, and darted to the opposite end of the room. He rushed after her.

'Don't madden me, child,' he muttered, and took her in his arms again. Again Madeleine broke away from him laughing.

'I won't come to you till—let me see—till you tell me if I took the fancy of Mademoiselle de Scudéry.' She was, when hard-driven, an excellent actress, and the question tripped out, light and mocking, as if it had just been an excuse for tormenting him. There she stood with laughing lips and grave, wind-swept eyes, keeping him at bay with her upraised hand. 'In earnest,' she cooed tormentingly, 'you must first answer my question.' For a moment, the pedagogue broke through the lover.

'Mademoiselle de Scudéry is an exquisitely correct lady, her sense of social seemliness amounts to genius. She could hardly approve of a hamadryad ... Madeleine!' and he made a dash for her. But she ducked and turned under his outstretched arms, and was once more at the opposite end of the room. The flame of her wish to know began to burn up her flimsy rôle.

'I—promise you—anything—afterwards, but—pray tell me—*did Mademoiselle de Scudéry make any mention to you of me?*' she panted.

''Tis no matter and she did, I....'

'Tell me!' And somehow Madeleine's voice compelled obedience.

'What strange *vision* is this? Well, then, as you are so desirous of knowing ... Mademoiselle de Scudéry ... well, she is herself a lady, and as such cannot be over sensible to the charms of her own sex——'

'Well?'

'Well, do not take it ill, but also she always finds it hard to pardon a ... well ... a ... er ... a certain lack of decorum. I told her she erred grievously in her judgment of you, but, it seems, you did not take her fancy, and she maintained'—(The Chevalier was rather glad of the opportunity of repeating the following words, for not being *in propria persona*, they escaped incivility and might be beneficial.) 'She maintained that your manners were *grossier*, your wit *de province*, and that even if you lived to be as old as the Sybil, "you would never be an *honnête femme*".... Maintenant, ma petite Reine——'

But Madeleine was out of the room—pushing her way through the lackeys ... then down the staircase ... then out into the street ... running, running, running.

Then she stood still and began to tremble from head to foot with awful, silent laughter. Fool that she was not to have seen it before! Why, the Sapphic Ode was but another statement of the Law she had so dreaded—that the spurner of love must in his turn inevitably be spurned! *Who flees, she shall pursue; who spurns gifts, she shall offer them; who loves not, willy-nilly she shall love.* As the words stood, the 'she' did not necessarily refer to the object of Sappho's desire. Fool, fool, she had read as a promise what was intended as a warning. *She was being punished for spurning the love of Jacques.*

What a strange irony, that just by her effort to escape this Law she had brought down on herself the full weight of its action! To avoid its punishment of her *amour-propre* she had pretended to be in love with Jacques, thereby entangling herself in a mass of contradictions, deceit, and nervous terrors from which the only means of extricating herself was by breaking the law anew and spurning love. Verily, it was a fine example of Até—the blindness sent by the gods on those they mean to destroy.

Well, now the end had come, and of the many possibilities and realities life had held for her, nothing was left but the *adamant of desire which neither the tools of earth can break, nor the chemistry of Hell resolve.*

CHAPTER XXXIV
OUT INTO THE VOID

So it was all over.

Had she been the dupe of malicious gods? Yes, if within that malign pantheon there was a throne for her old enemy, *Amour-Propre*. For it was *Amour-Propre* that had played her this scurvy trick and had upset her poor little boat 'drifting oarless on a full sea'—not of Grace but of Chance. After all, Jansenism, Cartesianism, her mother's philosophy of indifference, had all the same aim—to give a touch of sea-craft to the poor human sailor, and to flatter him with the belief that some harbour lies before him. But they lie, they lie! There is no port, no rudder, no stars, and the frail fleet of human souls is at the mercy of every wind that blows.

She laughed bitterly when she remembered her certainty of her own election, her anger against the mighty hands slowly, surely, torturing her life into salvation. She laughed still more at her faith in a kind, heavenly Father, a rock in a weary land, a certain caterer of lovely gifts. How had she ever been fool enough to believe in this? Had she no eyes for the countless proofs all round her that any awful thing might happen to any one? People, just as real and alive as she was herself, were disfigured by smallpox, or died of plague, or starved in the streets, or loved without being loved in return; and yet, she had wrapped herself round in an imaginary ghostly tenderness, certain in her foolish heart that it was against the order of the universe that such things should happen to *her*.

And as to Mademoiselle de Scudéry, she knew that the whole business had been a foolish *vision*, a little seed growing to grotesque dimensions in a sick brain, and yet this knowledge was powerless to stem the mad impetus of her misery.

How she longed for Jacques during these days, for his comforting hands, his *allégresse*, his half-mocking patience. She saw him, pale and chestnut-haired with his light, mysterious, beckoning eyes—so strangely like the picture by Da Vinci in the Louvre of Saint John the Baptist—marching head erect to his bright destiny down the long white roads of France, and he would never come back.

And yet, she had hinted to Madame Pilou that the fable of the dog and the shadow is the epitome of all tragedy. Somewhere inside her had she always known what must happen?

First, this time of faultless vision. And then, because—though hope was dead—there still remained 'the adamant of desire,' she began once more to dance. But with hope were cut the cables binding her to reality, and it was out into the void that she danced now.

EPILOGUE
THE RAPE TO THE LOVE OF INVISIBLE THINGS

αἴ σε μαινόμεναι πάννυχοι χορεύουσι τὸν ταμίαν Ἴακχον.

SOPH. AN. 1151.

'Art springs straight out of the rite, and her first outward leap is the image of the god.'—JANE HARRISON.

Some years later a troupe of wits, in quest of the 'crotesque,' were visiting the well-known lunatic asylum—'les petites maisons.'

'And now for the Pseudo-Sappho!' cried one. 'She, all said, is by far the most delicious.'

They made their way to where a woman sat smiling affably. She greeted them as a queen her courtiers.

'Well, Alcinthe. Mignonne has been drooping since you were here, and cooing that all the doves have left the Royaume de Tendre. Where is dear Théodite? Ma chère, I protest that he is the king of les honnêtes gens.'

The wits laughed delightedly. Suddenly one had an idea.

'Did not the ancients hold that in time the worshipper became the god? Surely we have here a proof that their belief was well founded. And if the worshipper becomes the god then should not also the metamorphosis of the lover into his mistress—Céladon into Astrée, Cyrus into Mandane—be the truly gallant ending of a "roman"?'

He drew out his tablets,—

'I must make a note of that, and fashion it into an epigram for Sappho.'

FOOTNOTES

[1] *Les petites maisons,* a group of buildings, used among other things as a lunatic asylum.

[2] As only Duchesses were privileged to sit in the Queen's presence, to say that some one had *le tabouret chez la reine* meant that they were a Duchess.

[3] Neuf-germain was notorious as the worst poet of his day.

[4] The great seventeenth century herald.